MURDER AS PREDICTED

A gripping murder mystery full of twists

LINDA MATHER

The Zodiac Mysteries Book 3

Originally published as
Gemini Double Cross

JOFFE BOOKS

Revised edition 2021
Joffe Books, London
www.joffebooks.com

First published by Macmillan in Great Britain in 1995
as *Gemini Double Cross*

Cover art by Dee Dee Book Covers

ISBN: 978-1-78931-854-8

PROLOGUE

May 2011

The house felt empty. As soon as she turned her key, she sensed it. She pushed the front door open and the draught excluder rasped loudly against the stone-flagged floor. When she came home from work, Monique was usually in the kitchen, chopping vegetables and listening to the radio. But this evening the house seemed strangely quiet.

'Hello-o, Monique? Where are you?' she called, peering into the empty sitting room as she passed.

The kitchen was also silent and tidy. The morning's mail lay in a pile on the table. Antonia sorted out her letters. Nothing very interesting. The envelopes addressed to Monique, she noticed, had been ripped open across the top. Antonia knew her sister would have been disappointed — she still scanned the mail every morning looking for something from John. From the outside of the envelopes, it was clear that, once again, there had been no word from him.

Sisters know too much about one another, she thought.

Monique was not in the kitchen garden or around the back of the house, although she had obviously been gardening earlier because smoke was still rising from the remains of a bonfire at the far end of the lawn. It seemed odd that she had made a fire just there. Antonia stared at it and resolved to ask her sister later whether the blackened grass would grow again.

Careful to keep to the paths because of her high heels, she walked around the house but still there was no sign. When the first whiff of pollen reached her off the fields, she began to sneeze and hurried back inside. She dug out her phone from her laptop bag and called Monique's number without feeling hopeful. Monique was inclined to ignore her phone when it suited her. Sure enough, it rang out and Antonia sighed in frustration, dropping the phone onto the polished hall table.

She found herself unable to settle, wandering from room to room clutching a mug of tea. She went over all the places her sister was likely to be but couldn't come up with many possibilities. For the last six months — ever since John had disappeared from the scene — she had hardly been out of the house. She had effectively given up her job as a librarian. She had simply stopped going to work and no amount of persuasion had been able to encourage her to return.

Perhaps she's gone shopping, Antonia mused, peering out of her bedroom window along the drive. Just recently her sister had taken to browsing in antique shops. Once or twice in the past week she had driven into Canterbury and had come home with a couple of ornaments.

Her hands around the cooling china mug, shoulders tense, Antonia reminded herself that she had spotted some other little signs recently that her sister was emerging from her depression. Monique had started to pay more attention to her appearance, plaiting her long brown hair and digging out her summer dresses. But the single most encouraging news had been her spontaneous decision to go to France the weekend before last to stay with their French relatives. This was surely the best indication that Monique was getting over John and becoming more independent again, Antonia said to herself. But her eyes remained fixed on the drive and the grey sliver of the lane beyond.

When the house phone rang, she hurtled downstairs to answer it.

'Yes?' she demanded. She was met by a heavy silence. Her palms were suddenly clammy on the receiver. 'Is that you, Monique?'

She heard a sigh followed by a whisper, which she didn't catch.

'Who is it?' She was about to put the phone down when the whispering became a giggle.

'Toni, Toni, it's me,' Guy's voice said, still laughing. 'Couldn't you tell, really?'

'Of course I couldn't.' Her heart was hammering. 'It could have been some awful pervert.'

'Instead it's this awful pervert,' Guy said, a smile in his voice. 'Were you really frightened?'

Antonia, caught between annoyance and relief, couldn't help but notice how even the sound of his voice was attractive.

Antonia frowned, not liking this conversation but drawn in despite herself. 'Yes — no, not really.' She rushed on to explain about Monique.

Guy cut her short. 'Not something else about your sister. I'm tired of hearing about her. Listen, have you thought any more about moving in with me? You'll go nuts yourself if you stay buried in the countryside any longer—'

'You know I'm tempted but . . .' Antonia twisted around in the hallway, looking up the stairs and back into the kitchen. 'Maybe if we made a plan, set a date for the wedding, that would give everyone more time to get used to the idea — including me.'

There was plenty of mileage in this subject and by the time Antonia put the phone down it was seven thirty. The antique shops would have closed two hours ago and Monique would have had plenty of time to drive home. Antonia tried her sister's phone again. It rang out.

'Monique where on earth are you? It's late and I know I'm probably being silly but I'm getting worried so just call me, OK?' She noticed how her voice sounded panicky despite her best efforts.

She carefully searched all the likely places where there might be a note. There was nothing in the kitchen or on the mantelpiece in the sitting room. She even looked in the dining room, which at present was being used to store some heavy dark furniture Monique had brought back from France. Nothing had been disturbed in there and there were no new messages on the notepad by the phone.

She looked at her watch again: seven forty-five. *Why on earth doesn't she use her phone like a normal person?* she asked herself. She paced around the kitchen. Maybe it had run out of charge. Perhaps Monique had gone out and the car had broken down? Perhaps she was stuck somewhere, unable to contact anyone? She pulled on her jacket. It was still light out, so she would get back in her car and go looking for her.

She suddenly realised she'd overlooked the obvious. Had Monique even taken her car?

She hurried out of the front door, leaving it slightly ajar. Her own car was parked in the drive, where she usually left it, ready for the journey to London in the morning, while Monique generally used the garage for her silver Toyota Yaris. She started towards it, almost jogging, despite the heels. Her heart was racing. Why had she just assumed her sister had taken her car? Why had she not thought to check?

She followed the curve of the paved drive past the paddock. The garage was dark and square in the gathering dusk. She clutched the key, which she had grabbed from the pot in the hall, but as soon as she gripped the handle, she realised it was unlocked. Her stomach sank. It was only then that she heard the sound of the car engine.

Breaking her nails against the wood, she grappled furiously with the doors before she could drag them open. Blackness and fumes engulfed her. The air was soupy with dizzying smoke, which grabbed the back of her throat. The car was there with the driver's door open and something long and white sticking out. They were her sister's legs.

Monique was sitting half out of the car, the car keys lying on the concrete floor at her feet.

Using all her strength, Antonia grabbed her sister under the arms and began to heave her out. Her sister's legs and feet flailed and banged against the door, but there was no responsive movement in the limp, heavy body. Antonia took a gulp of the fume-filled air and instantly felt heady and sick. She pulled, her sister's bare legs scraping along the ground, until Monique lay on the drive, her dress crumpled and twisted around her, her hair half out of its plait and her face an unhealthy red, revealing a deeper red stripe across her forehead.

Antonia felt desperately for a heartbeat then pelted back to the house to call an ambulance.

'Quickly — please, quickly,' she gabbled. 'Someone's killed my sister!'

CHAPTER ONE

Jo Hughes stood at the wide bay window of her flat feeling strangely nervous. It was out of character for her to be apprehensive about a consultation. Her notes were neatly lined up on the coffee table beside her laptop, along with the presentation folder containing the birth chart and written summary that she intended to give her client. The flat was as warm as she could make it on a freezing January morning. She'd had the gas fire on since she'd got up and had pushed the two easy chairs comfortably close to it. Really she couldn't have done any more preparation, she reminded herself, as she went into the kitchen to check she'd put the coffee on.

What worried her was the position of the planets over the next few months. This, combined with the sensitive, rather reckless personality the birth chart had revealed, meant she was going to have to give her client some difficult advice. In fact, the chart was one of the most disturbing Jo had ever studied. She had to find ways of warning her client to avoid risks and to let go of any personal crusades.

The character analysis had been strange too. Her client, Antonia Carlyle, was a woman with a fixation — according to the position of the planets when she was born. She was obsessive, driven. But driven to do what? Of course, the birth chart gave clues, suggesting the obsession might have something to do with a rift between a brother or sister, or past lover. Or possibly it was connected to her job. If she was a charity worker or nurse, dedicated to the point of self-sacrifice, it would fit in with the caring sign of Cancer being on the Ascendant.

Jo chewed her bottom lip. Her instincts told her the answer was not going to be that simple. This strange mission of her client's was likely to be something closer to her heart. And, because Neptune was personalised, it could get out of hand, making the outside world seem like a threat. As she returned to her discreet look-out post, a smart blue car drew up outside. A short, slight woman stepped out, looked around her at the quiet suburban street and then made purposefully for the Victorian house, in which Jo's flat occupied the top floor. Jo ducked out of view. She gave one more glance around the room. *Nothing else to do now*, she thought, *except wait.*

The shrill of the doorbell banished her oddly pessimistic mood and, bounding downstairs to open the front door, she felt more like her usual, rational self. The woman on the doorstep was a head shorter than Jo with a pale, pointed face, made more elfin by the large furry collar of her flying jacket. She looked smart and well-groomed and if Jo hadn't known she was thirty-four, she wouldn't have guessed the woman was eight years older than her. Jo introduced herself and the other woman looked instantly pleased and relieved.

'I'm fairly new to this area and I was a bit worried about finding your address,' Antonia said, following Jo up to her flat. 'But I've been really looking forward to meeting you. I've always wanted to have my horoscope read.' The woman paused on the threshold and looked around. 'What a lovely window, looking out at the tops of the trees.'

'I like the place,' Jo admitted, 'although it's hard to keep warm. Every year at this time, I think about leaving and wonder if I can afford to buy somewhere, but then the spring comes round and it gets more bearable.'

'I rent my cottage too. Now that we've supposedly got zero inflation, there's a lot to be said for it.' Antonia wandered over to Jo's bookshelves, touching the books and glancing around the room, seemingly reluctant to settle down. Jo offered coffee and went to the kitchen to fetch it. She had expected to be met by Antonia's lively energy but was well aware that, as with many Geminis, this confidence was only skin deep.

Ensconced in one of the armchairs when Jo came back with two mugs, Antonia looked even slighter without her outer clothes. She had a delicate, angular frame. She used her hands when she talked and her eyes never rested on anything for long. Her hair was a reddish blonde, pinned up in some complicated style. Her clothes — mainly black — were expensive and plain and her face was carefully made up to accentuate her high cheekbones and intelligent, dark eyes.

Jo took the other easy chair. 'Before I tell you about your birth chart, there's something I need to ask,' she began. 'Is there any particular reason why you wanted this consultation? I mean, what prompted you to seek me out?'

Many people sought the services of an astrologer when they had a difficult decision to make but Antonia had not been very forthcoming when she'd phoned to ask for a personal forecast for the year ahead. Now that Jo had seen the planets clustered in her Twelfth House, she knew Antonia would be secretive but thought it worth trying to get at her motives.

'It's a belated Christmas present to myself,' Antonia said with a little nervous laugh.

Jo sorted her notes, letting the silence stretch out. The other woman tapped her well-manicured nails against the side of her mug. 'Honestly, there's no particular reason. I mean, nothing serious anyway,' she said at last. 'Although I suppose you could say I'm having a few problems related to my job.'

Jo waited while Antonia shifted in the chair and went on, 'I used to work as a programmer in London until I was made redundant about a year ago. As I hated living in the city anyway, I thought I'd move away and I found a job in Warwick. There have been a few — well — problems, like I said.' She paused and Jo wondered if she'd been going to say more. 'I suppose I want you to tell me if I've made the wrong decision,' she finished, glancing down at her boots.

'I know because you've got your Sun, Mercury, Venus and Mars all in Gemini that you do like a challenging job. You loathe being bored. Is that what you dislike about your job?'

'Well, yes it is not as interesting as programming. Here I'm expected to be a jack of all trades. And it's my boss, Oliver Sargent,' she added. 'I don't really get on with him.' She was still suddenly, after all the fidgeting.

There were clear signs in the chart that Antonia was inclined to get emotionally entangled at work and Jo considered the complications lying behind this bald statement. Was Antonia contemplating an affair with this man, Sargent? Or getting over it? Or was he an office bully?

'When is his birthday?'

'The seventh of October. I know that means he's a Libra and Geminis are supposed to get on with Librans, aren't they? It's funny — both my parents were Libran and I got on with them marvellously. Oliver couldn't be more different. It's enough to make you doubt astrology, isn't it?' Antonia caught a breath. 'I'm rambling, aren't I?'

'Don't put too much faith in Sun Signs alone. There's more to it than that. And Librans can be devious. Maybe you just don't trust him—'

'That's true, I don't,' Antonia broke in. 'Oh, I'm sorry, you were saying . . .'

'That's OK, feel free to say whatever you like. This is entirely confidential.' It was not usually necessary to reinforce this with clients but Antonia seemed to be keeping so much back that Jo felt she had to make it clear. She turned to the birth chart, concentrating on the positive aspects like Antonia's intelligence, kindness and loyalty.

'You've probably got one or two really good friends among a whole load of acquaintances,' Jo said when she came to the planets in the Eleventh and Twelfth Houses. 'But you're inclined to use logic when forming judgements about people. People don't always behave logically. It could be you don't understand their motives as well as you think.'

Antonia was leaning forward in her chair. 'I have made some bad mistakes about people in the past,' she murmured.

Interesting. Jo decided it was time to touch on the darker side of her findings. 'To my mind, it seems you're on some sort of personal mission.'

Antonia frowned.

What could she say to get this woman to open up? She tried again. 'Perhaps it's an ambition you've held for a long time?'

Antonia dropped her eyelids, giving her narrow face an almost hooded look. 'I can't think of anything. I've always worked in IT and never really wanted to do anything else. I'm good at it.'

Jo was sure she was deliberately misunderstanding the question. 'I understand that you may not want to tell me,' she said gently. 'But if you know what it is, all the signs are that you should drop this quest. Let sleeping dogs lie. This year, Saturn is telling you to be careful and to put yourself and your own well-being first.'

Antonia sat back in her chair and appeared to consider this advice. 'Is there anything else I should watch out for this year?'

'Jupiter is transiting your Sixth House, which could mean a rift with a partner — either someone from the past or now.'

She groaned and rolled her eyes. 'That'll be Guy. My ex-husband. My little aberration.'

'Do you still see him?' There were definite signs in the chart that Antonia was vulnerable because of her poor judgement, that people would take advantage of her and maybe even put her in some sort of danger. Could Guy be the person to avoid?

'Yes, he still gets in touch now and again. But I always feel the less I know about what he's doing, the better. He's one of these men who seem intent on self-destruction. But unfortunately, I didn't realise it until after I'd married him. Nowadays when I see him, I just feel worried and depressed, so I try not to. He's a Pisces, by the way.'

'You're probably right. If he's been untrustworthy in the past, this is not the year to go for reconciliation.'

'There's no chance of that,' Antonia said with such firmness that Jo, for once, was in no doubt about her honesty. She followed it up with a winning smile. 'It was the old story, I'm afraid. I met Guy at work and he seemed so smart, so funny, so—' she searched for an apt description — 'so *in control*, which is a bad joke now. But I've never known anyone understand information systems like that man did. His thought processes were like lightning and he could decode anything. So,' her face took on a rueful expression, 'I fell in love with my boss.'

Jo's thoughts flew briefly to her own relationship with David Macy, who ran the PI agency where she sometimes worked. That was completely different, of course, as they were nothing more than friends.

The woman opposite her was looking wistfully into the middle distance. 'Guy had a great job too — this was about five years ago, when I fell for him. He was a sort of troubleshooter for other people who were developing software. And the firm knew he was good. They gave him a lot of leeway. Even so, it wasn't enough.' She sighed and her tone became ironic, world-weary. 'Constant searching for excitement can lead to all sorts of trouble, you know. And someone like Guy gets easily bored and searches out more and more diversions.'

'You mean like drink and drugs?' Jo was thinking of the traditional means of escape that Pisceans sometimes turn to under stress.

'Well, yes, those too,' she said. 'But Guy was bored with everything — with work, with me, with life really. Still is. We stayed together for two years and that was pushing it. We haven't actually divorced yet but it's just a matter of getting round to it. I certainly won't seek him out.'

Jo turned back to the chart. 'There's an indication of a rift in your family. Do you have any brothers or sisters?'

'I don't have much family. My elder sister died five years ago. Maybe that's a sort of rift. We were very close.' She paused and fiddled with the amber beads at her neck. 'Can I ask you something?' Jo nodded, and the woman shot her a quick, uncertain smile. 'Well, I do need your advice about a specific question. Is it ever right to give up? I mean, is there a right time to know when to quit? How do people ever know that?'

'Give up what? Your job?'

Antonia nibbled the edge of a painted fingernail. 'The trouble is, and I know this sounds stupid, but I feel someone is trying to frighten me away from Warwick.'

'Trying to frighten you? What do you mean?'

Antonia ceased fidgeting and fixed Jo with a steady gaze. 'You promise you won't think I'm totally off my head?'

'Of course I won't,' Jo said. 'Go on.'

'One of my cats was poisoned yesterday. Someone murdered him.'

'What do you mean? Why would anyone do that?'

'To get at me.'

This was said so dramatically that in normal circumstances Jo would have had trouble keeping a straight face, but she sensed the other woman's fear and stayed silent.

'Someone is trying to scare me off,' Antonia repeated, apparently unaware of how paranoid this sounded. 'That's why they killed poor Dylan — my cat. It was my fault for not keeping a closer eye on him. I should have known they could get at me through him.' Her eyes filled up and she rummaged in her handbag, pulled out a tissue and blew her nose quickly.

Jo guessed that Antonia had been longing to tell someone about this, and couldn't help but feel sorry for her. She was fond of her own cat and often thought he was the only male she could ever live with.

'The vet said she thought Dylan had eaten slug pellets. That's the most common cause of poisoning in cats, she told me,' Antonia said. She rested her pointed chin on one hand.

'Well, he could have picked up those pellets anywhere.'

'Not Dylan. He was a Maine Coon cat — a pedigree. I've got two and neither go far from the house. My cottage is on the outskirts of Ashow. You probably don't know it, it's a tiny village. At the back of me is the river. To one side, the land belongs to a farmer and he lives more than half a mile away. The nearest neighbour on the other side is two hundred yards away and she's another cat lover.'

'But even cat lovers put down slug pellets,' Jo said.

Antonia looked up sharply. 'Not in January.'

Jo had to concede this seemed unlikely. 'But you don't know it was slug pellets that killed him. Maybe the farmer is using another pesticide which is harmful to cats.'

'I've been living there a few months and the cats have been OK up to now, but I'll ask him. And I'll mention it to Betty too — she's my other neighbour.'

'If she's got cats herself, it might be as well to warn her to keep them in for a while if there is some dangerous pesticide about,' Jo said.

Antonia shook her head. 'Betty's cats will be all right. This was aimed at me. And I'm terrified in case . . .' She let the sentence remain unfinished.

'What?'

There was no response to Jo's prompting other than a slight shudder. She took a moment to consider this surprising turn in the conversation. It felt more like an interview that might take place in the PI office, where she sometimes worked, rather than an astrological reading. It seemed to be practical advice that Antonia was seeking so she closed her laptop. 'Why do you think someone would want to get at you by killing Dylan?'

Antonia's gaze slid away from hers. 'I don't know. I just feel someone is trying to frighten me, but I can't give you good reasons, so it's no use asking me. Talking doesn't achieve anything.' She glanced up with a closed expression which gave a hint of the determination below the surface. 'You've been very helpful and a lot of the things you said are absolutely spot on.' Antonia took her gloves out of her bag, clearly wanting to bring the consultation to an end.

'Are you sure?' Jo felt a little disappointed. The woman was paranoid and her strange, oblique references to danger were inexplicable and yet in those moments when she had seemed open and genuine, Jo had warmed to her. 'Are there any more questions you need to ask?'

'No, I have to think about what you've said. I've learned a lot. Maybe Guy's even worse news than I thought. But I think I'll stay around this area a bit longer.' Antonia held up the summary Jo had given her. 'It says in here that Geminis are better at starting things than finishing them. I ought to do what I set out to do.'

'What's that?'

She shrugged. 'Oh, you know, get on with my plans.'

'Well, don't forget it's a bad time to do anything rash or hasty,' Jo said. 'Just take it easy, no rushed decisions — especially in the first few months of the year.'

'No, and I'll look after myself better.' Antonia held out her hand. 'You've been really good — just by listening to me. Which has made me feel better. You don't get much chance of that when you live on your own, do you?' Before Jo had a chance to reply, Antonia rushed on. 'Anyway I must be on my way. And you must be busy this time of year. Everyone wants to know how the year will turn out for them. Does astrology keep you fully occupied?'

Jo didn't know whether she felt relieved or reluctant to talk about herself but she went along with the change of subject. 'Not all the time,' she admitted. 'I work for a private investigation agency in Coventry now and again.'

'Really?' Antonia looked impressed. 'Two intriguing jobs.'

'Yes, they beat the boring office jobs I had before. But they don't pay so well.'

Antonia pulled on her furry leather jacket. 'Money isn't everything. It must be fascinating working as a detective.'

'Not exactly.' Jo showed Antonia out. 'It's mainly tracing people who've absconded without paying their bills. But I'm not working for Macy and Wilson — that's the PI job — at the moment. And the way the astrology work is going, I may not have to work for them again.' She was aware that this was a grandiose claim but guessed she was unlikely to see her client again.

Antonia went down the path, hugging the folder to her. 'Thanks,' she called with an extravagant wave. 'I hope we bump into each other again sometime.'

Jo was not so sure she wanted to. Antonia seemed to be one of those Geminis who relish making life complicated.

CHAPTER TWO

Jo spent the next couple of days getting her astrology work up to date. She had a commission to cast a chart for a baby, which was very satisfying because she had the exact birth time. This meant she could be sure the chart was entirely accurate. She also worked on the horoscope column she wrote every week for a local paper. This week's was not a particularly easy one because the major planets in Capricorn were making life difficult for some.

On Thursday morning she had risen early and by nine thirty was engrossed in her column for the *Herald* when she had a call from Celia, asking her to pop in to see Mr Macy. Jo enjoyed a chat with Celia and agreed to call in that morning. Although she didn't want any PI work at present, she decided she should stay on good terms with them just in case. At least, that was how she rationalised her sudden urge to see David Macy. If there were any deeper-seated motives, she didn't examine them too closely. She worked until eleven and then walked into town.

The chipped plaque on the door frame read *Macy and Wilson — Private Investigation Agency* but Mark Wilson had left the firm years ago. Macy ran the agency with apparently minimal effort and a small staff of which Jo was a part-time member.

She literally ran into him at the top of the stairs in the office doorway. He was backing out, still speaking and not looking where he was going. The collision of bodies reminded her that her relationship with Macy was complex. He wasn't just her boss. They had been lovers once and she often entertained the idea of a repeat performance. She was sure Macy felt the same but they spent more time arguing than they did getting intimate.

He put a hand on her shoulder to stop himself falling down the stairs and she grabbed a handful of his warm shirt. 'Sorry — wasn't looking,' he muttered, then added irritably, 'Where did you spring from?'

Jo drew her hand back quickly, aware that the landing was in Celia's full view and she didn't miss a trick. 'Celia said you wanted to see me,' she replied, avoiding his eyes.

'Happy New Year, Jo!' Celia's voice boomed across the landing. 'We thought you'd deserted us, didn't we, Mr Macy? He was only saying—'

'Where the bloody hell is she — or words to that effect,' Macy supplied.

Jo crossed the reception area to be hugged to Celia's ample chest. 'Have you been busy with zodiac predictions?' she asked. 'Are we all going to have a wonderful year? Tell me that we are. Even if it's not true. Shall I get you some coffee?'

'All going well and thanks, that would be nice—' Jo began but was interrupted by Macy.

'But not so well that you don't still need us now and then,' he said.

Jo shrugged, glancing back at him. 'Well, if you haven't enough work for me . . .'

'We're keeping our heads above water without you, thank you.' Macy's dark eyes glinted amusement. 'I expect I can throw a few traces in your direction. That is, if you still remember how to trace people and serve papers.'

'Well, I've found you, and you can be pretty elusive—' Jo retorted.

'Don't bother with the coffee, Celia,' Macy cut across her again. 'I'll take Jo out to lunch.'

'Now there's an offer you don't get every day,' Celia remarked with a wink.

'We'll go to Brown's,' Macy said as they threaded their way through the bustling high street. Keeping pace with him as they ran up the stone steps to the terrace of bars and restaurants on the level above the shops, Jo thought he seemed unusually dynamic and said as much.

'New year's resolution,' he replied and Jo remembered that it was often hard to tell if he was serious. 'Or maybe it's the stars,' he went on. 'What do you reckon?'

'More fun than last year for you Cancerians. Mind you, this month is a bit tricky.' Jo explained about the cluster of planets in Capricorn.

'What does that mean?'

'Stress and setbacks — particularly in sexual relationships,' she added as she went ahead into the dim high-ceilinged bar.

'No change there, then. What would you like to drink?'

The bar was quiet as it was early for lunch. Students sat around talking or sitting over laptops and an old lady sipped her tea, her head in a paperback. Jo approved of Macy's choice. She liked the relaxed atmosphere.

They ordered their food and took a beer each to a table at the front of the bar. Jo sat down by the smoked-glass window and eyed Macy across the plastic tablecloth. His hair and eyes were the same dense shade of brown and as hard to read as ever. *Life would be easier if I didn't find him so attractive*, she thought.

'You've had your hair cut,' he remarked. 'It looks good.'

Jo was pleased but tried not to show it. Her dark curly hair was shorter and tidier than it had been for years after an impulsive visit to the hairdressers before Christmas. She picked up her bottle and tilted it slightly to him. 'Happy New Year. Now tell me why you're treating me to lunch.'

'You've got a nasty cynical streak.' He studied his long fingers on the tabletop for a moment then looked up at her again. 'All right, I'll tell you. I don't know what you're going to think about this. A woman came to see me last night. She claims to know you. Antonia Carlyle?'

'Oh, yes. I had a consultation with her last week. She's got a difficult time ahead and has had all sorts of problems, including a Maine Coon that died.'

'That's bad news in astrological terms, is it?'

Macy was straight-faced and Jo smothered a laugh. 'It's a cat. Just one of the many things that have apparently happened to her. Go on. What did she want with you? Did she tell you someone poisoned her cat on purpose?'

Macy frowned. 'Someone poisoned her cat? No, she didn't mention it. What did you think of her? She struck me as a couple of sandwiches short of a picnic.'

'I thought she was all there. Just a bit paranoid.'

Macy looked doubtful. 'Yes, well, the anxiety has really taken hold. She lives on her own and she's extremely *nervous*. She believes someone is out to do her harm.'

'Did she give any examples?'

'She's been getting obscene phone calls. Her briefcase was stolen, and she thinks her house was broken into, but nothing was taken. She hasn't been to the police because she says they wouldn't be interested, which I don't think is strictly true. On the other hand, she hasn't got much evidence for them to go on.'

'So what can you do to help?' Jo sat back as the waitress brought two plates of hot food. Jo addressed herself to her chilli and rice but not without an envious glance at Macy's plate. He had gone for the lamb tagine and the aromas reaching her were tempting. Around them, the bar was steadily filling up with the lunchtime crowd of office workers and shoppers, mostly loud and evidently very hungry.

'She wants a sort of minder — in a word.' Macy took up his knife and fork and tasted his first mouthful, taking his time over it. 'Yes, this is really good,' he said. He took a few more forkfuls before he relented with a half-smile and pushed his plate towards her. Jo helped herself. 'She wants someone to stay with her at nights and meet her when she leaves work every evening,' he went on. 'She's really jumpy — you know there have been some nasty attacks on women lately? She had chapter and verse on all those.'

Jo nodded. She saw what was coming and knew she didn't want the job. She returned to the territory of her own plate, as she decided how to respond.

'Antonia doesn't feel safe, for whatever reason. Real or imagined. She has to go on a course in Yorkshire soon, something to do with her work. She's particularly worried about it and wants someone to go with her. The thing is . . . she insists it has to be a woman. And she asked for you.'

Jo looked up from her meal. 'What did you say?'

'That I'd speak to you, of course. It would only be for a month.'

'How come? It sounds like a job for life to me. And I know she's not in for an easy time because I've seen what Mercury does in the next few months. On top of that, she's got a distinctly dodgy ex-husband, who's not quite an ex. Did she mention him?'

'No. In what way "dodgy"?'

'She wouldn't say,' Jo admitted. 'But she implied problems with the law, plus drink and drugs. Look, Macy, I don't want anything to do with this.'

Macy sighed. 'I had a feeling this was going to be an uphill battle. I told Ms Carlyle I wouldn't take on her case indefinitely but we could do it for a month and see how it went. I made it clear I couldn't tie up an operative on one job for any longer. She seemed happy with that.'

'So you did accept the job!' Jo sighed. 'I knew it. I knew you'd accepted it without consulting me—'

'I did not.' Macy frowned. 'I merely suggested those terms. But the job is a doddle. All you'd have to do is babysit this scatty woman in the evenings for a few weeks. I'd pay you full-time wages—'

'She's not scatty. Well, not from what I saw, anyway. In fact, I liked her and felt a bit sorry for her. She's had a difficult time. Her husband got bored with her, apparently, and her sister died young.'

'Well, maybe you could help her out,' Macy suggested. 'Honestly, it does sound like money for old rope. I don't know what you're complaining about.'

'I'm not complaining,' Jo said, keeping her voice calm. 'I just don't want the job.'

Macy looked out of the window, exasperated. 'You're being unreasonable. You'll be able to do what you want during the day, all your horoscopes and stuff. You'll only be working nights—'

'Only working nights?' Jo repeated. 'I'd have to move out of my flat and live with a complete stranger for weeks—'

'A month at the most, I said.' Macy's voice was rising too but nobody paid them any attention. 'And I'll pay you time and a half to take into account your working antisocial hours,' he added.

'You have accepted, haven't you?'

'No, I have not.' He pushed away his plate and threw down his napkin. 'I said I would talk to you. I'd forgotten you don't understand plain reasoning.'

'You're just trying to browbeat me into taking a job I don't want.' Jo's temper had subsided and she was almost enjoying the argument now.

'Who's browbeating whom?' Macy demanded. 'And if you were so against the case, why the hell did you tell the woman you worked for me? You even gave her the name of the firm.'

This made Jo pause for a moment. Had she unconsciously wanted to help Antonia? While Macy was speaking she had been thinking over the prospect of time and a half wages for a month and coming round to the idea. After all, the tax was due on the car soon and she would have heavy winter heating bills to pay. And she would still be able to do her astrology work . . .

'Who would look after my cat?' she said, stalling for time while she turned these thoughts over in her mind.

If Macy sensed her change of heart, he was far too astute to acknowledge it. He took a drink of beer. 'I would,' he said, surprising her. 'Claudius and I get on well. I'll go over to your flat and feed him if you give me instructions.'

Jo looked into his bland brown eyes. 'You and Claudius share the same level of low cunning,' she commented. 'And you both like your own way.' She swirled the beer in the bottom of her bottle. 'All right. I'll do it. When can I meet her? I've got to get more out of her than she's said so far. We don't even know why she feels threatened or if she suspects anyone.'

'I asked her, but she didn't give me a straight answer to either question. But you could make that a condition of taking on the case.'

'So you didn't accept it?'

Macy lifted his hands, miming his innocence. 'I told you I didn't. I said you would go and see her if you were interested. She works in Warwick.' He handed over an address written on a Post-It.

'Callendar Export Associates, Church Street, Warwick.' Jo stuck the note to the inside flap of her handbag. 'Will I be expected to protect her? I mean, would I be liable if anything happened to her?'

Macy considered this. 'Well, *I* might be liable, but I don't think you would be. I'll ask Julian to look at that. Maybe he can add something to the standard contract.' Julian Black was a local solicitor, for whom Macy did a lot of work. 'When you see Ms Carlyle and you've agreed what you're going to do, ask her to pop into the office to sign the contract.'

Jo agreed absently. Throughout the conversation, she had been thinking how stupid it was that she fancied Macy and he almost certainly fancied her but neither of them would do anything about it. For fear of rejection, she supposed, or — worse still — fear of getting too involved. Weighing up the odds, she decided that she must judge her moment and take a risk.

CHAPTER THREE

'Is that Antonia? It's Jo Hughes here. I understand you've got another job for me?' Jo didn't know how to describe it — minder or bodyguard sounded ridiculous. She wasn't cut out for either. She was tall but not heavy and only knew the rudiments of self-defence. Being independent by nature and the youngest in her family, she didn't see herself in the role of a protector. Obviously Antonia did.

'That's right.' Her voice sounded rushed and pleased over the phone. 'Nothing to do with astrology this time. I hope you don't mind me going to see your boss at the agency. I could have come straight to you but it seemed better to get things on a proper footing. I wouldn't want you doing anything as a favour . . .' She paused. 'It seemed a brilliant idea at the time.'

'I don't mind about that, but I'm not entirely sure what you want. Could we meet and talk about it before I say yes?'

'Of course,' Antonia said, her voice slowing a little. 'You wouldn't want to put yourself in danger at all.'

'That's right,' Jo agreed. 'Why don't I meet you at work when you finish?' she added, remembering what Macy had said about Antonia not feeling safe outside the office.

A sense of the other woman's relief came over the phone. 'That would be fine. I finish in an hour. I work at Callendar

Exports — did Mr Macy tell you? It's right by St Mary's Church in Warwick. Can you come back home with me and I'll cook something for us? You could stay tonight at least . . .'

Jo agreed, having half-expected this. She ended the call and shook her head at the ceiling. She had the feeling that Antonia was used to having her own way and, being a Gemini, she would be adept at getting it. She went into the bedroom and packed some overnight things into a holdall. Whether she stayed any longer than one night depended on Antonia's explanation, and she had promised to let Macy know her decision tomorrow. She stuffed a paperback into her bag, in case she couldn't sleep and, as an afterthought, added a packet of coffee. Antonia might only have decaffeinated or herbal tea. She looked the type.

She checked that Claudius had enough cat food and that the water heater was switched off and went down the fire escape to her car. It was a damp, cold evening — certain to be frosty later — and it took a couple of tries to get the old Renault started. Once the engine was turning, it took her twenty minutes to get to Warwick, driving fast, as she generally did.

Winding her way through the one-way system in the old town, Jo spotted Antonia's blue Mazda parked just off the road and pulled in beside it. She walked through a small garden into St Mary's churchyard with the rain misting her face and forming halos round the street lamps.

Jo knew Warwick reasonably well. Her first serious boyfriend had lived on the nearby council estate and she had spent many an adolescent Sunday mooching around the town centre. She had left for university promising to write and he had joined the Marines. They still sent exchanged Christmas cards. The town had not changed much in those eight years and remained a pleasant mishmash of old buildings with the impressive old church dominating the skyline.

Callendar Export Associates was distinguished by a discreet brass plaque on the plastered wall of a low house, which had a bare timber beam running across it. Jo pushed the doorbell. Nothing happened. She tried the front door and stepped into a narrow but well-lit hall. If it hadn't been for a side table stacked with leaflets about the firm and an official-looking calendar on the wall, she could have been in a private house.

A woman appeared from a door on the right. She was middle-aged and wearing a prissy matching cardigan and skirt. She held her spectacles in both hands and smiled warmly. 'Can I help you?'

'I've come to see Antonia Carlyle. She's expecting me.' Jo looked beyond the woman into the front room of the house, where she could see another woman hunched over a computer screen. The whirr of a photocopier could be heard in the background.

'Carry on along the corridor, turn right and sharp left. She's in the back room.'

Jo picked up a leaflet, from which she gleaned that the firm specialised in exporting antiques and other 'precious objects'. Following the directions as she read, she found her way to a cramped room. About six desks were squeezed into a narrow office. One or two people looked up when Jo came in. Most were packing up to go home.

'Over here, Jo!' Antonia's desk was in a quiet dark corner, surrounded by a clutter of computer hardware. 'I'll be two minutes, I've got to make sure this email goes today.' She finished typing, switched off her machine and packed all the items on her desk into a little tray. 'Now I just need to put these in my locker.' She disappeared through a door behind her desk.

Jo put her hands in her pockets and looked around, taking in the faded maps on the wall, the jumble of hardware, cables and files on cabinets and tables. Although the company had a prestigious location in what she assumed was a listed building, the interior of the office was dated and dusty and distinctly overcrowded. Jo felt glad she had left office life behind.

Two other office workers left together, calling good night and casting curious glances in Jo's direction. Jo smiled back at them and at anyone else who met her eye. One man, a white-haired, well-dressed, sun-tanned individual, gave her a quick smile back. He finished chatting to a younger man who was working at one of the PCs and came over to Jo.

'Hello — a stranger in the camp,' he said. She was aware of his very white, pleasant smile. 'How do you do? I'm Oliver. Are you a friend of Antonia's?' He held out a hand and gave hers a firm shake. Probably in his forties, he exuded an air of easy authority, but Jo knew it didn't necessarily follow that he was the boss. *Offices were a bit like the zodiac in that way*, she thought. *It was often not the showy, fire signs that had the most influence but the quieter ones ruled by the big, slow-moving planets.*

She introduced herself and explained she was waiting for Antonia. Eyeing him, she decided he must be a sunbed-basher with a tan like that. Or maybe a skier. He had the physique for it.

'Are you another IT geek like her?' Oliver folded his arms across his suit jacket as if he expected to chat for some time. He had a polished look about him. His hair — which was surely prematurely white — was sleek and well cut, his shoes were glossy and his hands and fingernails were scrupulously clean. 'Antonia is really rather good, you know. In the short time she's been here, she's revolutionised our reference system.'

'Everyone needs a good filing system,' Jo agreed, to keep the conversation going. She didn't want to turn away an opportunity to elicit information and hunted around for an intelligent question. 'What exactly do you export, by the way? Is it just antiques?'

'Mainly. As you probably know, Warwickshire and the Cotswolds are oozing with antiques shops and they provide the bulk of our business — but we take orders from all over the country.' He was regarding her with his head on one side. His eyes were so narrow, Jo could not make out what colour they were. 'Do you like precious objects?'

'I don't know much about them. I don't even watch *Antiques Roadshow*.'

He laughed and was about to say something else when Antonia reappeared, full of apologies for keeping Jo waiting. She paused momentarily when she saw who Jo was talking to. 'Can I do anything for you, Oliver?' she asked in a tone that managed to be both deferential and irritated.

'No, you go on home. I just stopped by to say hello to your friend.' Oliver began to move off then hesitated. 'Oh, Howard says his PC still isn't working properly—'

'I've promised to look at it tomorrow.' Antonia reached for her coat and handbag. 'See you then.'

'OK, fine.' Oliver grinned good-naturedly. As Antonia headed for the exit, he glanced at her straight-backed figure and flashed a telling look at Jo as if to say, *You know what she's like.*

Jo smiled back although, of course, she had not much idea. She followed Antonia through the warren of narrow corridors to the thick wooden front door.

'Is that your boss?' Jo asked. 'You don't seem to like him much.'

'Is it that obvious?' Antonia hesitated on the doorstep and glanced up and down the street before following Jo into the misty rain.

'Just an impression I got,' Jo said.

Antonia twitched her shoulders and plucked up the collar of her short swing raincoat. Jo turned into the churchyard, and she hesitated again. 'I don't usually go that way.'

'It's OK. It's reasonably well lit — and quicker.' Jo led the way along the path beside the graves with the other woman sticking to her side like glue. 'I've parked beside you. I recognised your car.'

'If you take the job, you can have the use of it during the day as long as you bring me to work and pick me up in the evenings,' Antonia said.

'Sounds like it's a chauffeur you want.' Jo kept her voice light but she couldn't help catching some of Antonia's nervousness and she found herself peering into the darkness as they crossed the unlit garden behind the churchyard. As they passed through the gateway and came under the white light of a street lamp, Jo saw Antonia's set chin and tense shoulders and guessed how she had steeled herself to take the shortcut.

'Do you think you will take the job?' Antonia asked in an overly casual tone.

'Not until you tell me the full story,' Jo said. 'There is a story to tell, isn't there?'

'Oh, yes. I'll cook something to eat and I'll tell you everything I can think of. It beats the soaps any day. I bought some pasta at lunchtime. Pasta's OK, isn't it?'

'Fine. I'll follow you to Ashow, then.' Jo went to her car.

She followed the tail lights of the Mazda, thinking about Antonia. Certainly she was frightened of something. The question was, did she have good reason?

CHAPTER FOUR

On a B road somewhere between Warwick and Coventry, Antonia took a sharp right and Jo followed her down a hill into the small village of Ashow. Jo had an impression of brick cottages close to the road and the lighted drives of grander residences. Antonia's place fitted neither category. She turned up a dark track, which zigzagged through trees and came out onto a patch of gravel in front of a cottage. The headlights picked out its whitewashed walls.

Stepping out of the car, Jo noticed the unfamiliar quietness. All she could hear was the drip of saturated greenery and trees rustling somewhere above. 'This is in the middle of nowhere, isn't it?' she commented. The cottage stood on its own. Its dim porch light was the only sign of life.

'Not really. Betty's house is just through those trees.' Antonia hauled two carrier bags out of her boot and locked the car. There was no gate to the cottage but an uneven path led between two small lawns up to the wooden porch. Jo waited while Antonia opened the door, thinking that this was not the best place to live for someone as nervous as she was.

'I know what you're thinking, but it's not the cottage that bothers me,' Antonia said over her shoulder. But Jo noticed her quick glances around her as she went ahead switching on lights. She didn't argue, reserving her judgement until she heard whatever it was Antonia had to tell her.

There was no hall. After the tiny damp-smelling porch, where Antonia picked up her mail, the front door opened straight into a sitting room that was surprisingly warm and cheerful. There were two sofas, both covered with various throws and cushions in terracotta or gold or tangerine. Rugs in similar bold colours decorated the plain carpet and the furniture looked old and well used but of good quality.

A large, vocal tabby cat ran up to Antonia, following her into the kitchen and winding itself around her legs. She bent down to make a fuss of it. 'This is Wilf. Brother to Dylan. I've not let him out since Dylan died and it's driving him mad. But I'm afraid in case the same thing happens to him.'

'Did you ask your neighbours if they had any idea what could have killed Dylan?'

Antonia began to unpack her shopping. 'Yes. Betty was horrified. As I expected, she would never put anything on the garden that was dangerous to cats as she's got four of her own. Plus two dogs and a goat, incidentally. Anyway, she's an organic gardener.'

'That puts her on the side of the angels, then.' Jo found herself a stool to sit on. 'What about the farmer? Was he using any pesticides?'

'I'm not so sure about him,' Antonia admitted. 'He got ratty when I asked him. The two nearest fields are pasture and he swears he doesn't put anything on them. It would upset his sheep, he said. He does spray his crops with all sorts of chemicals but those fields are much further away and I think Dylan would have had enough sense to stay out of a crop field. His nose would have told him it wasn't safe.'

Jo was not convinced but decided to keep this to herself. Maybe she could find out more tomorrow. *If* she took the job.

'Come on, I'll show you your room,' Antonia said, ignoring another loud wail from Wilf. She went to a latched door, which hid the staircase. The stairs creaked and twisted up to a narrow landing, off which were three doors. The front bedroom was Antonia's, a richly overdressed room, with frills on all the furnishings and a pile of lace cushions on the bed. A laptop with a blank screen sat incongruously on a chintz-covered table. Another door led to a tiny, basic bathroom and the third was the other bedroom. It was not as big as Antonia's and was simply furnished, which was more to Jo's taste. But it had dual-aspect windows, and there was an attractive double pedestal dressing table in one corner and a free-standing full-length mirror beside it.

'They were both my mother's,' Antonia said when Jo admired them. 'And the mahogany blanket box was her hope chest. I've managed to keep some of her things.'

Left to herself, Jo decided she liked the room and began to feel it wouldn't be so bad to stay here for a short while. Antonia — when not being paranoid — was congenial company. She put down her holdall and drew the curtains on all three small windows, stopping at the last one near her bed. She put her hands to the glass, blocking out the room light to see the river.

Through streaks of rain, she made out gently sloping fields and a band of trees that indicated the course of the Avon. Midway between the cottage and the river there was the dark line of a hedgerow. With the lighted room behind her, Jo felt strangely exposed, although her room was not overlooked and there didn't seem to be another building in sight.

She crossed the room to switch the light out and went back to the window. She swung it open in and leaned out, her palms on the wet sill. Her attention sharpened partly due to Antonia's nervousness, she peered out to see if there was any reason to feel uneasy. She still couldn't make out the river, although she could follow the line of it more clearly. Closer to the cottage, the hedgerow hid a lane and one part of the hedge looked denser, as if there was a shed or hen house behind it.

The night was chill and fresh. The gutter dripped from somewhere above her head. Shivering, she closed the window, drew the curtain and sat down on the bed. She told herself she was letting Antonia get to her. Searching through her holdall, she found a comb to tidy her curly hair and reapplied some lipstick and perfume. This was as close as she was came to dressing for dinner.

Antonia was frying onions, mince and tomatoes when Jo went back downstairs. Wilf was eating his dinner but he broke off to greet her by rubbing his face against her jeans, marking her out with his scent.

Jo reached down to pull his ears gently. 'Why did you give your cats Welsh names?'

'Because they're Welsh. I bought them from a lady who breeds Maine Coons in Pembroke.'

'I've got relatives in Wales. In fact, my father's Welsh–Italian,' Jo said. 'My grandmother still runs a little Italian café near Swansea.'

'Oh my God, you're part Italian and here am I cooking pasta for you!' Antonia grinned. 'I hope it's good enough. This'll help . . .' She tipped a liberal amount of red wine into the pan. 'Shall we drink the rest of it?'

'Fine.' Jo found two glasses and poured out the Chianti. 'So it's not living in the back of beyond that worries you,' she prompted, eager to hear why she was being offered this job.

'No, I used to live in the country when I was little. We lived near Canterbury and our house was on the edge of a village, like this one. I'm used to the quiet. Does it bother you?'

'Not really. Though I suppose I'm a bit of a townie,' Jo admitted. 'It must be a change for you too after London.'

Antonia added pasta to a pan of boiling water and clouds of steam hid her face. 'That was just a brief interlude, when I was married to Guy. We lived for a couple of years in Hendon when we both worked in London.'

'I'm interested in Guy. Could he have anything to do with your current problems?'

'No, he's not doing these things to me.' Antonia seemed certain.

'Why not? I mean, you left him, didn't you? Maybe he wants to get back at you?' Jo was guessing, trying to draw the woman out. It worked.

'Yes, I left him,' Antonia said with a hesitation in her voice. 'I suppose some wives would have stuck by him but — well, I'm not the type.' She glanced up. 'Anyway I don't want to talk about Guy. He's nothing to do with what's happening here, honestly.'

'All right,' Jo said. 'But just tell me, where is he now? What's he doing?'

'Probably drinking his way out of this world. It looked like it last time I saw him.'

'Which was?' Jo persevered despite the other woman's reluctance. She had already decided to make some enquiries of her own about Guy and the more she knew about him the better.

'Almost two years ago. He came into my office and made a scene. Shortly afterwards they offered me redundancy. I don't know if that was a coincidence but I was glad to leave. Anyway, it's all rather sordid and I'd like to draw a veil if you don't mind.' Antonia left the cooking and turned to Jo, her elfin face flushed from the heat of the stove. 'I must tell you about these awful things that have been happening to me lately.'

'Go on then,' Jo said, ready to enjoy this. Her host was a good talker once she got going.

'All right.' Antonia pulled up a stool for herself and took a gulp of wine. 'Well, I've lived here a year and nothing happened until about six weeks ago. I started getting funny phone calls—'

'Obscene calls?' Jo was all attention. At last, it seemed, she was getting to the heart of the matter. 'A man's voice?'

'Isn't it always?' Antonia sighed wearily. 'Some awful heavy breather saying he wanted to get into my knickers. That sort of thing. I took advice from the phone company and kept a whistle by the phone. I used it once or twice and never heard from him again. But it rattled me. And then I read about those sex attacks around here . . .'

Jo dug out a notebook from her handbag. She had learned from her days as a PI that it was useful to take notes if she wanted to remember details. And at this stage, it was impossible to know which detail was important. 'How many calls did you get? Was there any sort of pattern?'

Antonia raised her well-defined brows. 'Well, get you! I admit I'd not thought about that before. But I used to get a call about every other night and usually quite late — after ten, anyway. This went on for two weeks.'

'What next?'

'Well, as I told your boss, my work bag went missing. It's a typical sort of black, boring briefcase-type-thing and it disappeared from my car one night. I mean, who would come all the way up to this place and then just steal a briefcase? Why not take the car? That's what your average criminal would have done.'

'Maybe they thought it had a laptop in it?' Jo said. 'Did you report it to the police?'

'No, I never keep my laptop in the car. Due to years of having that drilled into me. So I thought the police wouldn't be interested because there was nothing of value taken. And anyway, it turned up a week later in the cottage.' She pointed to the worktop Jo was leaning on. 'It was sitting on there, unlocked, but the papers were exactly as I'd left them.'

'It turned up here?' Jo tried to keep the scepticism out of her voice. 'Are you sure you couldn't have just left it there yourself and forgotten about it?'

Antonia gave an exasperated sigh. 'Absolutely not. It was staring me in the face. I'm sure it was left there to taunt me.'

'OK. What was in it when it was stolen?'

'Just papers from work. My contract, a strategy document, a list of rates. The usual sort of stuff you print out. Like I said, nothing important. And when I got it back, they were all there — apparently untouched. Anyway, that's not the only thing. The next time someone broke into my car, nothing was stolen, and I often think someone gets into the cottage while I'm out. Things move around. My cyclamen plant was moved from the windowsill to the dresser. A whole pile of magazines I'd left in my bedroom were put on the floor in there—' she indicated the front room — 'and there are strange smells.'

'Smells?' This story was becoming less credible by the minute.

'Yes. I know this sounds really weird but twice in the last month the cottage stank when I came in at night. It smelled like rotten meat.' She wrinkled her nose at the memory and then went on, speaking rapidly as usual. 'The last time it happened, I found a dead rabbit on the doorstep. The first time I couldn't find any reason at all.'

'A cat could have left the rabbit there,' Jo pointed out. 'You said there were four next door as well as yours.'

Antonia was shaking her head. 'Then there was poor old Dylan,' she continued. 'That was the worst yet. It convinced me someone was out to frighten me into leaving.' She paused to taste the sauce. 'This is ready. Shall we eat?'

The quick change of subject was typical of a Gemini, Jo reflected, as she laid places for the two of them on a highly polished table in the next room.

The pasta was delicious and Jo enjoyed a few mouthfuls before asking her next question. 'Do you have any idea who would want to upset you, and why?'

'Yes,' Antonia answered. 'The man who killed my sister.'

At that moment, all the lights went out.

CHAPTER FIVE

'Don't worry. This happens all the time.' Antonia's voice was surprisingly calm. 'It's a fuse. No need to panic.'

Jo was a long way from panicking but she did feel slightly unnerved. Thick curtains pulled across the small windows made the room very dark and it was a while before she could make anything out. She heard Antonia get up from the table and go to the nearby dresser.

'I've got a torch and some candles here for just this eventuality.' Antonia's voice sounded strangely disembodied. 'The trouble is this place needs rewiring.' A drawer opened and shut and a torch clicked on, the beam glinting on a brass candleholder.

'What kind of fuse box is it?' Jo got to her feet. 'I might be able to fix it.'

'No, it's ancient. You won't be able to.' Antonia struck a match and lit two candles. 'It's one of those that are positively dangerous if you don't know what you're doing.' Concentric circles of torchlight bobbed across the room as she moved towards the sofa. 'I'll call Paul. He always comes to my rescue on these occasions. He used to be an electrician.'

'I could have a go at least.' Jo picked up the candleholder and looked around in the flickering darkness. 'Where is it?'

The torchlight jiggled on the wallpaper while Antonia's painted fingernail tapped the buttons on her phone. 'It's OK, honestly. Paul knows what to do. I'm only sorry this interrupted our dinner—' She broke off as the call connected.

Jo, seeing she was not going to be allowed to practise her basic electrical skills, sat down again and resumed her meal. Across the room, Antonia was speaking briskly and matter-of-factly into the phone, apparently confident that this man would come to her aid. And it seemed she was right.

'Paul will be along as soon as he can,' she announced, returning to the table. 'He's a taxi driver but I called him on his mobile. He says he's just got to drop off his fare in Leamington first.'

'That's nice of him.' Jo was more interested in Antonia's dramatic declaration before the lights went out. 'What were you saying? Your sister was murdered?'

The deep shadows thrown by the candlelight gave Antonia a scheming look. 'She was. A man killed her almost five years ago and I've been looking for him ever since. I've finally found him and now he's harassing me.'

'I know from your birth chart that you're tenacious and determined, but I said it could lead to problems,' Jo reminded her. 'You'd better explain from the start. First, tell me what happened to your sister.'

'Yes, of course.' Antonia nodded, her silhouette bobbing on the wall. 'I must tell you about my family. My mother was French, my father English. He worked for an oil company and they lived near Paris when they were first married. My elder sister, Monique, was born there.'

'What date?' Knowing the store Geminis set on family ties, Jo was not surprised that Antonia wanted to tell her the whole family history, but she was determined to find out the important astrological facts as well.

'The sixth of July — I have all the family birth dates written down somewhere. I will dig them out for you. My parents moved to Kent when I was born. I loved that house. . .' Antonia sighed nostalgically and paused for a sip of wine. 'When I was six, my father died. My mother couldn't really cope without him and she died a couple of years later. Monique was eighteen and just about to go to university, but she gave it up and stayed at home.'

'Couldn't a relative have looked after you?'

'We did stay with an aunt in Ashford for a while but we couldn't wait to get home. Instead of university, Monique qualified as a librarian and worked nearby.' Antonia set down her empty wine glass, which she had been playing with as she spoke. 'Would you like coffee? I can make it on the gas hob.'

Jo accepted and followed her into the kitchen, carrying her phone as a torch. She put it on the windowsill and ran the water to wash up. 'So what went wrong?'

'Nothing for years. I went to university in London and came home most weekends. When I got a job as a computer programmer, I commuted from Kent, so Monique and I stayed in our house. We were very close.' Antonia dried dishes half-heartedly, while keeping an eye on the coffee pot. 'Then about five years ago, it dawned on me that she had a boyfriend. She'd hardly ever been out with anyone. She was quiet and shy with men but I knew she had romantic dreams that some wonderful man would come along one day. Anyway, she had decided to join an online dating site and asked my advice about it sometimes. I didn't think she was having much success with it, then I gradually noticed John's name cropping up in conversations.'

'Cancerians play their cards close to their chests. Especially when it's something they care about,' Jo commented.

'Very true. Anyway, I'd started seeing Guy, so I was spending less time at home. Once or twice, I'd come home after ten at night and Monique would still be out. This was unheard of—' Antonia laughed — 'so I had to ask her what was going on. It turned out this man had been in touch and they had been going to auctions together. John Brooke was an antiques dealer and Monique loved antiques, so they had something in common from the start.'

They carried their coffee and a candle into the front room and spread out on a sofa each. 'Once she'd started talking about him, she couldn't stop. She showed all the signs of being in love. He sounded interesting, caring and considerate. The only trouble was, he wasn't around a lot of the time because of his job. Weeks would go by with Monique moping around the house and living for emails and messages. Then when she got a text from him, she'd be in seventh heaven for a bit. It was months before I finally met him.'

Antonia's triangular face was almost hidden in the shadows but Jo could see her slim fingers tugging rhythmically at the tassels on a cushion. 'By then, I'd begun to imagine he must be really old or incredibly ugly,' she went on, 'but in fact he was quite personable. In his forties — just a touch older than her, and a bit flash and cocky, I thought. Not the type I'd have thought Monique would go for, but she seemed utterly happy. He told her his dream was to own an antique shop. She had always wanted to travel — especially to India — and I gathered they started making long-term plans. I wasn't too surprised when they got engaged. But I'd still only met him once.' Antonia came to a halt.

'How long had they been seeing each other?' Jo asked. Wilf had settled himself against her legs and she had been stroking his glossy coat and listening carefully, not wanting to interrupt the flow.

'Six months.' Antonia sighed sadly, making the candles flicker. 'I hadn't realised how much Monique wanted to get married. She had all these plans for what the bridesmaids would wear and how she was going to make the cake herself . . .'

'I feel I'm getting to understand your sister a tiny bit,' Jo said when Antonia paused again. 'Monique seems typically Cancerian with her devotion to home and duty and her secret romantic longings.'

'Yes, that's right. But it all ended in tears. John never showed up again. She'd booked the church, she had the tickets to India on her dressing table and the wedding dress hanging up in her wardrobe. But there were no more postcards or messages. The number he'd given her became unobtainable — he disappeared off the face of the earth.'

'And Monique?'

'I came home from work one night and she wasn't in. I thought this was strange because, although she'd seemed to be getting over John and was going out on her own more, she was usually in when I came home. I waited and waited for her, like an idiot. I even talked to Guy for about half an hour and it was getting dark before I looked in the garage.' Antonia lowered her head. 'There she was, in her car with the engine still running.'

'Oh my God, how awful.' Jo bit her lip, seeing the scene vividly in her mind. 'So this John Brooke drove her to suicide—'

'No! He actually killed her.' Antonia's stern expression and flashing eyes held no shadow of doubt.

'What makes you say that? I thought he'd done a runner?'

'He must have come back and she didn't tell me. Somehow, he shut her in the garage and left the engine on.'

'But was the garage locked?'

'No. Unlocked. Obviously, he came back later and unlocked it.'

Jo shook her head. 'Too risky. No one would do that. He would have had to wait — I don't know — an hour or so and then come back to the scene of the crime.'

'You haven't seen the house,' Antonia insisted. 'It really *is* in the middle of nowhere. Honestly, the nearest civilisation is a quarter of a mile away. Anyway, while that pig Brooke was waiting, he burned everything she had of him — any pictures, letters, everything on a bonfire in the garden.' Antonia was breathing quickly and gripping the edge of the cushion. 'He killed her because he was afraid she would find out who he really was.'

Jo suspended her disbelief temporarily. 'OK, what did the police say about it?'

'They were marvellous straight after I found her, looked after me and just dealt with everything. But—' Antonia gave Jo a sudden fierce look, her hazel eyes picking up the candlelight — 'they insisted it was suicide. So did the coroner. And I'm telling you, it wasn't. They ignored all the evidence.'

'What evidence?'

Antonia leaned forward, ticking things off on her fingers as she spoke. 'First, there was no suicide note.'

'Yes, that's important,' Jo conceded.

'Second, there was alcohol on her breath. I noticed it when they brought her out of the garage and the post-mortem confirmed she'd been drinking. But Monique didn't drink much so it was easy to get her drunk. That's what Brooke must have done. Third, there was a bruise on her forehead.' She drew her fingers in a band across her own forehead. 'And she wasn't sitting the right way. Monique was shorter than me and always had the driver's seat really close to the steering wheel but it was pushed right back. She had her legs out of the car and the door open as if she was getting out.'

'What did they make of all these things at the inquest?'

'Oh, the police had good answers for everything. They said the effect of carbon monoxide impairs the judgement and she must have been confused. It also makes you dizzy, so they said she had knocked herself out. They didn't listen to me when I said Brooke got her drunk and then pushed her head against the wheel.'

'Had anyone seen Brooke around?' Jo interrupted.

Antonia sighed, flopping back onto the sofa cushions. 'No. I couldn't find anyone who'd seen him. Monique kept him very much to herself, even when they were going out together, so hardly anyone even knew about him.' She looked across at Jo. 'And at the inquest, the coroner made a lot of the fact that Monique had been taking tablets for depression. They even said *she'd* made the bonfire of all Brooke's things — and that she'd been trying to drown her sorrows . . .' Her voice trailed off tearfully.

'What a terrible thing to happen,' Jo said. 'I don't know how you got through it.'

'I just know she wouldn't have killed herself. Anyway, you don't know the half of it yet. When Monique died, I found out how much money she had given John Brooke. He must have spun some stories about this antique shop they were going to run together, because she had gone through all the savings in our joint account, including the money our parents left us. She had re-mortgaged the house and couldn't afford to pay it off out of her wages. On top of that, there were piles of credit card bills.'

'What did you do?'

'The house was repossessed and I had to sell most of the furniture. I moved to London, married Guy and gradually paid off the debts — with no help from him, I can tell you.' Antonia became more animated again. 'But I couldn't let it rest there, could I? I had to try and find him. I asked everyone who knew her if they could tell me John's address, or anything about him. I told the police what had happened to see if they could trace him. They made some attempt because of the debts he'd left but they didn't find him.' Antonia sat back against the sofa, tipping her head back as her words tailed off. When Jo remained silent, she resumed her thread, her voice tired but determined. 'It was years before I made any progress. For a while, I tried to forget all about it. Guy used to say it was making me ill. Then, just over a year ago, I went back to Kent to see some old friends and one of them told me he'd heard John Brooke's name mentioned at an auction.'

'Did he see him there?'

'No, but he knew John and Monique used to go to auctions together and he knew I was looking for Brooke. The auction was in Worcester but Hugh — that's my friend from Kent — went to the trouble of finding out where Brooke was having his purchases delivered. It was an address in Warwick.' Her eyes glittered with excitement. 'So I came here looking for him and, believe it or not, after a month or so, I found him—'

There was a firm knock at the front door and Antonia got up to open it. 'That will be Paul. We should have lights again in a minute.'

The interruption gave Jo time to think. She had little doubt that this quest for the sister's ex-fiancé was a bad idea — and not just because the horoscope had said so. She also felt, however, that having spent five years trying to trace this man, Antonia would not give up just on Jo's advice as an astrologer, or a PI, or even as a friend. A subtler approach might be required.

'What's happened now? Which fuse is it this time?' A man's voice, loud and jovial, drifted through to Jo. Paul, wiping his feet in the porch, sounded heavy and clumsy. 'I've told you this place gets more like *The Amityville Horror* every day. It needs rewiring.'

'I've told the landlady. You don't expect me to pay for it myself, I hope,' Antonia retorted spiritedly.

The man's presence was preceded by a strong waft of scent. It smelled like he'd been bathing in aftershave. 'I don't care who pays, but if you don't get it fixed there's going to be a nasty—' He stopped short as he came into the room and looked abashed when he saw Jo. 'Oh, excuse me, I didn't know you had visitors, Toni.'

Antonia stepped forward and picked up one of the candle-holders. 'This is Jo Hughes. She's thinking of taking the spare room and she's just come round to have a look at the cottage.' She moved the candle from Jo to the newcomer. 'Jo, this is Paul Bakewell, who comes to my rescue on a regular basis.'

Paul held out his hand a little awkwardly. 'Pleased to meet you, Jo. Any friend of Toni's — you know . . .' He had a soft handshake and a shy grin half-hidden by his beard. He was a bulky man, tall and well-rounded all over, especially the stomach.

'I'd have had a go at the fuse myself but Antonia wasn't keen,' Jo explained, wanting to dispel any idea that she was incapable of dealing with such problems.

'We'll soon have a bit of light on the situation, anyway,' Paul said. 'I've brought my bag of tricks.' He indicated his toolbox and strode into the kitchen. 'Downstairs lights this time, then?'

'Apparently,' Antonia answered, following him.

Jo stayed where she was, playing idly with one of the candles. From the kitchen she heard Antonia sneeze and blame it on Paul's aftershave. He made some comment and they both laughed. They seemed like old friends. In a few minutes, the lights came on and Antonia cried out, 'Bravo! You deserve a cup of tea for that.'

'Don't mind if I do.' Paul returned to the front room with a satisfied air. 'Then I'll have to be going. I've got to pick up a fare from Warwick station at ten.' He glanced at his watch and sat down on the sofa opposite Jo.

'You'll have to show me how to fix the fuse now the lights are on,' Jo suggested.

'No need,' he grinned. 'Just get on the blower and I'll come over.'

'No, we can't do that every time,' Jo protested. 'If I'm going to live here, I need to know how to mend it myself.' But Paul wouldn't hear of it, so Jo decided to have a look at the fuse box herself tomorrow and left it at that.

'What do you think of the haunted house, then?' he asked. She wasn't sure if he was joking.

'I like it, I've always lived in the town, so this would be a pleasant change.'

Paul sighed, looking round the room and shaking his head. 'Place is falling down, if you ask me. The landlady ought to be embarrassed to charge the rent she does. I worry about her living here,' he added protectively, nodding towards Antonia as she came into the room carrying a tea tray.

'That's why I want a lodger,' she said. She turned to Jo, 'I've made us some herbal tea. It'll help us sleep.'

Jo would have preferred more coffee but she took the cup and saucer, privately congratulating herself on guessing rightly that Antonia was a herbal tea drinker.

'What do you do for your living then, Jo?' Paul stirred sugar into his tea vigorously.

Jo explained she was an astrologer and he looked interested. His eyes were blue and almost lashless. His hair and beard were interspersed with grey and Jo guessed he was maybe in his early forties. 'That could come in handy,' he said cheerily. 'You might be able to tell Toni why she seems to be going through this unlucky patch.'

'I'd like to have a go,' Jo agreed. She noted that Paul Bakewell seemed to know about the various mishaps that had befallen Antonia and yet she clearly didn't want him to know the real reason for Jo's visit. Jo was happy to go along with this minor deception. In fact, she applauded it. 'I'm hoping to work on my astrology in peace and quiet here,' she went on honestly, 'while Antonia's at work.'

'From what she tells me, this might not be the best place for that,' Paul said, with a knowing look at Antonia. He drained his cup and checked his watch again. 'I'll have to love you and leave you now. Don't forget Saturday, will you, Toni? Rachel told me to remind you.'

As she saw him out, Antonia assured him she would come. They chatted for a while in the porch. When she closed the front door and turned to Jo, she was yawning. 'I must go to bed. I told you that herbal tea makes you sleepy.'

It hadn't had any noticeable effect on Jo, who was used to going to bed much later. She was content to go up and read her book for an hour or so — but not until she had got some more information out of Antonia. 'You were at a crucial point in your story. How did you find John Brooke?'

Antonia gave a quick, self-satisfied smile. 'Not only did I find him, I managed to get a job working for him.'

'You mean he's the man I met? Oliver Sargent?' Jo exclaimed, remembering Antonia's cool manner towards her boss. 'But why don't you go straight to the police? Even if they don't believe he killed your sister, there was all that money he conned out of her—'

'I told the police down in Kent, but they obviously think I'm batty.'

'Well, we'll try again with the police here,' Jo said. 'You'll have to tell them about these odd things that have been happening as well.'

'There's no point.' Antonia started to rinse the cups and tidy up, indicating that the evening of confidences was coming to an end. Jo decided to content herself with asking how Antonia had managed to trace Sargent.

'It so happened that shortly after I found out John Brooke might be in the Warwick area, I was made redundant. That was one of the things that spurred me on. Guy and I had split up and I had nothing to keep me in London, so I came here. At first I stayed in a bed and breakfast near the racecourse and spent my days going round the antique shops looking out for Brooke. Then the landlady told me she also lets this cottage, and I really liked it. Still do. It took another month or so to find Brooke and then it was purely by chance that I recognised him in a restaurant. I found out he needed an IT expert and applied for the job.'

'Weren't you worried he would recognise you?'

'He'd only met me once, and that was five years ago. Since then, I've changed my name and grown my hair long, so I was pretty sure.' She hesitated. 'At least, I was almost certain he doesn't know I'm Monique's sister. But now Dylan's been killed and the place has been broken into and it's too much of a coincidence . . .' She looked at Jo with pleading eyes. 'I'll go bananas if you don't help me out, Jo. You and Paul are the only people I can count as my friends.'

Jo found Antonia's story hard to believe but decided this was not the time to say so. 'I'll see what I can do.'

'Paul's nice, isn't he? A bit under the thumb, though. Rachel, his wife, is really fierce. They've invited me over for the day on Saturday, as you heard.' She finished on another yawn.

'I have to tell my boss tomorrow whether or not I'll take the job,' Jo said, not willing to change the subject. 'It's difficult to say yes or no until I've heard the whole story. Have I?'

Antonia stacked the crockery in the kitchen cupboards, closely followed around by Wilf, who was after more food. 'Pretty well. You understand why I'm nervous now? I hate being on my own with Oliver with the doubts going around in my head. What if he's found out about me and wants to get rid of me, like he did Monique?' She turned to look at Jo. 'You will help, won't you?'

'I'll sleep on it. Is that OK? I'll tell you tomorrow,' Jo promised. 'One other thing,' she added, while she thought of it, 'who has keys to this place apart from you?'

'No one. Apart from the landlady, Mrs Pumfrey. There's a spare one for you in the dresser. Will you come with me to work tomorrow?'

'Of course.'

They parted on the landing. Jo went to her room, still replaying everything Antonia had told her. She knew she must try to persuade Antonia to give up this crusade on behalf of her sister.

Feeling wide awake, she went to the window before settling down to her book. The view was the same as before: dark, rainswept fields leading to a hedge and beyond that, the river. But something struck her as different. She stared at the hedgerow. Earlier she had noticed a denser patch of shadow in the line it followed. Now it had gone. She wondered if it could have been a car with its lights out. Although there might be many good reasons for a car to have been parked there, the idea occurred to Jo that someone had been sitting in it, looking up at the cottage.

CHAPTER SIX

Jo had never been a very good sleeper and after going to bed early she woke up at three fifteen feeling like she had slept all night. She knew if she switched on the light and started reading she would be awake for hours, so she lay with her eyes closed and tried to will herself back to sleep. She might have succeeded if she hadn't heard the scrunch of gravel outside.

Remembering her earlier feeling of being watched, she lifted her head and listened. She thought she made out another footstep, again from the front of the cottage, but more muffled this time. Disentangling herself from the sheets, she went to the window that overlooked the drive.

She moved the lace curtain aside slightly and saw the short, square lawns, weakly lit by the porch light, the two cars parked side by side on the pale gravel and the dark shrubbery behind them. Everything looked as it should. There was no movement except the tops of the trees rippling against the city-tinted horizon. The bushes around the drive, where the shadows were most dense, would be the obvious place for someone who wanted to stay out of sight. Still nothing moved.

She pulled a jumper over her head and waited, straining her eyes. One part of her mind told her to go back to bed. If she was going to do this job, it would be no use her becoming as neurotic as Antonia. She sighed and changed position, lifting the curtain a little higher to see the far side of the drive. A shadow stepped quickly back into the bushes.

She let the curtain fall and struggled into her jeans. She pulled on her boots, jerking the laces together, and ran downstairs, the carpet muffling her steps. She remembered where Antonia had left the torch and snatched it up, together with her own keys from her handbag, which she bunched in her hand, the shafts sticking through her fingers. She knew that as soon as she stepped into the lighted porch, she would be visible to anyone outside but to switch off the light would alert them even sooner.

Outside, she stood for a moment staring at the spot where she had seen someone move. The shadows were still. She started to walk over there, directing the torch beam at the bushes and straining for any sound. At her third step, a car started up in the drive.

She turned and ran towards it. Tyres scrunched on stones as it pulled away ahead of her and out of sight. It had to go slowly because of the bends in the drive and she kept on running. Even so, she had no chance of catching up with it and as she panted round the last bend, she saw the tail lights turn left. She ran to the end of the drive and stood, holding her stomach and staring uselessly at the empty lane.

Jo walked slowly back to the cottage, still clutching her keys, although it seemed fairly certain the intruder had gone. Flicking the torch beam around, she noticed a passing place on the drive where the car had been parked. There were deep tyre marks in the gravel where it had pulled off at speed.

There was no sign of Antonia when she let herself back into the cottage. Jo imagined she must have slept through the whole thing but paused at the door of her room and peered in just to make sure. By the time Jo was lying shivering in her own bed, she had developed a plausible theory about the intruder, which she decided to put to Antonia the next day.

* * *

It was not until they were on their way to Antonia's office that Jo felt sufficiently awake to broach the subject of the prowler. She had fallen into a deep sleep at about half past five, only to be awoken by Antonia's alarm at seven o'clock. She sat blearily through breakfast, grateful that Antonia was not so lively first thing in the morning. It was a definite point in her favour that she ate her muesli in silence, engrossed in the news sites on her phone, because Jo was incapable of being sociable until she had consumed her third coffee.

As Antonia drove to Warwick they chatted about the weather and the traffic, and Antonia asked if Jo had slept well.

Jo took the opportunity to expound her new theory. 'Not really. I heard someone outside in the small hours. Did you hear anything?'

'No. Not a thing. What was it?'

'I thought someone was hiding in the bushes but they got in their car and drove off when I got outside. I saw the car turn out of the drive—'

'There was a car on my drive?' Antonia sounded alarmed.

'Yes. I've no idea what kind — except it was a biggish saloon. I only saw its lights, but I'm pretty sure the driver was prowling around at the front of the cottage,' Jo said matter-of-factly. 'Do you think it could have been your friend the taxi driver?'

'Paul? What makes you think that?' Antonia kept her eyes on the road.

'Well, he'd still have been working then, I suppose. I just thought maybe he'd come back to see you and when he saw my car was still there, he gave up.' Jo paused and Antonia said nothing. 'You weren't expecting him, then?' she added.

'You think Paul and I are having an affair?' Antonia asked. When Jo did not answer straight away, she went on, her voice rising, 'Well, I can disabuse you of that idea. He's married, for heaven's sake. And his wife is a friend of mine.'

There was a toot from the car behind. They had waited too long at a roundabout. She negotiated it in silence and then added in aggrieved tones, 'How could you think such things about me?'

'I don't know you very well,' Jo pointed out. 'And the fact that he's married wouldn't make much difference to a lot of people—'

'Well, it does to me!'

Jo was not perturbed by the other woman's reaction, although she was mildly annoyed with herself for falling out with a would-be client. Anything she said at the moment might make matters worse, so she kept quiet until they reached the office.

'Do you still want me to meet you this evening?'

'Of course.' Antonia sounded surprised but still cool. 'I'll see you here at five.' She walked briskly through the low front door without a backward glance. Jo got into the driver's seat, shaking her head over Antonia's outrage. She seemed unusually volatile, even for a Gemini.

When she had woken up that morning, she had decided to take on the case. There was the possibility that Antonia's story about her sister wasn't entirely true and the strange things that had happened to her could be coincidental or invented by an overactive imagination. But the intruder had been real enough and the sight of the car turning out of the drive had made up her mind to try to find out what was going on.

She drove back to her flat to feed Claudius and pack sufficient clothes for a week or so. Then she made herself a cup of coffee and took up her phone. Settling down on the wicker chair, she rang Macy to let him know she would accept the case. She gave him a brief version of what Antonia had told her, while Macy sat at his desk and munched on a doughnut.

'Antonia sounds even more of a fruitcake than before,' Macy remarked when Jo had finished. 'But provided you can cope with that, it still sounds an easy job to me.'

'I've already managed to fall out with her,' Jo admitted. 'But I like her and can stand to share a house with her for a short while. I'm going to try to persuade her to give up this daft crusade on her sister's behalf and move house — and preferably jobs, too. Once she does that, she'll feel safer.'

'You don't think she's making the whole thing up just to get attention?'

'Some of it perhaps. But there was definitely someone snooping round the cottage last night. Anyway, you wouldn't be saying that if she was a man. Women are always considered neurotic if something odd happens to them.'

'You can't accuse me of being sexist. My opinion of both sexes is equally low,' Macy said. 'What's this about someone snooping?'

'I think it was a boyfriend of hers hoping to find that I'd gone — although she denies it. She wants me to be a mixture of chauffeur, confidante and chaperone. But so far, that doesn't seem too onerous.' Jo paused for a sip of coffee. 'I'm going to insist she lets the police know what's happening. I'll go to the station with her this evening.'

'Good idea,' Macy said. 'They hate to be left out of things and you never know when they might come in useful. My contacts in the Warwickshire force aren't as good as in West Mids, but DI Kevin Macnally is still there, I think. I'll give him a ring to say you're coming in.'

Jo promised to call into the office to pick up a contract for Antonia and give Macy her spare key so that he could feed the cat. Before she rang off, she thought of a couple of questions she needed to ask him. 'Remember you said you'd give me all the backup I needed if I took on this case?'

'I said nothing like it, but go on, what do you want?'

'Could you ask one of your chums in London about a Guy Carlyle? Used to work in computing — was quite a high-flyer, some sort of consultant, troubleshooter type, if Antonia's not exaggerating, but not anymore.'

'Loads to go on there,' Macy said sarcastically. 'I suppose it would be beyond you to find out the name of this firm.'

'I'll try. I can probably get a last known address too,' Jo promised. 'But if I knew it all, I wouldn't have to ask, would I? Carlyle is Antonia's not-quite ex-husband and she's being mysterious about him. And, by the way, have you ever heard of this Oliver Sargent — the man she thinks killed her sister?'

Macy, although not a Coventrian, had lived in the city for years and had made it his business to know about local people. If Sargent was a successful businessman or criminal, Jo knew there was a good chance Macy would have heard of him. She mentioned Callender Exports as well, in case he knew anything about the firm.

Macy had to admit he didn't. 'I don't know Oliver, but the Sargents are an important family in Warwick. Adam Sargent owns the Royal Hotel and there's another Sargent who's a county councillor. Chances are Oliver's a relation, in which case you might have a hard time persuading the police that he goes around shutting unsuspecting women in their garages. I would think twice about taking on someone with his connections, but I'll see what I can find out about him.'

This was a start. Jo promised to keep in touch with Macy and after she put the phone down stood for a moment, sifting her thoughts. She knew it was not going to be easy to persuade Antonia to give up trying to get revenge on her sister's ex-lover. Geminis could be surprisingly obstinate. It would be a good idea, therefore, to find out what she could about Oliver — especially his past — to see if there was anything to confirm Antonia's suspicions.

And, she thought, as she packed her laptop and astrology notes, she would have to keep an eye on the cottage, check that the locks were up to scratch and have a good look around the place. She realised, as she was carefully selecting which jumpers to pack, that she was putting off the moment when she would have to go back to there. Something about the place made her uneasy.

She sighed, grabbed a handful of hangers and laid the clothes on top of the case. She wrestled it closed and dragged it downstairs, with hardly a backward glance at her precious flat. If she lingered any longer, she knew she would feel worse. She drove back to the cottage with a stoicism that was typically Virgoan.

CHAPTER SEVEN

When she saw the cottage looking idyllic in the bright morning sun, Jo wondered why she had thought there was anything sinister about the place. The sound of her key in the lock brought the cat running to meet her and the living room looked as cosy as when she had left it. She had to remind herself that last night she had been convinced she was being watched. After she had unpacked her clothes and books and had eaten some peanut butter on toast, she decided to have a look around the outside of the cottage to see if she could find anything to confirm this suspicion.

She slipped out of the front door, having first tempted Wilf into the kitchen with the promise of food. Hunched into her coat for warmth, Jo walked round the overgrown garden, which sloped gently down towards the river. Dense, tangled hedges on three sides gave adequate protection against intruders from the back of the cottage. It seemed the only access was from the drive. Following the lane, she found a track that led down the side of the cottage. As rounded the house, she could see the upstairs windows — her own bedroom and the bathroom, she realised. Antonia's room overlooked the front of the house. She was sure a car had been parked there last night, but, she supposed, it could have been for perfectly innocent reasons.

The farmhouse, the nearest building to the south of the cottage, was a good half-mile further down the lane. There was no one about, but on her way back she met Antonia's other neighbour. Betty's house was not set as far back from the lane and Jo saw the elderly woman tying up a shrub in the front garden. A goat tethered on the lawn watched her approach balefully.

Jo said hello and explained she had just moved in next door. Betty straightened her back and gave her an appraising glance. 'I'm glad to hear that. You couldn't chop this thick branch off for me, could you? If I hold it here.' She handed over the secateurs. 'The damn winds are wrecking my roses. I don't prune them enough, you see — I'm too afraid of killing them off.'

Jo approached the task gingerly, partly because she was no gardener and partly because of the enormous thorns on the rose bush.

'It's nice to have another young face about,' Betty said. 'Now chop this one for me, if you don't mind. Do you see, where it's all broken? It's so much easier with two. It will be good for Antonia too,' she added, switching subjects again. 'She seems a bit nervy to me.'

Jo withdrew her hand quickly to avoid a vindictive branch. 'I know,' she agreed. 'She's been having a few problems — her car was broken into and she thinks someone has been in the cottage too. Have you been bothered by anything?'

'Not at all. Not a thing,' Betty shook her head. 'Terrible about her cat, wasn't it? She told me the vet said it had been poisoned, but I doubt that anyone could make a cat eat something it didn't want. It was a pedigree, you know, and they fall foul of all sorts of strange diseases. Give me moggies any day.'

Jo made an excuse to leave before Betty could persuade her to do some more gardening. It surprised her to find Betty was sceptical about Dylan's poisoning. It echoed some of her own doubts. But no matter what reservations she might have, if she was going to take this job on she felt she had to assume Antonia's story was true. Just in case it was.

It didn't seem she was going to be able to make much progress on how the cat had died, but she was determined to find out who had been snooping round the cottage. On her way to Callendar Exports that evening, Jo was pondering how best to discover as much about Oliver Sargent as possible when she spotted him getting out of his car in the car park by the church. His tall, spare frame and silver hair were distinctive under the street light. She pulled in beside him quickly and he recognised her. He stood waiting, holding his briefcase and trench coat while she got out of the car, and greeted her in the same friendly, urbane manner.

'Hello, have you come to meet Antonia? She'll be about ready to finish for the day.' He glanced at his watch. 'Whereas I'm only just starting — or so it seems. I've been in Birmingham all day being nice to people. I think they call it "collaborating with stakeholders". Now I'm going into the office to do some proper work. Are you going up there? If so, we can walk together — if you don't mind?'

Jo said she didn't and they fell into step together. Oliver was one of those men whose charm seems effortless. Although he was distinctly not her type — and about twenty years older than her — Jo had to admit his fastidiously smart appearance, piercing eyes and faint soapy smell were appealing. She had no trouble imagining the effect he would have had on a woman like Monique.

'I see Antonia lent you the Mazda. You are honoured. Have you known her long? I only ask because I know she's relatively new to the area and still settling in.'

'We used to work in London together,' Jo said, her powers of invention working on a suitable story.

'Oh yes? She had a really good job there, didn't she? I sometimes wonder how long she'll stay with us. We're probably a bit of a stopgap for her. Personally, I think she's daft moving here when she could probably get a better job in the big city. But she says she likes living in the sticks. She's got a nice little cottage, I understand?'

Instead of volunteering any additional information, Jo asked a question of her own. 'Have you worked in Warwick for long?'

'I'm a local. A Midlander through and through. Born and bred in Warwick, went to school in Shrewsbury and university in Brum.'

'Not much of a traveller, then?' Jo remarked, finding his slightly flirtatious manner infectious.

'I went to Crete for my holidays, will that do? I tell you what, why don't I send you my CV?' This was said in the same smooth tones but Jo heard the rebuke. She felt quite pleased to have nettled him. 'But where would I send it?' he went on. 'Do you work in Warwick?'

'I'm a civil servant.' Jo found it was a good policy to lie as little as possible so she fell back on her old job. 'I work in Coventry.'

'Do you like it?' He turned his narrow gaze on her.

'It's OK. I like Coventry. I was born here and have come back to live here so that must prove it.'

They reached the office and he bounded energetically up the stairs. Probably to smarter accommodation, Jo thought, as she went along the narrow corridors to Antonia's room. If she was going to have to be a chauffeur, there would have to be better arrangements about meeting, she decided. Antonia was not at her desk. A softly spoken ginger-haired woman who sat nearby told Jo she was in the storeroom and gave her directions.

She found Antonia in a basement room searching for something among a mountain of boxes and old files. She apologised for not being ready. 'And I'm sorry I was offish this morning. I shouldn't have taken offence like that.' She turned to Jo. 'I can't afford to upset you. You're the only one I know who is on my side.'

And that's because you're paying me, Jo thought. 'That's OK,' she said. 'Now, about the case—'

'Will you take it on?'

'With certain conditions, yes.' Antonia brightened at once and Jo continued, 'First, you must come with me to the police station tonight so we can tell them all that's happened to you.'

'It won't do any good,' Antonia said, 'but I'll come.'

'The second thing is more difficult. I want you to promise that you'll consider giving up the idea of proving Oliver Sargent was your sister's fiancé.'

Antonia didn't reply immediately. She continued to scan the cardboard boxes on a shelf and eventually selected one, tucked it under her arm and led the way out, locking the door behind them. 'I'll think about it,' she said at last.

Jo was prepared to leave it like that for the moment. 'If you're happy with those conditions I'll get you a contract to sign and you can tell me a bit more about what it is exactly you want me to do. Not just giving you lifts to work, I'm sure.'

'I want you to stick with me as much as possible so I won't feel nervous. I know you can't be with me here at work, but that's not so bad because I'm surrounded by other people. And I really don't think Oliver—' she dropped her voice on his name — 'would foul his own nest. But there are a few things coming up which I'm especially apprehensive about. Today's Thursday, isn't it? Next Friday there's a ball run by the Chamber of Commerce and I'm expected to go, along with everyone else from work. Would you come with me?' She stopped in the corridor outside her office.

'A ball? I can't promise I've got the right clothes.'

'You can borrow something of mine. We just need to put in an appearance.'

'Won't your colleagues think it a bit odd that you're going with me?'

'They know I've not been in the area long and I don't know anybody else,' Antonia explained. 'Anyway, I don't mind what they think quite honestly. And if they jump to the wrong conclusion, at least it might keep some of the men at arm's length.'

'What else is in your social diary?'

Antonia hesitated. 'The other major thing is a health and safety course in Yorkshire the week after. I've found out Oliver is attending a management course there at the same time. That was what finally prompted me to go and see Mr Macy.'

'And you want me to look after *your* health and safety while you're on this course?'

'I'd only want you to be around outside work hours. I'm sure you'll be able to book a room in the hotel where the course is being held . . .'

Jo agreed to go with her. In turn, and somewhat to Jo's surprise, Antonia willingly kept the first part of her side of the bargain and went with her to the police station later that evening.

Detective Inspector Macnally, a quiet man with appraising green eyes and a classic policeman's build, patiently sat and listened for an hour or so while Antonia recounted the various things that had happened to her. She refused to come entirely clean — she did not mention Sargent or her reason for being in Warwick. 'I didn't want to prejudice their thinking,' she said to Jo afterwards. 'It's their job to find out who's doing these things. I thought I'd let them approach it with an open mind.'

Macnally had taken notes and promised to include the cottage on one of the PC's beats for the next month or so. Jo came away reasonably content. They had made contact and even if Macnally only knew half the story, she could get in touch with him again if necessary.

* * *

Over the next few days, Jo set her mind to tackling her new job. She made sure the cottage was secure, installing a burglar alarm and window locks. She had another go at finding out what had happened to the cat, but the nearby farmer was as unhelpful as Antonia had said. Having seen how far his crop fields were from the cottage, however, she revised her opinion that Dylan could have wandered over there. She spent a few fruitless but pleasant hours tramping around the garden and down footpaths along the river looking for evidence of slug pellets.

She also went to see the landlady, Mrs Pumfrey, a colourless, phlegmatic woman who ran the bed and breakfast by the racecourse where Antonia had first stayed. Mrs Pumfrey received the information about the prowler and the dead cat in doubtful silence. She had large tinted glasses that rested on the bags under her eyes and smoked three cigarettes during the short conversation. Jo got the distinct impression that Mrs P didn't want to know about Antonia's problems.

'As far as I'm concerned, people are entitled to their bit of privacy,' she said. 'I tell that to all my guests and tenants — particularly the women. Your friend Antonia asked me not to give her address to anyone and I haven't.'

'She appreciates that. You see, she feels someone's out to get her.'

'I know that, dear. She told me all about it and said if anyone came round asking for her, not to tell him anything. You might tell her, in fact, a shifty-looking bloke did call the other day and I said I'd no idea where she was.'

'What was he like? In what way shifty-looking?'

Mrs Pumfrey twisted her mouth to one side while she thought about this. 'Oh, I don't know. Tall, thin, scruffy. Could have been one of those private detectives — but I know she hasn't got money trouble, she pays her rent on the dot every month so I'm not worried.'

'When was this? What did he say?'

'Just said he was looking for her. He wouldn't leave a name so that made me suspicious right away. This would be last week — Thursday or maybe Friday afternoon.'

The landlady couldn't shed any more light on her visitor but before she left, Jo got her assurance that there were no other keys to the cottage apart from the one Mrs Pumfrey kept locked in her cash box.

That evening Jo told Antonia that a man had been asking for her at Mrs Pumfrey's. Seeing her alarmed expression, Jo added quickly, 'Don't worry. Mrs P said she didn't know where you were. But who do you think it could have been?'

'Oliver Sargent, of course, trying to harass me. It figures because I had to give Mrs Pumfrey's address in at work as I didn't want them to know this one. Although I know that's silly because he could find out where I live quite easily. He only has to follow me . . .' When she became anxious Antonia talked even faster. She started to line up the containers in the kitchen cupboard, making sure they were in a neat row.

'And if Sargent is doing the other dirty tricks, then he must know you live here,' Jo said. 'So why go to Mrs Pumfrey's place?'

'It's the way he thinks, you see. He's fundamentally devious. He's sent someone round to Mrs Pumfrey's to ask for me, knowing it would get back to me. It's all part of his campaign of harassment.'

Jo sighed. She was in the middle of putting away the shopping they had bought on the way home. As she rearranged the packets in the small freezer, she tactfully tried to tell Antonia of her reservations. 'I've been here a few days now and there haven't been any funny phone calls or strange visitors,' she began.

'But someone called on Mrs Pumfrey.' Antonia was pacing restlessly round the kitchen. 'Don't you see? It's the very fact you're here that is keeping Oliver so quiet. But I know he hasn't given up. He means to get rid of me one way or the other. I still hate being near him — even when there are people around.'

'Well, you could always leave that job,' Jo pointed out.

'Then he would have won.' Antonia shook her head stubbornly. 'I've still got to prove that he and John Brooke are the same man. Oh, by the way,' she added brightly, 'I've found out his birthday — and Paul's.'

'At last. What are they?' Jo knew she was being diverted but she had been after this information for a while.

'Oliver's birthday is the sixth of October.'

'Slap bang in the middle of Libra. They're usually pretty harmless types. They favour harmony and peace.'

Antonia shook her head. 'Not him. I wouldn't put it past him to lie about his birthday, seeing as his whole life's a lie. Anyway, Paul's date of birth is the second of August. What does that say about *him*?'

'A Leo? Bossy, pompous, pushy. But they make good friends.'

'I could have told you that. Do you know he offered to go with me to the ball tomorrow night? He hates things like that but he knows I'm nervous about it.'

'He can willingly go in my place.'

'No, I'd rather you came.' She looked up from the plastic carrier bags she had been systematically folding and unfolding. 'Jo? You're not getting fed up, are you? Don't let me down, will you?'

Jo closed the freezer door and turned her attention to the fridge. 'No, I won't.'

She wouldn't have admitted it, but Antonia had hit on a Virgoan weakness: the need to be needed. For all her misgivings about taking on this case, she couldn't help being fond of Antonia, with all her eccentricities. She supposed she would stay around until the end of the month. After all, she hadn't been required to do much so far. She had spent the last few days expecting things to happen and nothing had.

Nevertheless, she couldn't shake off a strong feeling of apprehension.

CHAPTER EIGHT

Oliver Sargent was proving elusive. He was never around anymore when Jo went to meet Antonia from work. She tried asking Antonia's colleagues about him and found he was generally well liked and respected. She also asked discreet questions of one or two antique dealers in Warwick about Callender Exports and they thought well of the firm and of Sargent. In fact, no one had a bad word to say about him except Antonia.

She fell back on astrology to tell her more about him, but without knowing his year or time of birth she had only his Sun Sign to go on. The worst things she knew about Libran men were that they could be inconsistent and shallow, but it was hard to see Sargent in the villainous role Antonia had cast him in. On the face of it, a Libran man and Gemini woman should get on well together.

In Paul's case, she could work out roughly where the planets had been when he was born. She saw straight away that he and Antonia would be sympathetic to each other because they both had Venus in Taurus.

Jo knew from Antonia's chart that she was not a typical Gemini. She was more secretive than most and her integrity was doubtful too. But there were things about the chart that drew Jo closer to her. With both Jupiter and Mars in the Eleventh House, it was clear she really valued her friends, for example, and was loyal to them. She had high ideals and a quick brain. There were all sorts of signs of nervous strain and depression as well and Jo was doing some further work on the progressed chart to see, among other things, when these bad fits of the blues were likely to strike.

She was looking forward to spending another hour or so on it before Antonia came in. She didn't have to collect her from work today because Paul had offered to bring her home. His wife was away visiting friends, and he had asked her to his house 'for a coffee', Antonia blithely informed her. Jo had raised her eyebrows but said nothing. It seemed patently obvious to her that Paul's interest was not platonic. However, Antonia didn't see it. Or didn't admit to it anyway.

When Antonia came home only half an hour later than usual Jo began to doubt this cynical view. Her clothes were as neat as always and her hair still in the complicated chignon. She breezed in, divesting herself of her leather jacket, scarf and boots. 'I've had an easy day. Everyone was going on about the ball tonight.'

'Including Oliver?' Jo enquired, looking up from her work.

'Oh, yes. Oliver was *most* gregarious. He's going to buy all us drones a drink.' Antonia made a face.

'Do you want a coffee? You could hardly have had time for one at Paul's,' Jo remarked.

'Yes, I did,' Antonia responded with bright-eyed innocence. 'I'll just have some fruit because there'll be food at this ball tonight.' She jumped up and made for the fruit bowl.

As she reached over Jo to take an apple, she saw her birth chart and Jo's neat notes. 'Oh, I thought you'd already done mine?' she asked. 'What's up? Is anything terrible going to happen to me this month?'

'Well, a progressed birth chart is like a diary — you have to keep checking it to see what's going on,' Jo explained. The truth was, the outlook for the rest of January and February was fraught. However, Jo was sufficiently experienced to be able to field such questions. 'As for this month, you need plenty of time to relax and take it easy. So if you don't want to go to this shopkeepers' shindig tonight, you don't have to.'

'Actually, I do feel a bit under the weather. Maybe I'm getting a cold.' She searched around in the dresser for a box of tissues. 'But I do want to go out tonight. It's no use trying to persuade me not to just because *you* don't. Now, we've got an hour so we can have the bathroom for half an hour each. Do you want to go first?'

Jo wanted to finish her work so she opted to go last, which meant she had to rush to get ready. Antonia had lent her a smoky-blue silk dress, which only just fitted. She was still doing it up when Antonia called from downstairs, 'Jo! It's quarter past seven. Shall I call a taxi?'

'No. I'll drive,' Jo called back. 'I don't mind not drinking.' As Antonia seemed to be in a hurry, she rapidly finished her make-up, slipped on her one and only pair of high-heeled shoes and went downstairs. Antonia, draped from head to foot in a chocolate brown velvet cape, was idly eating grapes and reading the newspaper. Before they left, she grabbed another handful of tissues and spent the first half of the journey describing her cold symptoms. Jo listened tolerantly, having grown quite fond of Antonia's idiosyncrasies, including hypochondria.

The ball fulfilled all Jo's pessimistic expectations. The hotel was bland and forgettable and so was the food. The people were all young fogeys who were only interested in their cars and houses. Antonia seemed quiet and edgy, even among the people she worked with. Oliver spent a few minutes chatting to her little group, but he paid no particular attention to Antonia. Jo thought him charming and distant. It was looking more and more like the whole story about him was a figment of her client's paranoia.

Jo kept an eye on her all the same. This didn't prove too difficult at first but after a few drinks Antonia became livelier and spent quite a bit of time with a hearty young solicitor called Rod. Jo, having discouraged his friend, watched them dancing together and wondered if it was a good moment to slip out. She needed to call Macy. There had been a message from him on her voicemail, but it had been characteristically enigmatic.

At ten o'clock, while Antonia and Rod were clamped in each other's arms on the dance floor, Jo decided to pop outside to make her call where it was chilly but less noisy. For once, he answered first time although he sounded tired.

'Are you still working at this time?' Jo demanded cheerfully.

'Accounts,' came Macy's flat tones. 'What are *you* doing? I've been expecting to see you. You haven't picked up the contract for that batty woman yet. Do you know she hasn't paid us anything? And I don't suppose she will until she's signed a contract.'

'All right, I'll pick up the contract tomorrow. I don't know what I'm doing on this case.' Jo felt a sudden urge to tell him all her troubles. 'Antonia's really odd. Nothing's happened and I sometimes feel she's making the whole thing up — about Sargent and her sister and all that. And others I'm not so sure. Did you find out anything about him?'

'Not much, but from what I've heard he's Mr Clean — respectable local business man, Rotary Club member, school governor—'

Jo groaned. 'Don't go on. A regular pillar of the community. That's just what I thought. I think Antonia and I will have to have a talk. We'll have plenty of time for it. We're off to Yorkshire on Sunday for a week.'

'You'll enjoy that. It sounds to me as if she's in more danger from your evil temper than she is from any mysterious malefactor.'

'What about Guy? Her ex? Antonia wasn't very keen to tell me but I found out where she and Guy used to work and their old address. I left a message with Celia the other day. Did you get it?'

'Yes, and I phoned a London firm which sometimes puts work our way. They're going to see what they can find out.

I'll let you know. Anything else I can do for you?' Macy finished drily.

Jo thanked him. Their conversation lifted her out of the enforced boredom that had been gradually getting to her and she ended the call grinning stupidly at the outside wall. She would have liked to talk for longer but was aware that she'd left Antonia on her own.

When she returned to the ballroom, the smile froze on her face. There was no sign of Antonia.

Jo did a quick circuit of the room, noticing with relief that Oliver at least was exactly where she had last seen him, sitting with some glamorous women who were all partnered by men in dinner jackets. Empty wine bottles were clustered on the table and they looked like they were enjoying their own private party.

Jo left the ballroom and threaded her way through the knots of people standing in the corridor. She was heading towards the toilets when she saw Antonia coming out clad in her long cape, clearly ready to leave. She was looking round, her face pale and tense, and didn't notice Jo until she went up and touched her on the arm. 'Are you OK? I went off to make a phone call and when I came back you'd gone.'

Antonia's eyes focused on her. 'Actually I'm not feeling too well. It's this cold,' she sniffed. 'I think I'll go home. Do you mind?'

'Mind? No, I'm delighted. Don't you want to say good-night to anyone?' They made their way to the revolving door.

Antonia pulled up her velvet hood. 'I'd rather not.' She spent most of the journey blowing her nose and fiddling with a pack of tissues she found in the glove compartment.

Jo swung into the drive. 'Nothing happened to upset you, then?'

'No, nothing happened,' Antonia said. 'I just felt a bit dizzy. I still don't feel too good . . .' Her voice trailed off as Jo parked the car and they went up the path to the cottage in silence. She seemed subdued and the way she fumbled with the key made Jo think maybe she wasn't making it up after all. Certainly she did look pale and forlorn, dwarfed by the huge velvet cape and standing in the middle of the bright lounge.

Jo offered to make her a herbal tea but Antonia refused. 'The best thing to stop a cold is orange juice, paracetamol and menthol inhalation.' She made for the kitchen, where she took down a first-aid box and sorted out the things she wanted. 'I'll be all right in the morning. You may as well go to bed,' she advised, pouring herself a large orange juice.

Making herself a coffee to take upstairs, Jo watched Antonia, still in her evening clothes with her head shrouded in a tea towel, taking in lungfuls of menthol over a steaming bowl. Something was not quite right about the evening but Jo couldn't put her finger on it just then. She dismissed the thought and went up to bed.

CHAPTER NINE

When Jo woke up it was still dark but it felt like morning. Her trusty phone said 6.05 and she lay back in the comfortable knowledge that it was Saturday and there was no need to take Antonia to work. She was just drifting pleasantly back to sleep when she heard the quiet but distinct sound of the front door closing.

Was Antonia up already and going outside? With that cold? Or was somebody letting themselves in?

Jo hauled herself out of bed to investigate. Nothing was to be seen from the side window, which gave a good view of the front lawns. The garden was still, and totally dark. Not even the porch light illuminated it. From the windows overlooking the side and rear of the cottage, the scene was equally black. Yawning, Jo went back to sit on her bed but she felt uneasy. A sliver of light under the bedroom door showed that Antonia had left some lights on. Trying not to think of the warm bed behind her, Jo put on some clothes and opened the door, listening carefully.

Antonia's bedroom was empty, the bed undisturbed. Below she could hear someone moving about casually, easily. She went downstairs and, as she lifted the latch on the door into the kitchen, Antonia was coming into the room, white and tired-looking but cheerful. She was holding a box of light bulbs.

'Morning, Jo. The porch light has gone out. I was just going to put a new bulb in.' She searched through the box.

'Isn't it a bit early for home improvements?' Jo asked. Then, following her into the lounge, she added, 'How are you this morning?'

'Not bad, actually. Inhaling the menthol really helped. Hope I didn't spoil your evening, though?' Antonia opened the front door and began to fit the new bulb.

'I was ready to leave.' Jo said. She noticed a bed made out of cushions and blankets on the sofa.

'I couldn't sleep so I sat up reading,' Antonia explained. 'Did you keep an eye on Oliver last night? He seemed to keep himself to himself.'

'He didn't come anywhere near us.' Jo went back into the kitchen to make herself a coffee. 'Are you sure he's the same man who went out with your sister? He seems perfectly OK to me and I understand he's well respected locally.'

'I know.' Antonia nodded seriously. 'That's part of his deviousness. But he's watching me all the time.' She paused to blow her nose on some kitchen towel. 'By the way, I'm going to Paul's later. He's coming to collect me in the taxi. He's working till noon but I said I'd help Rachel with the lunch. Will you pick me up at around five o'clock?'

Jo agreed vaguely, still not properly awake. Despite her cold, Antonia seemed in good spirits and cheerfully went off with Paul after breakfast, leaving Jo with the day to herself. After a brief visit to Macy's office to pick up Antonia's contract, she spent most of the time at her flat reading a new astrology book she had ordered and watching the last half of a film on television. She went to meet Antonia at five o'clock as planned and found Paul's house, on a large estate just outside Warwick, without any trouble.

The neat semi-detached looked similar to those around it except for a more interesting front garden, an oval lawn fronted by a tidy privet hedge and surrounded by conifers from gold to blue in various shapes and sizes. It didn't appeal to Jo's taste but it was clearly well thought out and looked after.

Paul, looking domesticated in a cardigan and slippers, invited her in as Jo had been hoping he would. It was worth trying to find out a bit more about him because of his interest in Antonia. She had already managed a discreet look at the back of his taxi as she passed and decided that it could have been the car she had chased down Antonia's drive.

'We're just about to have a cuppa and a piece of cake,' Paul said. She followed him down the narrow hall, noticing Antonia's flying jacket thrown carelessly over the end of the banister.

Antonia looked very much at home, hugging her knees on the tan leather sofa in the lounge, her boots kicked off. She grinned up at Jo and patted the seat beside her. It was an overheated room, which ran the length of the house. At one end was the wide, squashy sofa opposite a large television and a flickering gas fire in a stone surround.

Paul lowered himself into an armchair next to Antonia. 'Rachel's just bringing the cake—'

'Her chocolate cake is legendary,' Antonia interrupted him, beaming at Jo like a child keen to show off her friends. 'She says it's the reason why Paul married her.'

Jo, unbuttoning her coat and studying her surroundings, felt distinctly claustrophobic. Every surface she laid eyes on, including all the nooks and crannies in the ugly stonework, was cluttered with china animals. A fancy display cabinet in one alcove was filled with larger animals. The other alcove was adorned with rows of horse brasses and though the room was big, all the seats were at one end. She stretched out her legs and knocked the coffee table, making the teacups rattle.

'I've just been telling Paul about our visit to the police station,' Antonia said. 'That inspector was very patient, wasn't he? He heard us out even though I could see him thinking I was absolutely neurotic.'

'At least you've told them now. I've been after you to do that for weeks. Well done, Jo. You seem to have succeeded in twisting her arm.' Paul nodded at her from his comfortable armchair.

'I don't suppose they'll do much,' Antonia went on, 'Detective Inspector Macnally said I could contact him any time I felt uneasy but I'd feel really bad if I did—'

'I should think so,' another woman's voice cut in impatiently. 'I'm sure the police have got more important things to do.' Rachel was carrying a cake stand, which she plonked unceremoniously in the centre of the coffee table.

The most striking thing about her was her white-blonde hair. She wore it long and unstyled, the ends bobbing about just above her shoulders. It was the kind of hair you expected to see on someone much younger. In fact, Rachel looked older than Paul. Mid-forties, Jo speculated. She had a long, ruddy face with a beak of a nose and wore round, wire-rimmed glasses. She stood tall, straight and thin, like a tense Olive Oyl gone blonde.

'This is Jo, Toni's new lodger,' Paul said, and Jo guessed he was trying to be conciliatory, but Rachel was not to be deflected. She barely glanced in Jo's direction and poured out some tea while continuing to address Antonia. 'I'm surprised you had the nerve to go to the police, to be honest. After all, nothing's happened. It's not as if you've even been burgled. Help yourselves to cake,' she added offhandedly.

Jo felt obliged to defend her own idea. 'Someone did break into Antonia's car twice,' she pointed out. 'And the first night I was there, I saw someone prowling round outside.'

Rachel sat down in an armchair across from Paul's. She regarded Jo appraisingly over her teacup. 'You actually saw someone, did you?'

'That was what finally decided me to go to the police,' Antonia explained. 'It seemed incontrovertible evidence that all the other things were connected.'

'Well, it was worth a visit to the cop shop anyway.' Paul looked from one to the other. 'No harm done, is there?' He leaned forward and helped himself to a generous portion of cake.

'At any rate, I expect things will improve now you've got your friend staying with you,' Rachel remarked. 'It takes a bit of getting used to, living on your own. I sometimes feel on edge when Paul works nights. I'm always imagining someone's going to creep in through the back door with a machete.' She gave a sharp bark of embarrassed laughter. 'I keep a poker beside my chair in case.'

Antonia chose to ignore Rachel's hint that she was imagining things. As soon as she could, she turned to Paul and started to talk about a new computer game that they had played together. This left Jo munching Rachel's cake and wondering how to start a conversation with her. The older woman sat upright in her armchair, staring into the middle distance, her long legs crossed and a slipper dangling as she joggled one leg absently.

'Have you lived in Warwick long?' Jo asked. She had detected that both she and Paul had Estuary accents rather than the familiar Midlands intonation.

'Ten years,' Rachel said. 'More tea?'

'No, this is fine, thank you. Do you work locally?' Jo tried again.

'At Sainsbury's, stacking shelves,' Rachel said, surprising Jo, who had pictured her behind a desk in a fusty old office.

Jo returned to her cake, finding conversation too difficult. What with Antonia's rampant paranoia and this woman's frosty blue gaze, she felt she and Paul were the only normal ones there. He and Antonia were making arrangements to meet for lunch next week when Rachel abruptly got up and left the room. Antonia and Paul continued to talk quietly, heads bent over his phone, which left Jo feeling distinctly supernumerary.

Jo interrupted to ask Paul where the bathroom was and he gave her brief directions before turning back to Antonia and some YouTube video about the game. She left them to it and went upstairs as directed. Glancing into the kitchen at the back of the house, she saw Rachel with her arms in the sink, washing up, her unusual blonde hair hanging down over her face.

The bathroom trick was one Jo often used when bored. Even if she had no desire to use the lavatory, she sometimes liked a few minutes on her own when the company of other people got her down. She also took the chance to peer around. It was not very interesting, being clean and tidy. The male and female toiletries were kept strictly separate in two cupboards, Jo noticed, and there were no plants or ornaments, just a bowl of lurid pot-pourri on the windowsill.

She looked down on a small but well-laid-out garden. She made out the curving, bushy beds in the twilight. Either Paul or Rachel was a far more ambitious gardener than their neighbours, who just had plain rectangular lawns.

Long experience had taught Jo not to extend her bathroom time for more than a few minutes or people asked embarrassing questions. All the bedroom doors were closed so she was unable to indulge her natural nosiness any further and reluctantly started downstairs. She was on the landing at the turn in the staircase when she saw a figure bending over the coats in the hall. Leaning over the banister to see better, she looked directly down on the crown of Rachel's head. She could see the uneven parting in the white-blonde hair. With the door of the lounge firmly closed behind her, Rachel had her hand inside Antonia's jacket. Jo watched, transfixed, as the woman's long, thin fingers lifted up the jacket, looking for something underneath. Rachel found Antonia's handbag and flipped it open, rifling through the contents.

Lipstick, compact, hairbrush were passed over. Out came Antonia's purse. *Surely she isn't going to steal some money?* Jo wondered. But Rachel discarded the purse after a quick search and picked up the leather credit card wallet. She flicked through this, stopping to take out one or two cards and slide them back in again. This was then abandoned as she made a swift check of the other pockets in the bag. *What is she looking for? Does Rachel suspect Paul and Antonia are having an affair, and is she now looking for proof?*

All this was carried out in a matter of a minute or so. Rachel worked with a silent determination, intent on what she was doing and apparently confident she was not going to be disturbed. When the search — seemingly fruitless — was over, she went back into the kitchen. Jo watched her disappear from view, then went downstairs noisily. By the time she was back in the lounge, she had already decided not to say anything about the incident. Jo knew by now that it would only end in an argument. Antonia would undoubtedly defend her friends, and anyway, more might be gained by keeping the information to herself, Jo thought.

Antonia had finished her tea and was ready to leave. On their way out, Jo made an excuse to seek out Rachel. 'I just wanted to thank you for the tea and cake,' Jo said, leaning round the kitchen door.

'Are you off now, then?' Rachel was in the middle of drying the dishes and didn't try very hard to be pleasant. Jo thought she detected a martyred air. She was aware of Antonia and Paul laughing together in the hall and Rachel was certainly aware of them too. She banged down the roasting tin, picked up a saucepan and dried it with vigour.

'I noticed your garden,' Jo said brightly. 'Looks like someone works hard on it.'

'Yes, that would be me.' Rachel stared down at a stain on the pan. Jo noticed that her eyelashes were almost white, like her hair. 'My mother was an avid gardener, so I suppose it's ingrained.'

'Oh, so you're the gardener, are you?'

'Yes, Paul's not interested. Never was.' Rachel had a way of speaking as if she begrudged letting go of the words.

'I don't know much about it,' Jo prattled on. She was aware that Paul's voice behind her had dropped to a low mutter and was answered by a breathy giggle from Antonia. Rachel's chilly eyes travelled over Jo's shoulder. 'But now I've moved into the cottage, I suppose I'll have to do things in the garden. Antonia tells me she has trouble with slugs. How do you get rid of them?'

Rachel gave her a sharp look. 'There are literally hundreds of ways — eggshells, salt or you can make a solution, mashing up dead slugs with water and pour that onto the soil—'

Jo gave an involuntary shudder. 'But aren't they old wives' tales?' she said. 'Surely slug pellets are the best?'

Rachel regarded her imperviously. 'The most effective, yes, but also the most expensive. Personally I find a bucket of the dead slug mixture does the trick.' She put down her tea towel and pushed past Jo. 'I suppose I'd better say goodbye.'

Paul and Antonia were standing close together at the bottom of the stairs, talking quietly. Rachel had gone out of her way to invite Antonia over, which Jo thought was odd. *Or on the other hand, perhaps she believes if she gives him enough rope, he'll hang himself.* The phrase jumped into Jo's head unbidden and for some reason made her shiver again.

As she followed Antonia along the garden path, she turned and looked down the passageway at the side of the house, where she could see a garden shed. *I bet I'd find slug pellets in there*, she thought. *It wouldn't prove that Rachel had killed Antonia's cat. But there's a possible motive if Rachel wants her to move back to London . . .*

Jo reversed the Mazda out of the drive. The back of Paul's car was now lit up in the headlights. 'Does Rachel drive?'

'Yes, she has to use Paul's taxi, which she says is a total embarrassment, but they can't afford another car.'

'How did you meet them?' Jo asked when they were on their way home. Antonia, so much younger and smarter than the staid couple, had seemed conspicuously out of place and it was hard to imagine how the three of them had struck up a friendship.

'I met Paul through an advert in the paper,' Antonia said airily.

'What advert was this?'

'I must have told you. I put an advert in the local papers — you know, the lonely hearts column — when I first came here. Something along the lines of, "Shy, professional woman seeks caring man for friendship, possibly leading to romance."'

'You never told me you advertised!' Jo shook her head in disbelief, trying to keep her attention on the road. 'You could meet all sorts of creeps doing that kind of thing!'

'I know. I did,' Antonia said with some feeling.

'But didn't it occur to you that one of those creeps could have been your obscene caller? And the source of all your other problems? I can't believe you haven't told me who they were.' Jo flicked on her indicator and roared past a slow car, transmitting her irritation to the accelerator.

'I did think of that. Of course I did.' Antonia sounded affronted. 'And you can have their names, if you want. I only went out with three anyway. But I had to advertise and I wanted to do it locally and not online because I wanted to tempt John Brooke out of the woodwork by pretending to be rich and available. Hence the flash car, et cetera.' She waved an explanatory hand.

'Why would Paul reply to your ad? I thought he was happily married?

'He is. He and Rachel are perfectly content together. But my ad said *friendship* wanted as well as romance. I used almost the same wording as Monique did. Paul was just looking for a chum.'

'Has anyone ever told you how naıve you sound sometimes?' Jo snapped, swinging the car into the drive and taking the first bend too fast.

'No. I suppose you're going to tell me it's a typical Gemini trait,' Antonia said with a touch of sarcasm. One of her better points, Jo reflected, was that she never made any comments about her driving, even when it was really bad. 'But as I'm paying you, I think I'm entitled to withhold information if I choose.'

'You've not paid a penny yet, as you damn well know,' Jo retorted. 'And if you do refuse to tell me what the hell is going on, I won't be around much longer.' Both women now sat glaring at each other. 'And while I'm on the subject, this whole thing is a waste of my time. You don't have anyone after you — you just can't stand being on your own and I'm not prepared to be your chauffeur!'

Antonia had looked away during this speech and was staring through the windscreen. When she spoke, she dropped her lofty tone. 'I *am* worried. Oliver *is* after me. I know it. But I understand you might be getting pissed off. If you'll just come to Yorkshire with me tomorrow, I'll think again afterwards. Either I'll get someone else or I'll cope on my own. But I just can't stand the idea of being on this course among strangers and Oliver being always around.'

Jo, who was cooling down, took the keys out of the ignition and sighed. 'All right. We go to Yorkshire,' she agreed. 'But you must come clean. I want the names and addresses of everyone who responded to your advert.'

'I didn't deliberately keep them from you but I'm sure they're not important. I know who wants to frighten me off and it's not them.'

They got out of the car and walked side by side to the cottage. Jo was glad she had delivered some home truths and Antonia seemed suitably subdued.

Inside the porch, Antonia stooped to pick up an envelope. She hesitated before turning it over and then, with a quick apprehensive look at Jo, tore it open. She drew out a single page of paper, read it quickly, her teeth biting into her lip, and thrust it at Jo, white-faced.

THIS IS A WARNING. DON'T POKE YOUR NOSE INTO OTHER PEOPLE'S BUSINESS.

The letters had been cut from a newspaper. Jo put it back in the envelope and followed Antonia into the cottage. 'It's a bit melodramatic, isn't it?' she commented. 'Someone's been watching too many old films.'

'It's awful.' Antonia, sitting hunched on the sofa, looked up at Jo with tears running down her face. 'He's been here again while I was out. That means he's watching us all the time.'

'I know you feel bad,' Jo said sympathetically. 'We'll take it over to DI Macnally later and see what he can do. After all, it's our first tangible proof that you're being harassed.'

Antonia was in no mood to look on the bright side and Jo went into the kitchen to make her a cup of tea. When she brought it out, Antonia was on the phone to Paul, sobbing hysterically. Jo sighed, put the tea beside her and went to look around outside the cottage in case there were any signs of the person who had left the note. There had been ample time for it to be delivered — she and Antonia had been out of the house since eleven that morning.

Nothing was visibly amiss outside and gratefully Jo went back into the warm room. Antonia seemed calmer but was still on the phone. Re-examining the note, both the envelope and the lined paper were cheap and thin, the single page had been folded four times to fit the envelope and some of the letters were peeling off. The print looked familiar and Jo rooted around in the magazine rack for a local free paper. Holding them side by side, it was easy to see the letters had been cut from the local *Citizen*.

DI Kevin Macnally seemed most impressed when Jo told him this later, but she had a sneaking suspicion he was patronising her. He kept the note, so Jo was glad she had studied it thoroughly. It didn't seem appropriate to ask him for a photocopy, especially as Antonia was still distressed. She didn't say much but looked even more worried when Macnally asked her who she thought had sent it.

'What will you do?' she asked. 'I know who it is but I don't want him to know I know.'

DI Macnally ducked his large head to look her in the eyes. 'We'd normally take the note round his house and ask him if he sent it. Then — whatever he said — we'd tell him it's caused you a lot of worry and we'll be keeping an eye on your house so he'd be wise not to go anywhere near it.'

'No, I don't want you to do that.' Antonia was adamant, and refused to divulge Sargent's name even after Jo had pointed out the sense of what Macnally had said. Jo threatened to tell Macnally herself but this had no effect and a slight shake of the head by the policeman warned her not to carry out her threat. She supposed it was Antonia's complaint after all and it was up to her to name names.

'Then there's nothing I can really do for you,' Macnally said. 'Except to continue to keep an eye on the place.' Having established this, he seemed keen to get rid of them, and though he remained polite and patient, they weren't in the station long afterwards.

* * *

'I'm sorry to be such a wimp, but you must see how it would look if the police took that note round to Oliver's? He would know I suspected him, which terrifies me. But I'm really grateful, Jo. I don't know how I would have coped on my own.' They were back in the cottage with the remains of a takeaway dinner in front of them. 'Things have started happening again, haven't they?'

Jo had to agree. Antonia had gone from receiving obscene phone calls to a prowler and now an anonymous note — on top of the other incidents that were harder to prove. 'Don't forget to give me the names of the men who responded to your advert,' Jo reminded her.

'I've got a folder with the emails in. You can have that,' Antonia promised. 'But I only went out with Norman, who was a plumber with a deaf mother, Stuart, a bit of a wide boy, and Paul. The others were non-starters. They didn't sound like they could possibly be John — usually because they were too young — so I never bothered to contact them again.'

Nevertheless, when Antonia handed over a folder of emails before she went to bed, Jo sat down and looked through it carefully. Each email had been printed out and clipped to a corresponding photograph. A couple sounded vaguely interesting and one or two others positively disgusting, but she couldn't judge which of them, if any, would be likely to have been harassing Antonia. She would have to interview each one. If only she had known about this earlier, she could have made a start.

As she slid the last note back into the folder, she noticed another sheet caught under the paper clip. It was a single A4 sheet showing photocopies of newspaper articles, mostly one or two short columns from local papers. The date and the name of the paper were printed underneath in Antonia's black italics. There were six articles in all, each one about attacks on women that had happened locally. One woman had been sexually assaulted in a bus shelter about five miles away, another attacked late at night on a road leading out of Warwick. The most recent was a woman who had been raped just before Christmas on her way home from late-night shopping.

Jo felt slightly nauseous by the time she'd finished reading. She slipped the piece of paper into the folder and wondered why Antonia had gone to the trouble of cutting out the clippings and copying them. Did she suspect Sargent of these attacks? If so, why hadn't she mentioned it? Or was it just another example of her nervousness?

The home phone rang, and Jo jumped. She put down the cuttings and reached for the receiver. After she'd said the number, there was no immediate response.

She was instantly alert. 'Who is this?'

There was a sound at the other end of the line like a snuffle or a smothered giggle.

'Who's there?'

'That's not you, is it?' A man's muffled voice spoke at last.

'This is Jo Hughes. Who do you want?'

There was another long, breathing pause. 'Antonia? Is she there?'

'No, she's not. Who are you?'

The line went dead.

Jo replaced the receiver. It had been hard to tell anything about the man's voice. It hadn't sounded at all familiar. Of course it could have been an innocent caller, who simply didn't want to leave his name.

Jo mentioned it the next morning when Antonia was packing for their trip to Yorkshire.

'Hardly anyone has this number,' Antonia said. 'It must be that pervert who used to call me. I'm sure that's something to do with Sargent.'

She was equally unhelpful about the newspaper cuttings, just murmuring vaguely about liking to 'keep tabs on what's going on locally.' Jo couldn't get any more out of her and decided it was something else she'd need to follow up later.

She explained to Antonia that she had to pack some additional clothes herself and she also wanted to check on her flat. Antonia agreed to pick her up from there in about an hour. In fact, it was barely half an hour later when she turned up at Jo's front door and Jo was reminded, yet again, of a Gemini's characteristic dislike of their own company. Fortunately she had already managed to throw a few extra items into a bag.

She took a quick glance at her chart before they set out, but it did not make her feel any better. She told herself that Mercury moving through her opposite sign of Pisces could just mean delays and trouble with communications. But the nasty square between Mars and Saturn was unmistakably bad news.

CHAPTER TEN

Even before Antonia set foot in the hotel, it was obvious she wouldn't feel at ease there. It was modern and purpose-built, with a cluster of low buildings laid out around a brick-paved courtyard dimly lit by white globe lanterns. Some of the rooms and the lighted windows of the restaurant looked out over the central. 'Not much privacy either. And it's so isolated—'

'You can see the lights of the village down there.' Jo, trying to be encouraging, pointed down the road they had just turned off. 'There's bound to be a pub in Whitby and the coast is only a few minutes' walk away. We may even have sea views.'

'I wonder where Sargent is,' Antonia muttered, as they went through the main entrance. It wasn't long before they found out. Jo was bending over the reception desk, signing in, when she heard Sargent's plummy accents behind her.

'Antonia, this is nice, seeing a friendly face. We'll have to keep each other company. Like two souls washed up on a desert island together.'

Jo turned round to find him looking down on Antonia with a grin that could only be described as wolfish. He was as well turned out as ever and seemed very relaxed. Antonia, on the other hand, had gone pale. 'Not quite on our own,' she was saying. 'My friend Jo is staying here too.'

'Oh, really?' Sargent's grin grew wider as his shrewd gaze took in Jo. 'Oh yes, so she is. Well, hello again, Jo. What brings you here?'

'She's walking,' Antonia said before Jo could answer. 'Along the cliffs.'

Jo tried to make the best of this rather lame excuse, which they had concocted earlier. 'I like coastal walking,' she said. 'And it's an excellent time of the year for birdwatching.'

Sargent's eyes became so narrow they almost disappeared altogether. 'Very bracing,' was his only comment, then he added pleasantly, 'Would you both care for an aperitif with me when you've had time to settle in?'

Jo refused politely for Antonia's sake, although her own instinct would have been to accept. She always worked on the premise of trying to find out as much about people as possible — especially if she didn't entirely trust them.

Their rooms on the third floor did not have views of the sea as Jo had hoped. They were singles next door to each other, as she had requested, and both looked out on the moorland that surrounded the hotel on three sides, the fourth side being the main road. Jo's room was small but comfortable with a cafetière and a supply of decent coffee on her dressing table.

Antonia was less contented. 'I won't be able to call you if anything happens.' She was sitting on the edge of her bed, looking miserable. 'At the cottage, you're always in shouting distance.'

Jo had thought of this. She had paid a visit to the shops before leaving Coventry and bought a baby monitor. She had seen one in use when her nephews were babies and the more modern versions were even more sophisticated. With the transmitter beside Antonia's bed and the receiver plugged into the socket in her own room, Jo could effectively be on duty twenty-four hours a day.

'It's not exactly high-tech surveillance but I think it will do the trick,' Jo said after she had set it up.

'Not a bad idea,' Antonia admitted. 'If Oliver comes knocking on my door, I'll yell into this and you can deal with him.' She examined the white plastic transmitter with its cute rabbit transfers.

'I'm afraid the bunnies couldn't be avoided,' Jo said. 'And of course my phone will be on twenty-four/seven and doesn't leave my side. You'll even be able to get me while you're on your course, if you need to.'

'I'm still worried about him being so near.' Antonia frowned. 'Didn't you see the way he looked at me downstairs? He knows I'm scared and he just wants to taunt me.' She looked around her room. 'There isn't any way he can see me in here, is there? What do you think he's doing now?'

Jo crossed the room and drew the curtains, having looked out briefly to ensure Antonia's room was not overlooked. 'I'll go and find out where his room is,' she offered, 'and where he'll be tomorrow. Hopefully you needn't have anything to do with him. Where is your course being held?'

Antonia dug out some papers from her holdall. 'The Cromwell Suite. Don't leave me on my own too long, will you?'

Jo reassured her, thinking it might be better if Antonia abandoned the course and went home, if being near Sargent was going to affect her like this. It would be better still if she could be persuaded to give up the whole idea of proving Sargent was her sister's killer and get a job somewhere entirely different, but this seemed unlikely.

The woman on reception was quite chatty and friendly. According to her badge, her name was Yvonne and Jo spent a bit of time talking to her, claiming to be a colleague of Sargent's who wanted to look him up. Yvonne seemed to have time on her hands and was very ready to listen. She even gave out his room number, which was more than Jo had expected, and said he was booked all week on a course in the Cromwell Suite.

'He's on full board so he'll be eating in the restaurant every night. Do you want me to put you on a table close to him?' the receptionist asked with a broad grin.

'No, better not.' Jo smiled back. 'Don't want to appear too obvious.'

'Oh, I'm not one for subtlety, me,' the woman laughed. 'Hit 'em over the head or ten to one they don't notice you.'

Jo thought there was probably something to be said for this approach but she didn't have time to pursue the discussion. She thanked Yvonne and headed back upstairs. She took the door to the second floor and made a quick detour past Sargent's room, ready to produce a look of pleased surprise if she should bump into him. It was on the same side of the building as hers and Antonia's but on the floor below and at the other end of the corridor.

Antonia remained quiet and tense during dinner and turned down the idea of walking to the village afterwards. She didn't want a drink in the bar either — although Jo had hoped this might relax her — or to try out the fitness centre. Left with no other options, they retired early to their separate rooms.

Fond as she was of Antonia, Jo couldn't help feeling relieved when she was finally on her own for the night. Antonia's obvious unease was not exactly restful. Tired by the journey, Jo was dozing in front of the TV when she heard Antonia's voice, alarmingly close at hand.

'Jo! Jo! Come here.'

It took Jo a moment to realise the sibilant sounds were coming from the baby monitor. *It works, then*, Jo thought.

She pulled on her trainers and hurried to the next room. Checking her phone, she saw it was only ten o'clock. She rapped on the door, said her name and was let in quickly.

'There's someone out there,' Antonia announced, clearly agitated. She pointed to the window.

'What were you doing looking out?' Jo strode across the room. The curtains were slightly parted, not as she had left them. She told Antonia to switch the lights out and peered through the gap.

'I felt sure I was being watched,' Antonia said breathlessly at her elbow, 'I was convinced.'

'But they couldn't see you through the curtains.'

'It didn't matter, I knew he was there. I had to look and—' she caught her breath — 'I saw him. There was a light down there like a torch. He must have been standing outside my room.'

Jo could just make out a path around the hotel and what looked like a tall hedge beyond that. There was no sign of life now but she collected her own torch from her room, put on her coat and went out to have a look.

She found the tarmac path and the hedge of conifers that ringed the hotel buildings and walked slowly around it. She didn't see signs of anyone or any marks in the grass by the path below Antonia's room. Craning her head back, she could see the dim light around the curtains and, next door, her own room starkly lit up. Moving her eyes downwards and counting windows, she found what must be Sargent's room, also brightly lit and with the curtains drawn back. She waited a while with her torch switched off and one hand on her phone, looking up at his room and occasionally glancing over at Antonia's.

After a minute or so, she saw Sargent cross in front of the window wearing nothing but a towel round his neck. It looked like he had just washed his hair. Her cheeks coloured in the darkness, and she turned and walked back to the main entrance of the hotel, feeling uncomfortably like a peeping tom but also slightly excited by the sight of Sargent naked — he was certainly in good shape for a man of forty-five or so. If it had been Sargent lurking outside Antonia's room, he'd have had to get back very quickly, strip off and shower in a matter of minutes. Would he do that on the off chance someone might see him from outside? It seemed so unlikely.

On her way in, Jo stopped at the reception desk, where Yvonne was still on duty, and asked if the hotel employed any security guards. They might come in useful and it might also explain who had been wandering around the grounds with a torch. She drew a blank on this, however.

'There's no need to worry about anything like that,' Yvonne said. 'You're not in London, you know.'

'There are just hotel staff on duty at night, then?' Jo asked.

'Yes, but we don't have any problems with break-ins and the like. We're safe as houses up here. If you need anything in the night, just give me a bell.'

Jo thanked her and went up to see Antonia, who still seemed uneasy. She remained convinced that her room was being watched and she was the same in the morning — on edge and withdrawn over breakfast, eating very little and glancing across at Sargent every so often. He was apparently oblivious behind his paper at a table in the corner.

'I want you to keep an eye on him all the time,' Antonia murmured to Jo. 'When I go out to my course, you stay here and make sure he doesn't follow me.'

Jo agreed but, seeing how anxious Antonia was, suggested that she consider going back home instead of attending the course. 'It can't be that important,' she reasoned. 'It's not as if you're going to stay with Sargent's firm.'

Antonia shook her head. 'I know, but the course is useful in its own right. I'll always be working with IT and nowadays you need to know the health and safety legislation. Anyway—' she gave Jo a sudden meaningful look — 'I think I'm bringing things to a head by coming here. He's going to make a move. Then I'll have my proof.'

There was no time to get her to explain further as she had to go upstairs to fetch her notes for the course. She told Jo she would go straight to the course room, which was in a conference room across the courtyard. Jo could see the entrance from the restaurant window. She stirred her coffee and covertly watched Sargent, who paid no attention as Antonia left the room. From where Jo sat, she could see down to the main glass door of the hotel and was able to watch Antonia cross the courtyard to the featureless building opposite. Sargent still did not move and Jo felt herself relax. She stayed there, fetching a top-up of coffee from the buffet, until Sargent left for his course. He gave her a charming smile on his way out and Jo smiled back, thinking of her unexpected view last night.

In her lunch hour, Antonia met Jo in reception as arranged and Jo suggested a walk before their meal, thinking it would do Antonia good to get away from the place for a bit. She agreed, saying it had been stuffy in the course room, and asked the receptionist if he would look after her notes for her. As he took the ring binder, he noticed her name on the front. 'Oh, are you Miss Carlyle?'

'Mrs Carlyle, yes.'

'A man was asking for you earlier,' the young receptionist said, 'but he didn't leave a name, just said he would find you . . . Did I do the wrong thing?'

Antonia was gripping the edge of the desk and staring at him. 'A man? What man? What did he want?'

'Can you remember what he looked like?' Jo asked in more reasonable tones and the receptionist turned to her.

'I told him Mrs Carlyle was in the Cromwell Suite and would be there till lunch,' he said. 'I said that if he wanted to leave a message I would ensure it reached her but he said it didn't matter. There was nothing unusual about him, a businessman, you know.' The boy seemed to be floundering when it came to a description.

'Was he another guest?' Jo asked.

'I don't think so,' he said. 'But I see so many people . . .'

'What — what did he want?' Antonia demanded.

The receptionist was looking increasingly harassed. 'I honestly don't know. Were you expecting someone? You didn't leave any instructions.'

Jo took pity on him and steered Antonia out. 'I'll see if I can find out some more this afternoon but it couldn't have been Sargent,' she said, leading the way across the main road and down the lane, which she guessed led to the coast path. 'Whatever else you said about him, you couldn't describe him as ordinary-looking . . .'

Antonia shot Jo a suspicious glance. 'You like him, don't you? I saw you looking at him at breakfast.'

'No, I don't. I don't know him,' Jo answered.

'But you don't believe me, do you?' Antonia's pace quickened and she kept her head down. 'If you did, you wouldn't fancy him. I told you. He *killed my sister*.'

Jo felt her own blood pressure rising, no doubt affected by Antonia's tension but she kept her voice even and quiet. 'I'm prepared to believe you. What do you think I'm doing here?'

'Of course it wasn't Sargent asking for me at the hotel. He's too clever for that.' Antonia strode along at Jo's side, not looking to right or left. 'He's got other people working for him so he can watch me all the time. I felt it when I went over to the course room this morning.'

'Did you see anybody? Because Sargent was still sitting at his table—'

'I told you,' Antonia interrupted, 'he's got someone else doing his dirty work now. They're just waiting.' She sighed. 'For what? I don't know.'

Jo was no psychologist but to her, Antonia was sounding like she had a classic persecution complex. She decided it would be wise to change the subject. 'Did you bring the list of people on your course like I asked you?'

Antonia produced a piece of paper from her pocket and handed it over silently.

Jo studied the list of names, which meant nothing to her. 'Do you know any of these people?'

'Not a soul,' Antonia responded. 'They are all from small businesses all over the country. Mostly earnest IT types and almost all men, as you can see.'

It was a blustery day, the wind from the sea buffeting them as they walked along the worn path. Jo had the sense to say very little and enjoyed the noise of the sea pounding on the rocks below and the steady line of the grey horizon. Antonia seemed to be calmer by the time they went back to the hotel, and Sargent was nowhere to be seen when they were having lunch, which probably helped.

* * *

That evening, Jo had an idea that she thought might help to calm Antonia's nerves. She had been for a swim during the afternoon and had noticed a large glassed-in sauna area at the back of the pool. After dinner she suggested a swim and a sauna, and Antonia seemed quite keen, on condition she checked Sargent wouldn't be there. Jo agreed and went to seek him out while Antonia fetched their swimming costumes.

Sargent had left the restaurant about half an hour before them and she guessed he might be in the bar. Sure enough, she saw him near the back of the long, narrow room, deep in conversation with a woman in a business suit. Someone he'd met on his course, perhaps.

'I bet she's rich,' was Antonia's rather sour comment when she heard this. She was more interested in the sauna than the swim and after only a few minutes in the pool they presented themselves at the desk the other side of the turnstile, where they were given big white towels and a range of different saunas, ice showers and plunge pools to choose from. Antonia chose one of the dry heat cabins and Jo, thinking she ought to stay close by, went in with her, although she would have preferred a Turkish steam room.

She found she could not stand more than a few minutes of the oppressive heat, and had to leave for the obligatory cold shower. She took a soft drink and sat where she could see the door to the cabin. After a while a couple came out, which left Antonia in there on her own. Flicking over the damp pages of a magazine she had picked up, Jo kept one eye on the wooden door and wondered how she could bear the heat for so long.

She was wondering about the various states of undress of people around her — some were wearing swimming costumes, others went around naked, like the slim woman with straight blonde hair, and one man strolled past fully dressed in jogging top and bottoms, even wearing a baseball hat back to front. Slightly overdressed, Jo was thinking, when she was startled by banging and shouting from the cabin. Antonia's voice screamed something unintelligible from behind the door.

Jo jumped up, swerving to avoid colliding with a large naked man who was in her way. From the cabin she could hear strangled cries.

A young, slight attendant reached the cabin first and bent down to get Antonia out. Jo could see her half-lying just inside the door. Between them, she and the attendant helped her out. She was bright red and crying loudly, 'Someone locked me in there! I couldn't get out. It was l-locked!' Tears and sweat coursed down her face.

'It wasn't locked, honestly.' The attendant turned to Jo as if appealing to reason. He was about twenty, short, thin and fair, and his face was as white as his overalls. 'None of the doors lock.'

Jo cut short his explanation and asked him to fetch a glass of water. Antonia was sobbing quietly and shaking as Jo led her to a seat and wrapped a dry towel around her shoulders. 'Calm down. Don't try and say what happened. You can tell me later. Take deep breaths.'

The incident had caused a minor sensation in the sauna room and a little crowd had gathered. The young attendant returned with a glass of water. 'She must have just panicked,' he said, thrusting the glass towards Antonia and stepping back. 'There are rules printed on the inside and outside of the sauna cabins and recommended times to stay . . .' His words faded out as he caught Jo's hard stare.

'Please could you fetch the manager,' Jo said. 'Or someone else who knows what's best to do. My friend was stuck in there for some time.'

While he was still dithering, the young attendant was rescued by a tall, self-possessed woman in a similar white uniform. 'Can I be of any help?' she asked. 'I'm Moira Lee, the manager here.'

Jo explained what had happened. Antonia was still sobbing.

'As long as she wasn't in there for hours on end, she should be OK,' Moira Lee said. She turned to Antonia. 'I'll get you some more water. How are you feeling? If you can manage it, I suggest you sit in the tepid pool to cool down slowly.'

Antonia, who was calmer but still visibly shaken, thanked her and allowed herself to be led to the small pool. 'I couldn't get out,' she murmured. 'I would have died in there, could have had a heart attack — or—'

'Not at all. Our attendants observe who goes in and out of the cabins. They would not have let you stay in there too long. But I will have the doors of all the cabins checked, just in case,' Ms Lee promised. 'Perhaps you stood up too quickly to leave — the heat can make you dizzy, you know. Maybe you felt weak and then got a bit frightened. It's quite understandable,' she added in a voice which implied that indeed it was. But only in lesser mortals.

'Do you mind if I have a look at the door now, all the same?' Jo asked.

Ms Lee appeared surprised but agreed. Leaving Antonia sitting with her feet dangling in the tepid pool, rather forlorn and draped in towels, Jo walked back, past the plunge pool and the entrance to the showers, to the cabin Antonia had used. She swung the door to and fro on its hinges, watched by the attendant. The door showed no signs of sticking or jamming. The wooden door jamb and sill were smooth and unmarked. The door handle turned easily. Jo stepped back, puzzled. It seemed Antonia had indeed panicked for no reason. There was no lock, as the attendant had said, and from inside and out the door gave no resistance.

Feeling the sceptical gaze of the attendant upon her, she walked slowly back, her mind full of all kinds of doubts, to Antonia still sitting limply by the pool, her hair dark with sweat, her face puffy with tears. As soon as she saw Jo she became animated, shaking her wet hair off her face.

'Jo! We've got to leave,' she hissed, wild-eyed. 'He's getting worse. He's trying to kill me now!'

CHAPTER ELEVEN

At first, Antonia wanted to go straight back to Warwick, abandon the course and even leave her job. Jo thought it would be better to sleep on it and make a decision in the morning. She had accepted Moira Lee's explanation as the most likely version of events, at least for the moment, but Antonia still maintained that she had been locked in. 'I struggled and struggled with that door and I am telling you, it didn't budge,' she said, pacing around the narrow bedroom.

Eventually, Jo realised it may be better just to drive straight back, as she couldn't see either of them getting any sleep. But when she suggested this, Antonia frowned at her, clutching her towelling robe closer. 'Why have you suddenly changed your mind?'

Jo sighed, at a loss. 'No reason. Just — maybe you're right, that's all.'

'But that would be giving in.' Antonia sat down on the side of the bed and chewed a fingernail. It was 11.40 p.m. when she insisted on ringing Paul to tell him the whole story and became almost hysterical again on the phone. Jo busied herself checking that the baby monitor was plugged in and the windows were locked.

'Paul's coming up first thing in the morning!' Antonia announced when she finished the call. 'Isn't that marvellous? He believes I am in danger, no question about it,' she added defiantly, getting back into bed and pulling her knees up to her chin. 'He understands I can't relax here.'

'That's good of him,' Jo agreed. 'Have you got anything to help you sleep tonight? Can I make you one of your herbal teas?'

'There's some homeopathic sleeping remedy in my make-up bag in case of emergencies. Isn't Paul kind to drive all this way to see if I'm OK? He's going to set off as soon as he's finished work and so he'll be here before breakfast. He's a good friend.'

Jo concealed her irritation about Paul's expected arrival. 'You may as well try and get some sleep, otherwise you'll be knackered by then,' she suggested. Antonia always became more helpless in his presence and he might well persuade her to leave first thing tomorrow. Jo wanted to go back to the sauna in the morning to check the place again and question the staff.

'I can't possibly sleep.' Antonia lay down, still looking tense and dishevelled. 'Not while I know Oliver Sargent is so close and could be at my door in minutes. God knows what he's doing—'

'I'll go down to his room and see if I can find out exactly where he is,' Jo offered. 'If you know he's in there asleep, maybe you'll feel better.'

Antonia seemed mollified by this and dosed herself with some of the sleeping remedy, which seemed to consist of rubbing oil on her pulse points.

Jo went quietly down the back stairs in her canvas pumps. This plain, functional staircase was also used as a fire escape and she had identified it as not only the quickest but also the most discreet route to reach Sargent's floor. She taxed her mind to come up with a good reason for knocking on Sargent's door at 11.45 p.m. The only excuses she could come up with sounded like pickup lines. Overlaying this difficulty was the left side of her brain, which argued that the whole exercise was a waste of time because Sargent had been nowhere near the sauna and in any case, Antonia could not have been locked in. Nevertheless, for duty's sake, she approached his door and raised her hand to knock, hesitating because she was still without a proper excuse.

'Are you going in?' The voice from behind startled her, although she knew it wasn't Sargent because of the strong Yorkshire accent. She turned to confront a young, lanky waiter who was grinning at her.

'I was just—' Jo was about to produce an explanation when she realised that the waiter was carrying a wine bottle and two glasses.

He smirked. 'You can take these in for me if you like.'

'No, you go ahead,' Jo said with icy politeness, 'I seem to have the wrong room.' She moved away from the door but hovered long enough to see the wine taken in by an unusually flushed and rumpled Sargent. The muted sound of the television could be heard from the room and Jo was sure she heard a woman's voice just as the door closed. She wondered if it was the same woman she'd seen him with earlier in the bar.

'Looks like you missed the boat there, chuck,' the waiter remarked and Jo returned rapidly up the stairs, reflecting that dignity was a luxury a PI couldn't afford. Antonia was still awake so Jo gave her the news that Sargent had gone to bed and not necessarily alone. She didn't add her opinion that she thought this was unlikely behaviour for a man who had just tried to murder someone.

'I always heard these management courses were an excuse for musical beds,' Antonia commented, sounding more relaxed. 'I wonder what the guys at the office would make of his behaviour if they knew.' Jo made no comment but was relieved that Antonia seemed reasonably content and so she left, making sure first that the transmitter was plugged in and switched on.

* * *

She did not sleep easily. Although it seemed most likely that Antonia had simply panicked in the sauna, Jo found herself going over and over the incident as if she was looking for another explanation. She finally drifted off to sleep in the small hours and was awoken by the phone by her bed ringing. The room was pitch black and Jo had to grapple for the receiver, knocking over her water glass. 'Yes?' she croaked.

'Is that Jo? Antonia's friend?' The voice was familiar but Jo couldn't place it.

'Yes. Who's that?' Her own voice sounded thick and sleepy.

'It's Paul Bakewell. I just rang to say I'm on my way. I told Toni I would call when I set off but I'm a bit worried because she didn't answer the phone. Is she OK? She seemed really upset earlier on.'

Jo had retrieved her own phone and discovered it was five thirty in the morning. 'She's all right. She took a sleeping remedy type of thing so the phone probably didn't wake her.' Jo swallowed a yawn. 'What are you ringing at this hour for anyway?'

'Toni insisted on me calling as soon as I was on my way.' Paul's voice was patient but unapologetic. 'Listen, could you just check she's OK and if she wakes up, tell her I'll be there in a couple of hours.'

Jo agreed with a poor grace. She put the phone down and bent her ear towards the baby monitor. It was sensitive enough to pick up most sounds in the room, including breathing. The first prickle of panic touched Jo's scalp when she found the machine was utterly silent.

As she pulled on her dressing gown, her brain was shocked wide awake by the realisation that if Paul had been ringing Antonia's room or her phone, she should have heard it through the baby monitor. She was sure it would have woken her. Either he hadn't called or the monitor wasn't working.

She rapped on Antonia's door. She didn't have a key to the room. She had asked for one when they arrived, but the hotel had refused. When Antonia didn't answer her knock, she rattled the door handle and knocked as loudly as she could without waking the whole corridor.

Surely that remedy wouldn't make her sleep this deeply? Jo thought. Ceasing to care about the other guests, Jo shouted Antonia's name. The palm of her hand hurt from thumping against the wood and doors along the corridor began to open. Someone shouted at her to be quiet.

When there was still no response or sound from Antonia's room, Jo dashed to the main stairs, which were the quickest way to reception. On her way down, she met Yvonne, the receptionist. 'I need a master key,' Jo explained hurriedly. 'My friend in room 506 is not answering the door. She may be ill.'

'It's all right, I've got it,' Yvonne responded and followed her up the stairs. A few hotel guests were standing in the corridor on the fifth floor, curious about the noise. Jo looked round quickly, hoping Antonia would be among them. But she wasn't. The receptionist advised people to go back to bed, slipped her master key in the lock and went in.

Jo stepped in behind her, flicking the light on. She saw the empty bed and white sheet trailing onto the floor. Antonia was not in the room. The bathroom was also empty. Her next glance was towards the bedside monitor — it was still plugged in but was switched off at the socket.

The receptionist was looking at Jo. 'Looks like your friend's gone out.'

The dressing table, which had been scattered with Antonia's make-up only a few hours ago, was cleared of everything except the folder of hotel stationery. The make-up bag lay open in a drawer, its contents spilling out along with some more of Antonia's clothes, which were surprisingly rumpled. Jo riffled through the hangers in the wardrobe while Yvonne watched, wearing an expression that said, *I've seen it all now*. Her leather jacket and boots were missing. Some clothes were in a jumble on the floor of the wardrobe but they were not among them. The sky was just starting to grow pale, and Jo wondered what could have possessed Antonia to leave her room.

'Has anything been stolen?' Yvonne asked. Previously the woman had been cheerful and friendly but Jo was aware that this was now the early hours of the morning and she was eliciting increasing suspicion.

'Her handbag is missing, her boots and her leather coat,' Jo said. 'It looks like you're right, she has gone out. I don't suppose you saw her?' The receptionist shook her head. 'Then I think we should call the police.'

'Let's not be hasty.' Yvonne shot Jo a look that was loaded with meaning. 'Maybe your friend has gone to visit someone else who's staying here.'

'But she's taken her coat,' Jo murmured, allowing herself to be ushered out of the room. She walked past a couple of old guests in their dressing gowns who were still hanging around in the corridor, agog with curiosity, and followed the receptionist downstairs. 'The thing is, my friend thinks she's in danger. She believes someone locked her in the sauna last night,' Jo explained. 'You can ask your spa manager about it. And maybe Antonia really is in danger. I don't think she would have left her room voluntarily. I'm very worried for her safety.' Jo couldn't put words to the feeling of anxiety rising up inside her.

The other woman returned her look, her plain, open face apparently incapable of surprise. 'What do you want me to do? If your friend reports something has been stolen, we can consider calling the police—'

'But I'm worried about where she is!' They had reached the front desk and the receptionist retreated behind it. 'Have you been on this desk all night? Has anyone been past you? You might have seen her on her way out. She's got reddish-blonde hair and she's a bit shorter than me.'

Yvonne shook her head. 'I haven't seen anyone. There's only me and Eric about. He's the night porter and about as much use as a chocolate teapot. He's supposed to check the corridors at nights but he spends most of his time doing crosswords.'

'Please call the police,' Jo said. She leaned on the desk, aware that her palms were leaving sweaty marks on the high gloss. 'Or I'll call them myself.' Faced with this ultimatum, Yvonne agreed and Jo thanked her. 'I'm going to carry on looking for her,' she said and hurried off upstairs.

'Don't wake any of the guests!' Yvonne called after her.

Jo got dressed quickly, pulled on her coat and left the hotel by the nearest door, which was a fire exit at the bottom of the stairs. If Antonia had gone outside, this was probably the exit she would have used. If not, the receptionist would surely have seen her. Outside it was lighter than Jo had expected and she could see the courtyard with the low-pitched roof of the fitness centre ahead. There were a few lights still on in the grounds but the buildings around her were in darkness.

The first place to check was the car park. Antonia still had keys for the Mazda and might have driven off somewhere if she couldn't sleep. But the car was where Jo had parked it, so she walked briskly around the grounds, peering fruitlessly into the dark conference rooms. In the fitness centre, the swimming pool glittered vacantly.

She jogged to the main road and looked in each direction. A car sped past toward Whitby as she stood there, heart racing and legs jelly-like and uncertain. Once the rush of the car had passed, nothing stirred except a chill, damp breeze.

No matter how sleepless and stressed she was, the notion of Antonia wandering off into the countryside alone was unimaginable, so Jo retraced her steps to the hotel. Yvonne confirmed the police would be here 'in a minute', but waiting for them seemed inexplicably wasteful so she carried on searching, trying the deserted bar first and then the restaurant, which was also empty but set for breakfast. Hearing voices from the back of the dining room, she pushed the swing door and stepped into a dingy, clinical kitchen, where the breakfast chef and the kitchen porter were drinking tea.

'I'm looking for my friend. She's a guest here. A blonde woman, a bit shorter than me in a leather jacket with a fur collar. Have you seen her?'

The chef gave her an early morning look, white-faced and narrow-eyed. 'I've only come up the stairs and I've not seen a soul.' He pointed to the floor. 'I live in,' he added by way of explanation. He turned to the man in overalls beside him. 'How about you? Can you help the lass?'

The kitchen porter shook his head, blinking from behind round glasses. 'I came on my bike ten minutes ago. Didn't see any blonde women about.'

Jo thanked them and left. It was nearly half past six and there was nowhere else she could think of to try except Oliver Sargent's room. It was hard to imagine Antonia going there voluntarily but what if she had been under duress? Jo felt she had to try everything.

She knocked on Sargent's door and his answering voice sounded muffled. There was a long pause before he appeared, clutching a thick towelling robe around him. 'What is it?' he repeated, his face more creased and folded than she remembered.

Jo explained and he raised his eyebrows, seeming more alert. 'Well, she's not here,' he said with a ghost of a smile. 'Maybe she went out to see the sun rise. If she doesn't turn up by breakfast time, you'd better come and see me and we'll decide what to do.'

Jo disliked his authoritarian tone and had no intention of consulting him about her next move. She murmured something, which could have been taken for agreement, while straining to see past his wide shoulders into the room. He opened the door a little wider, almost as if inviting her in, while at the same time, his expression hardened. Meeting that look, Jo took a step back.

'You'd better go and sort out your little problem, hadn't you?' he said, his eyes not wavering. 'Because you're just wasting time here.'

It was only a few moments that passed between them but the tension rooted Jo to the spot while her mind raced.

What to do for the best? What would help Antonia? What had she missed?

She headed back to the reception area, where she discovered to her relief that two constables had arrived. They were being shown into the bar by Yvonne, who also promised them coffee. Sitting around a little table near the shuttered bar, the smell of last night's alcohol in the air, Jo directed her explanation to the older of the two, a woman, who introduced herself as PC Kenny. The officer had a quiet, economic way of speaking. 'Why does Antonia believe herself to be in danger?'

Jo gave her a quick summary of the sauna incident and Antonia's fear of Sargent. She knew that without this background information the police would be unlikely to do much.

'Where do you think she is?' PC Kenny waited, eyes on Jo and very still.

'Outdoors somewhere. She took her coat and boots. Probably within walking distance because she didn't take her car.'

'We'll ask around in the village — there's always a couple of bods about early,' the other officer chimed in, already looking towards the door. 'We'll head off there now but we'll keep an eye out on the way. And you'll let us know, won't you, if she turns up?'

'We'll do our best to find her and give you a ring later,' PC Kenny said.

Jo watched the two figures walk down the drive with a growing sense of despair. She told herself that Antonia would show up at breakfast with some vague, irrational reason for going out in the early hours of the morning. Or she would just appear around the corner, unaware of all the commotion she had caused. Common sense demanded that she would turn up soon. But the slow minutes were ticking towards unreality and any sense of optimism was becoming shakier. She was glad the police officers had taken her seriously. She tried to believe that those two competent individuals would find Antonia, would just come across her somewhere — Jo didn't care where. And they would bring her back, like firemen plucking a kitten out of a tree.

But Antonia, for all her irritating dizziness, was not that helpless and daft, Jo reminded herself, trying to force herself to think logically. For one thing, Antonia had switched off the transmitter by her bed so she could slip out. And for some reason, she had left her belongings in a mess. Perhaps she had been looking for something in a hurry? So she must have had some destination in mind. The question was, had she left on her own?

Jo picked up her coat and put it on again. Yvonne had gone off duty now, to be replaced by an unfamiliar man in the hotel uniform who looked down his nose at her as she went past.

It was now almost fully light outside and cold and fresh. There was a sparkling frost and the sage green of the steep hills was deep and chilled. No one was about. Jo, needing to be doing something, walked along the main road, trying to keep the feeling of dread from seeping into her mind.

CHAPTER TWELVE

She heard the dog barking first. The sound would have carried for miles in the still morning air. Then they appeared, dog and man, over the brow of the hill, running on the frozen grass. Jo stood still on the path that led to the clifftop where she and Antonia had walked the day before. As the man ran heavily towards her, it was as if she had always had a deep, buried feeling that it would end like this.

'Excuse me! Excuse me!' the man bawled, his breath clouding his face. The dog barked and pranced ahead. When he was still a couple of metres away, the man began to explain at the top of his voice, panting, 'There's someone laying under the cliff. She must have fell off onto the rocks and she doesn't look too good. Can you fetch an ambulance?'

'Yes,' said Jo, her voice high and strange. She took out her phone and started to dial while she was speaking. 'Are you going back to her? I'll follow you.'

The man nodded, still out of breath. He was red-faced, duffle-coated and middle-aged. The dog, a sprightly Jack Russell, turned when he did. The man pointed behind him. 'There's a path down a bit further along. It doesn't look like much can be done but I'll go back anyway.'

Jo was already treading close behind him when the call connected and she gave the details. Her voice sounded perfectly calm but after the call, she started to run, catching up quickly with the man and his dog. They both had a surprising turn of speed and she had to slow to a walk when she reached the cliff path, clutching her sides and looking over the edge, where the black shiny rocks swayed dizzily below.

The man, for all his bulk, had started to scramble down and Jo half-tumbled after him, picking her own route, sweating inside her coat. The brown sea looked choppy and cold and, she saw in glimpses, the sand below the cliff was wet. She was swerving dangerously close to an edge to peer over when the dog appeared through the bushes. She picked a steep path down, slipping occasionally on the worn stones, with the dog following. At a sudden drop, she jolted awkwardly over a boulder and saw, not far below, the bald head of the duffle-coated man bending over Antonia.

Her friend lay in an oddly defensive position, almost curled up. There was a complete stillness about her, even at this distance, which Jo didn't like, and the left arm was crooked under her head protectively. Jo kept running, somehow stumbling down, the heedless dog dashing ahead now.

The man said something but it just blended into the constant crashing of the sea. She came slowly to Antonia's raised shoulder, feeling through the blonde hair for a pulse on the neck and her fingers touched blood, wet and warm. She stepped back, shaking, sobbing. Her chest felt tight with pain, the tightness spreading to her throat and head. The sobs of disbelief and loss were stuck in her. She found a rock to sit on, horribly conscious of every small detail. Antonia's body lay in front of her.

The police arrived before the ambulance and made the sense of dread marginally more bearable with their ordinariness, their common-sense words. Jo spoke to the same police officer as before, PC Kenny, who thankfully didn't need to be told a lot of things. Jo wanted to stay with Antonia, insisted on it. She had some vague idea that it was her duty. She saw the body tied onto the stretcher and carried across the sand to an easier path further along and then up the cliff to the ambulance. PC Kenny walked beside her all the way and led her to a police car.

Jo got in unquestioningly, wishing she could just stop thinking. Each thought was worse than the last. She had half-imagined the police car was following the ambulance but she never saw Antonia again.

* * *

Jo was taken to the police station and given a cup of tea while people bustled around and talked over her head. She saw the man in the duffle coat nearby and wondered where his dog was.

Eventually she was shown into an interview room by PC Kenny, who introduced her to a small man with a brown, crumpled face and a virtually non-existent chin. DCI Gammon was curt and unsmiling and he got straight to the point. 'I will be in charge of the investigation into Antonia Carlyle's death. I need to know everything you can tell me about her. Everything you can think of. Now I need you to confirm your name and address and what you are doing here. PC Kenny tells me you're staying at the St George Hotel?'

Jo had already decided to tell the police everything and launched into her story, while inwardly reflecting that Antonia would not have approved — she had always liked to keep something back. The detective hardly interrupted at all but made copious notes, which Jo guessed must be more from habit than anything else as the interview was being recorded. Jo noticed how the jaded gaze from across the table became a little sharper when she said she was working as a PI.

'Of course,' he said when Jo had finished, 'we don't know that anyone else was involved in Ms Carlyle's death.'

'But what about what I've just told you?' Jo demanded, taken aback.

Gammon didn't answer this, preferring to study his notes. After a while, he looked up. 'Did you believe your friend's story?'

'Not all of it all of the time,' Jo admitted, 'but it looks like I should have done.'

He pushed the top back on his gel pen and gathered his loose notes together. 'If what you say is true, it's not your fault this happened,' he said in the same matter-of-fact tone he had used throughout the interview, 'so if you want some advice, don't take it all on yourself.'

Jo was not quite ready to leave it there. She was feeling steadier and the detective's brusque manner had a calming effect on her. There were things she needed to know too. She kept her voice level. 'How did Antonia die?'

DCI Gammon frowned, his weary face creasing up even more. 'As far as we can say at this stage, she died from the fall. Hit her head on the rocks. Some bones were clearly broken.'

'Do you know when?'

He shook his head automatically but the hooded eyes across the table regarded her for a minute and he added, 'Can't say, of course. But likely a matter of hours, that's all.' He glanced up at PC Kenny, who took her cue and got to her feet.

'But you are treating her death as suspicious?' Jo asked before she could be ushered out.

'Suspicious, yes,' DCI Gammon said. 'Now, PC Kenny will show you where you can get a fresh cup of tea and some breakfast.'

Eating breakfast was out of the question but she managed a couple of cups of coffee in the tiny canteen while she waited to sign her statement. About an hour later she was driven back to the hotel in a police car and escorted in by the two constables. The first person she laid eyes on as they entered reception was Paul. Her heart sank.

He made straight for them, white and anxious and full of questions. Jo was saved from the awful job of telling him what had happened by the merciful PC Kenny, who took him to one side to break the news. The other constable explained to the hotel manager that the police would need to interview some of the guests.

Jo stood in the midst of this, feeling an overwhelming need to be on her own. She knew she should be planning her next move, trying to finish the job at which she had singularly failed. But now that Antonia was dead, there seemed to be no point.

'Jo! You were supposed to be looking after her!' Paul came up to her, his face uncomfortably close and distorted with grief. 'How did it happen? How did he get to her? Why did you let her go out on her own?'

Jo stayed calm. Nothing Paul could say could make her feel worse. 'We don't know she did go out on her own,' she said.

'What do you mean?' Paul's voice rose hysterically, his face going from white to red. He jabbed a finger. 'What do you know? The police said she went for a walk, she fell. She would never have gone out on her own—' The capable arm of PC Kenny clamped itself around Paul's shoulders as she murmured calming words.

'All I'm saying is, no one knows yet,' Jo kept her voice steady while her body was stiff with tension.

'Why don't you both have a bit of a rest?' PC Kenny suggested. 'You've been up half the night, Mr Bakewell, I'm sure the hotel will find you a room—'

Jo escaped to her room gratefully but not before she had been warned by the other constable not to leave the hotel. Her body felt unreasonably tired as if she hadn't slept for a week and her neck was like a twisted cable. But when she got to her room, she couldn't relax. She felt cold and apprehensive and kept shivering convulsively. She paced up and down, her mind wouldn't settle and she started to make herself a cup of coffee more from force of habit than because she really wanted one. It occurred to her suddenly to call Macy. A dose of his caustic realism would do her the world of good.

With fingers that still weren't very steady, she pulled up his number. She registered it was eight twenty-five but it felt like it could be any time of the day or night. The phone rang and she willed him to pick up.

'Jo?' He always answered the phone in a tone that gave little away.

'I've got something terrible to tell you.' She waited a breath for this news to travel the distance between them. 'It's Antonia. She's dead. I found her body at the bottom of a cliff this morning.'

'You found it? Have you told the police?' Macy's voice was practical, clear.

'They know all about it. I've just come from an interview at the station.'

'What are you doing now?' Macy asked.

'Sitting on the bed waiting for the kettle to boil. As soon as I've had my coffee, I'll go and ask some questions—'

'Go to bed,' Macy advised. 'Forget the coffee. What's your room number?'

'505. I'm perfectly all right, you know. There's some people in the sauna I've got to interview.' This had been one of her plans before Antonia had died and she felt she ought to do something.

'Wait until I get there. I'll see you in a couple of hours or so. If you want to do something useful, turn up the heating and tell room service to bring up a bottle of brandy and stick it on your expenses.'

For once, Jo did as Macy said. Almost. She went to bed without a coffee as he had recommended but when she woke up an hour or so later, it felt too pathetic and awful just to lie there waiting for him to turn up. Besides, there was always the chance he might not. She got up and showered, trying not to think of Antonia as if she was still there, next door, dependent, wanting a lift somewhere, peculiarly vulnerable but sparky.

As she was putting on clean clothes, she remembered Macy had told her to order some brandy. She doubted if it would make her feel better but she did anyway. It cheered her up slightly to see the expression — half disgust, half admiration — on the face of the man who brought up the bottle and two glasses.

Before she could pour herself a glass, Macy arrived, looking untidy and cold in his shirtsleeves. 'God, that was an awful journey. And I was stuck behind a horse box for the last twenty miles.' His eyes alighted on the brandy. 'Exquisite timing, I see,' he commented. 'How are you? You look OK.'

'I feel awful. But better than I did.' She poured a small drink for both of them. 'It's my fault, you know, there's no getting away from it.'

'Just because Antonia thought something bad would happen to her and it did, does not mean you are to blame.' Macy flopped into the armchair. 'What happened to you anyway?'

'Me? I was just asleep in bed. Antonia must have gone out at about five o'clock this morning. It wasn't even light then. I didn't think wild horses would have got her out of that room on her own but she'd never have left it with Sargent either. He's on the floor below, by the way.'

'I'm only getting this in bits and pieces,' Macy complained.

For the second time that day Jo told Antonia's story, including what had happened to her sister to make her so suspicious of Sargent. More than ever, she wondered how much Antonia had left out. It looked like she would have to fill in the gaps herself now.

When she got to the incident in the sauna, Macy opened his eyes. 'Do you think someone tried to shut her in there?' he asked. 'It seems a thoroughly unreliable method of killing someone.'

'I don't know. Maybe they just wanted to frighten her. Antonia was nearly hysterical, though.'

'A habitual state of mind with her,' Macy murmured.

Jo ignored this and went on, 'She wanted to go straight home but I convinced her to stay.' The reasonable arguments she had produced were painful to recall and she came to a halt.

'What are you going to do?' Macy asked into the silence.

'I was planning to go back to the sauna today to find out what exactly happened. There was a bloke and a woman on duty last night and I was going to speak to them to see if they saw Sargent — or anyone else — about.'

Macy didn't seem to be concentrating on what she was saying. He looked around vaguely. 'I don't know what I'm doing here.'

Jo didn't know either but he was like a slice of normality and she was glad to see him. Unable to say this, she said instead, 'You could tell me what you think of Sargent. We ought to try and have a word with him too. I saw him at about half past eleven last night. He was in his room and I think there was a woman with him. Not Antonia,' Jo added. 'She was up here at the time. This morning at about six thirty I knocked on his door and he was there. He seemed sleepy but that's how you would act if you wanted people to think you'd been asleep all night.' She took a breath. 'Thanks for coming,' she said, not looking at his eyes but at his long fingers resting on the arms of his chair.

'I suppose it might be interesting. But it was bloody freezing when I got out of the car and I don't think I've got a coat. Have you got a jumper or something?'

With Macy pulling irritably at the sleeves of one of her jumpers, they went over to the sauna together, through the swimming pool area, which was fairly quiet. The sauna was not as busy as the night before. Through steamy glass windows she could see a few people sitting around in white towels, reading or just lying back and listening to the classical music being played softly through speakers. Jo saw straight away that the young attendant she had met last night was behind the desk. He was talking to a customer ahead of them. Jo thought he was probably booking a session until he turned round and she realised it was Paul.

His face hardened when he saw them. 'I thought you'd scuttled back to Coventry with your tail between your legs,' he muttered to Jo.

'Not yet.' Jo lifted her chin. She didn't want a show-down with him, but she was prepared for it if necessary.

Paul looked from Jo to Macy and addressed his next words to him. 'If you're the sucker who employs this girl, I ought to tell you she has made a complete balls-up.'

'Thanks for your comments,' Macy said, 'but I trust my staff, not your judgement.'

Paul took a step towards Macy. 'I'll see your firm in court for this.' His face red with strain, he stormed off, watched by the wide-eyed assistant. Jo glanced at Macy, who gave her a nonchalant shrug. Gathering her composure, she turned to start the interview she had planned, privately wondering what else could go wrong.

CHAPTER THIRTEEN

After a start like that, Jo thought, the interview could hardly get much worse and she was right. Her credibility had taken a severe dent in the eyes of the young man behind the desk, who had heard every word. When Jo questioned him about what had happened last night in the sauna, he didn't divulge anything except to repeat that the doors to the cabins didn't lock. His boss was not on duty so she had to give up.

'Paul must be making his own enquiries about Antonia's death,' she said to Macy on their way back to the hotel.

'Perhaps I'll offer to do that for him,' Macy said.

'I know it would be your ideal to get paid twice for doing the same thing but I somehow think Paul's faith in private investigators has been shaken slightly.'

'You're probably right.' Macy sighed. 'Let's eat anyway. It's so damn cold up here it's making me hungry. Then I might go over to the police station to see if I can find out any more from them.'

'I ought to talk to Sargent,' Jo said. 'Not that he'll tell me exactly what he was doing last night, but at least I can try.'

She felt more up to the task after a sandwich. She found out from the hotel receptionist that the police were interviewing people in one of the conference suites and it seemed logical to assume that Sargent might be among them, so, after Macy had driven over to see if he could charm some information out of DCI Gammon, she walked over to the low building that was next door and identical to the one in which Antonia's course had been held.

A group of about eight people were sitting waiting in a large dingy room, which had no windows and inappropriate-looking gilt-legged chairs set out cinema-style. No one spoke. A couple of people were staring at their phones and there was a waiting-room atmosphere. Jo wondered who to approach as Sargent clearly wasn't there. One woman was conspicuous by being less conventionally dressed than the others in their sober business clothes. She was sitting with her arms folded over a couple of layers of bright sweaters. A long, crumpled skirt reached her socks and boots.

Jo sat down beside her. 'Are you waiting to be interviewed?'

'Yes. Isn't it awful?' She regarded Jo with a considering expression. 'You're a friend of hers, aren't you? I've seen you at breakfast. I noticed you because I'm interested in auras and your friend had a very intense indigo aura.'

Jo had a friend who was a crystal healer and occasionally would venture an opinion on auras, so she wasn't too taken aback by this. 'I didn't know. What does that mean?'

'You only get it on people who feel things deeply — a sensitive soul. But with your friend, I got a distinct impression that her main feeling was fear—' The other woman stopped, her wide brown eyes regarding Jo seriously. 'I'm sorry. I'm being thoughtless. You must be extremely upset.'

'Yes I am,' Jo said. She gave a somewhat shaky sigh. 'But — well, I need to know what happened to her. Were you on the same course?'

'Yes. My name is Petra Lancaster. I didn't know Antonia very well. She seemed quiet but I didn't think she was unhappy enough to . . .' She let the words trail off.

'You think she committed suicide?'

'That's what people are saying. Or was it an accident?'

'Nobody knows. The police are treating it as suspicious,' Jo answered.

'Really?' Petra's eyes grew wider. She turned suddenly to the man sitting beside her. 'Stefan, you talked most to Antonia yesterday, didn't you?'

The man looked up reluctantly from his book, took off his reading glasses and frowned at Jo. 'We were in the same syndicate group but we just talked about work. She seemed bright. Do you know what happened? They're saying she threw herself off a cliff.'

'I don't know. She may have been pushed. She was out on the cliff path early this morning and I don't somehow think she would have gone out on her own. I don't suppose you were around at five o'clock, were you?'

'I was awake then,' Petra said, 'but I didn't leave my room.'

'Whereabouts are you?'

'On the second floor. I got up to finish my assignment. I have to do all my studying in my own time and the thing is, I can't take it in if I'm not fully awake so I like to get up, have a shower and do a few minutes' meditation to get me in the right frame of mind. I'm doing an Arts degree to get out of boring IT.'

'The police said Antonia died between five and six o'clock, so presumably she left her room at around quarter to five or before. Did you hear anyone about?'

'There were some cars coming and going outside. My room has a very picturesque view of the car park.'

'Did you look out?'

'I just heard cars moving about.' Petra cast her eyes to the ceiling and considered the question. 'When I went to the window, there was nothing happening.'

'What do you mean?' Jo persisted. 'What exactly did you hear? It's important. I was supposed to be looking out for Antonia.'

Petra looked hard at Jo. 'I can see your colours too, you know. They're rather muted at the moment.'

'That doesn't surprise me. The way I'm feeling, I'd have thought any self-respecting aura would have packed up and gone.'

Petra nodded. 'You probably just need to get this sorted out,' she said. 'Then your aura will bounce back. Anyway, if it helps you, I'll tell you what I remember — but I warn you, it's not very exciting. I got up at five o'clock with the alarm. I made myself a cup of tea almost straight away and that was when I heard a car engine starting up below. I didn't look out then.' She paused, chewing a thumbnail. 'It was when I heard another car engine and a man's voice that I got a bit more curious. But the kettle was boiling, so I filled the teapot and then went over to the window. All I saw was a man with white hair walking towards the hotel.'

'With white hair? What else did you notice about him? How tall was he? Where was he heading?'

'Towards the side door. As for his appearance, I don't know,' she said. 'Looking down on someone it's impossible to judge their height, isn't it? But he had broad shoulders and he was wearing a trench coat, hands in his pockets, head down. His hair was untidy. He seemed lost in himself—'

'There's a man on your floor with white hair — Oliver Sargent. Was it him?'

'Is he the one with the wolfish smile?'

As she was speaking, a uniformed policeman came into the room with a list of names. He called one out and a woman in a loud salmon-pink suit stood up from the back row. As the PC waited for her to enter the interview room, he noticed Jo and came over to ask what she was doing here.

'Actually, I was looking for Oliver Sargent,' she said.

'You're Jo Hughes, aren't you?' This took her by surprise — she didn't think she had ever seen the constable before. She supposed being involved with Antonia's death gave her a certain notoriety. 'I wouldn't bother with Sargent if I were you,' the PC advised. 'Why don't you head back to your room now?' He courteously held the door open for her and she left regretfully with Petra staring after her.

Still hoping to see Sargent, Jo tried the bar and the dining room but he wasn't there. She even knocked at his bedroom door but there was no answer. Then on her way up to her room, using the stairs as usual, she bumped into him coming down. He looked as suave and well-groomed as ever.

'Jo. How are you? Isn't it dreadful?' His expression was grave and concerned, silver eyebrows drawn together. 'When I heard the news, I couldn't believe it. You know you spoke to me before breakfast? When you couldn't find her? I didn't realise something like this had happened—'

'Neither did I,' Jo said, striving to keep her voice emotionless.

'I should have come and helped you, I'm sorry. Is there anything I can do now? I wasn't quite with it then, I'm afraid—'

'That's funny, because I've just been speaking to someone who thinks they saw you in the car park at about quarter past five this morning,' Jo said, keeping her eyes on his.

Sargent looked at first as if he didn't know how to take this. Then his Libran charm froze into something altogether tougher. He pointed a finger at her and took a step closer, his manner icy. 'That's an extremely mischievous lie that you've been told and I would like to know who said it. However, I suspect you won't tell me because you have made it up—'

Jo began to deny this but he spoke over her, raising his voice. 'I know you must feel bad, as you were in a position of some responsibility, as I understand it. But you should think very carefully about what you are saying.' He stepped around her and resumed walking downstairs, his manner composed, then turned his head back. 'If I hear you repeating that rumour around the place, your little firm will find itself with a defamation case that will sink it like a stone.'

Watching his unhurried walk downstairs, Jo reflected that being threatened with two lawsuits in one day must be some sort of a record for her. She decided not to mention the latest threat to Macy when he returned from the police station.

He had little news: an inquest would be held in the next few days and they expected a verdict of accidental death. Antonia had died just before dawn, according to the unofficial estimation, and the cliff path was not lit. If she had gone out for a walk on her own, it was quite feasible that she could have slipped and fallen. The police were trying to find anyone who had seen her but, from what he could glean, they had not turned up any witnesses. And, he pointed out, there was no suicide note, which was significant.

Jo had a sudden memory of the pages of hotel stationery lying on the dressing table in Antonia's room. Surely there had been some sheets missing? Did that mean there was a note somewhere? And yet surely Antonia could not have killed herself? 'I don't suppose there's any chance of them letting us have another look in her room?' she asked.

'Not a hope. The hotel have got strict instructions not to open it to anything but a badge.'

Other bleak practical details were bothering Jo, as she tried to explain on the way to the restaurant. 'Do you think the police will know who to contact? I don't think she had any family. She did mention an aunt in Ashford, who she stayed with when she was little and some relatives in France, I think. I told the police about her aunt but the woman may be dead by now. As far as I know, there's no one else.'

'She must still be alive because the woman PC — what's her name — Kenny — told me the funeral will be held in Kent.'

The restaurant was busy and Jo, who now felt she knew most of the guests by sight, noticed some unfamiliar faces. One livid, bearded face was only too recognisable. Paul, eating at a table on his own, studiously avoided any eye contact as she and Macy passed. They found a table as far away as possible.

'DCI Gammon is not exactly forthcoming,' Macy said after they had ordered their meal, 'but he's an old hand — not prepared to waste a lot of time avoiding questions that he may as well answer. So he told me a few things which didn't do any harm and refused to say anything else.'

'What did he say?' Jo asked. Macy hesitated. 'Go on, you can't keep anything from me. This is still my case — and it matters.'

The waitress returned with their dinner plates. 'I just thought I might wait until after we'd eaten,' Macy suggested. But Jo insisted on knowing any news he had straight away and he acquiesced. 'She died of a broken neck,' he went on, while the waitress tried to find room for side dishes of vegetables, 'due to the fall. No indications that she was pushed.'

'But there would have been so many bruises from the fall,' Jo argued. 'It's about a fifty-foot drop from that cliff and there were rocks below . . .' She paused and swallowed, trying to detach herself from her feelings. She regarded her plate, on which lay a pallid chicken breast in a pool of equally colourless sauce. All vestiges of appetite departed. 'She was right all along, you know,' she said to Macy in a low voice. 'She knew she was in danger and I didn't believe her enough.'

Macy was selecting a floret of broccoli from the serving dish. 'You're getting depressed, and I'm not surprised in this place. Limp vegetables and an atmosphere like a whist drive on a wet Sunday.' He glanced around at the quiet diners, many of them business people eating alone. 'How have you stood it so long? There's a pub in the village, isn't there?' He stood up, abandoning his steak. 'They're bound to have some crisps.'

As Jo followed him out, she took the opportunity to ask him where he intended to stay the night. Addressing this question to his back meant she avoided his appraising brown eyes.

'I've got my own room now. But I'm not staying in this godforsaken hole indefinitely. I suggest we go back to civilisation tomorrow.'

Jo was non-committal. 'I'm not sure the police will let me anyway.' They walked down the road to the village and she told Macy what she had found out from Antonia's fellow course members.

He couldn't make much of it either. 'If it was Sargent in the car park, it doesn't look good for him, but it could have been anyone with white hair. One of the staff coming to work, for instance.'

They mulled over the case over a couple of bottles of beer without making much progress, until Jo made a conscious effort to change the subject. 'How is work apart from this case?' She was hoping to get Macy to talk about himself, which was never easy.

'Not very good,' Macy admitted, to Jo's surprise. 'There's been a dearth of process serving lately. Some of the credit control people have started to take on that work. And if they offer a package to the companies—'

As he was speaking, Jo's attention was caught by the sight of some familiar straight shoulders and striking white hair. Oliver Sargent was paying for two drinks at the bar. She watched as he carried two short glasses to a booth in the corner behind her. She pointed him out to Macy, who had a better view, and hissed, 'Who is he with?'

'A woman in a light jacket. I can only see the back of her head and shoulders but she's tall and broad.' Macy watched for a moment longer. 'She's got heavy features, a strong chin, dark hair — shortish.' He held the tips of his fingers against his chin to indicate the style.

'A bob.'

'That's right. She's thirty-something, attractive.'

'Older or younger than you?'

'Older, definitely. She's at least thirty-five. They're quite preoccupied with each other.'

Jo risked a quick glance round and saw a sleek, dark brown head nodding, close to Sargent's. The woman's shoulder, just in view, was clad in salmon pink. A slim briefcase rested beside her court shoes. 'I've seen her before,' Jo said. 'Sargent was drinking with her in the hotel last night and she's on Antonia's course. She was waiting with the others to be interviewed. In fact, the police called her name while I was there.' She scrunched up her face, trying to remember what it was. 'Something unusual like Corinne or Catriona . . . Rutledge,' she said at last. 'She could be the woman Sargent was with last night.'

Macy shook his head. 'DCI Gammon said Sargent was on his own all night, according to his statement.'

'I'm sure he wasn't. I heard a woman's voice when the waiter took in a bottle of wine and two glasses at quarter to twelve.'

'Perhaps he's lying to protect her.' Macy gave the corner booth another glance. 'She looks married — she's got that well-heeled, protected look about her.' Jo gave him a sceptical glance and he added with a sheepish smile, 'Plus, she's wearing a ring.'

'But it would be in Sargent's interest to tell the police if she is his alibi. Maybe he's trying to get her to agree to give her name,' Jo suggested.

'They look like more than good pals.' Macy finished his beer. 'Shall we go over and ask some uncomfortable questions?'

'I'd rather try and speak to her on her own tomorrow. You'll just antagonise them if you butt in now. Let them think we don't know their secret.'

'All right. We'd better go before they see us.'

On their way back to the hotel, it was impossible not to think of the last time she had walked the route with Antonia. Her mind kept replaying their conversations, searching for hidden depths and hints about information that Antonia might have kept to herself.

Macy broke into her thoughts. 'There's something I've forgotten to mention until now. You know you asked me to find out about Antonia's husband, Guy Carlyle? I've managed to trace him. It wasn't too difficult, actually. He's still living at their old address in Hendon.'

'It would be useful to speak to him. He might be able to fill in some of the gaps Antonia left unexplained.'

'I've got a number for him but the PI firm who did this work for me have been round to the house and can't get an answer there. His neighbours say he hasn't been there for a week or so.'

Jo subdued a sudden impulse to look over her shoulder. 'Antonia always insisted her problems were nothing to do with him. But what if she was wrong? What if he has been trying to find her? She assured me she didn't give him her address at the cottage, so I wouldn't be surprised if that was him who called at her landlady's. If he managed to get her phone number, maybe he's been calling her at the cottage. If he's found out we came up here . . .' Her words tailed off and she shook her head. 'Hold on, I'm letting my imagination run away with me. Why should Guy want to seek out his ex-wife?'

Macy sighed. 'Money?' he suggested. 'You don't know why Guy lost his job? He was arrested for computer hacking. Apparently he was very good at it and was selling on all sorts of personal information to dubious sources. He stood trial two years ago.'

'So that's why she left him.'

'Well, the timescale fits. He avoided going to prison by the skin of his teeth. Just a large fine and a suspended sentence. And a ruined career, of course.'

'She told me he'd started drinking—'

'And drinking costs money — which he doesn't have any of,' Macy pointed out. He came to a halt. In the quiet Jo could hear the shifting, restless noise of the waves against the cliffs and smell the cold sea below. They stood in silence for a long minute. Without any words or thoughts to distract her, Jo noticed his physical closeness and suddenly felt very alive.

'I don't want to think about all this,' Macy said, his voice soft and serious. 'You know what I would like to do?'

Although they weren't touching, it seemed the salt air around them had drawn them close. It felt like they were the only people for miles. Jo had a spontaneous thought that the usual rules didn't apply. She felt for Macy's hand and found his wrist, the friction of fine hairs against her finger tips.

'I wish I'd brought a coat. You didn't tell me it was freezing up here.' Macy put an arm around her shoulders. 'We've still got the brandy. Shall we go to bed with it?'

Jo couldn't see much of his face in the dark but she felt the comfort of his shoulder against her head. She put a hand on his waist, feeling his body through the thin jacket and didn't care that in the morning, she would probably regret both the brandy and the bed.

* * *

She went to his room carrying the brandy bottle and feeling quietly excited. 'This is hardly the thing to do the day your friend dies,' she said, her voice tight.

There was only one light and Macy was sitting on the side of the double bed, still fully dressed. He reached for her free hand, drawing her to sit down beside him. His dark hair was falling into his eyes as it always did when he looked down. 'Poor Jo, you've had a hard time.' He took her hand and held it to his chest.

Remembering the last time they had made love, Jo expected passion not gentleness. But then Macy always surprised her. That was one of the things she liked about him.

Liked? There was more to it than that, wasn't there? Was she being honest? Her mind ran on, doubting and questioning as usual.

Macy's eyes looked almost black. She made a conscious effort to close down her thoughts and kissed him. Placing the brandy bottle down by the side of the bed, she brought up her other hand to touch his rough face and silky hair.

CHAPTER FOURTEEN

The next morning Jo had no regrets. Macy had been so tender, it had been possible to think he really cared. She reminded herself in the shower that it was daft to think this way. Still no regrets but, as the warm water poured over her head, all her doubts returned. What did she really know about Macy? He hadn't even been completely upfront with her about having been married. She'd found out by looking through old letters in his office. And what about Antonia? Wasn't it more important to spend her time trying to discover what had happened to her and why she had been right to be so frightened?

Macy, lounging in the double bed in his room where they had spent the night, said he didn't want any breakfast so Jo went out on her own. She knew that when she got back their relationship would be on its usual footing — mostly business but with the enticing possibility of sex. She supposed it suited her.

In her own room, she tried to call Guy on his London number. There was no answer so she went down to breakfast and, collecting her orange juice and croissants, noticed Petra Lancaster sitting by herself. Her long hair was snatched back from her face and she was tucking into a full breakfast with her habitually serious expression. Jo asked if she could share the table and Petra nodded. 'I can't wait to get out of this place,' she said. 'It really feels almost haunted to me. Not in a spooky sense but just a feeling of unease. Do you know what I mean?'

Jo found herself thinking of the immortal souls of those people who took their own lives and had to shake off this melancholic idea. She reminded herself that Antonia almost certainly hadn't committed suicide. 'The police have finished with you then?' she asked. 'Did you see them yesterday?'

Petra nodded, spearing a forkful of vegan sausage. 'I told them everything I told you. They showed me some pictures of Oliver Sargent and I recognised him from seeing him in here—' she gestured around the restaurant with her fork — 'in fact, I think he's been here when I've stayed before. But I couldn't say he was definitely the man I saw in the car park.' She scanned the room. 'I can't see him now. He's Antonia's boss, isn't he?'

'That's right.' Jo dunked her croissant in her coffee and wished everyone she interviewed was an Aquarian like Petra, who had no axe to grind and seemed to anticipate her questions. 'Do you know a woman called Corinne or Catriona Rutledge? I think she's on your course.'

'Carina? She's not on the course. She's the trainer. She runs a small company that does a lot of the training here. She's on to a good thing, from the number of people who come on these courses. She must be making a bit. But could you stand it? Not just the repetitive aspect of teaching the same thing week after week, but health and safety is so boring, all those rules.' She gave a mock yawn.

'Where is she?' Jo glanced around. 'I haven't seen her about much.'

'She doesn't stay here. She commutes from Harrogate every day. Why do you want to know about Carina? She goes out of her way not to be interesting because it would be too unconventional.'

'I saw her in the pub last night with Sargent and they looked more than friendly.'

Petra's unruly eyebrows shot up. 'You're joking! She doesn't seem the type to have an affair — although with her job she has all the opportunities, doesn't she? Meeting businessmen who are a long way from home and anyone who knows them.' She took a sip of tea and thought about it further. 'But she seems so uptight and serious. An affair might do her good, actually—'

'She is married, then?' Jo asked when able to intrude on the conversation Petra seemed to be having with herself.

'Yes, she said so. I imagine a little man in the background mowing the lawn and eating her microwaved dinners.'

'Do you know where I can find her? Is she coming in today?'

'No need for her to.' Petra drained her cup. 'No course, is there? Carina said that the police investigation is proving too disruptive but personally I think she was just looking for an excuse to finish the course early. She's left already and I'm going too, right after I've finished this. You might find her company in Harrogate I suppose—'

'Or I could try the hotel,' Jo said, thinking aloud. 'If she's always holding courses here I bet she leaves an address at the desk. Or at least a number.'

Petra was studying her. 'Your colours seem brighter today. Is it anything to do with that sexy man in the crumpled suit? I saw you together at dinner last night and I could tell he was pouring pheromones in your direction.'

It was slightly disconcerting to think other people might find Macy attractive. Jo had always thought he was an idiosyncrasy of her own. She was wondering how to reply when Paul Bakewell walked closely past their table, conspicuously ignoring her.

Petra followed Jo's gaze. 'Now there's a stranger. I've not seen him before but he seems angry. His auric field is all reds.' She sighed and buttered herself a piece of toast. 'You ought to let me take you to Harrogate. It's on my way home and my boyfriend lives there so I can tell you where to find things. And I'm hypersensitive today, so I might be of some use to you. I think the Moon must be in Cancer.'

'It is, as a matter of fact,' Jo said absently as she thought over Petra's suggestion. She stalled her questions about astrology and decided to go along with it, arranging to meet her at reception in an hour.

It didn't take Jo long to find out Carina Rutledge's address. She knew the company details from the training folder which Antonia had been carrying around and a quick search online produced an address in Harrogate. While she waited for Petra at reception, she saw that Yvonne was back on duty and took the opportunity to ask if she could have another look at Antonia's room. As Macy had predicted, the request was firmly turned down.

'You have to be joking.' Yvonne shook her head. 'We've got strict instructions from the police. They're going through everything up there with a fine-tooth comb and they've asked for all the information we've got on Mrs Carlyle.'

'But you don't keep a lot of information about guests, do you?'

'No,' Yvonne admitted with a grin. 'There's only the booking details, billing info, you know, and the phone log.' She nodded towards a sheaf of printouts, which she must have placed ready for the police.

Jo glanced at the sheets and then at Yvonne. 'The phone log? You couldn't let me—?' As Yvonne was already shaking her head, Jo smiled and tried again. 'But if you could possibly just get me a morning paper . . . ?' She pointed to the stack of newspapers, which were on a table behind the desk, some distance from where they were standing.

'I suppose I'd have to get it for you.' Yvonne sighed and began to walk slowly towards the papers.

With a quick look round, Jo snatched the list from behind the desk. The printout of the booking details was not revealing and she quickly turned to the sheet showing all the calls Antonia had made and received in her room.

Antonia's mobile had struggled to pick up a signal in the hotel so she had been forced to use the hotel phone a couple of times. There were no calls made on Sunday but her call on Monday night to Paul's mobile phone after the sauna incident was shown. Below that, at 2.10 a.m. was a call from a Warwick number.

'What paper did you say, madam?' Yvonne asked from the corner of the room.

'One near the very bottom of the pile, please.' She memorised the Warwick number and replaced the sheaf of papers on the reception desk as Yvonne returned with the *Daily Express*. It was not exactly her preferred morning reading but she thanked Yvonne warmly and asked her to put it on her bill.

She came away with more doubts than before. It was now clear that the baby monitor had been switched off before two a.m. — otherwise the incoming call would have been audible. It was difficult to see why, unless it was to ensure Jo didn't hear it, which was a disturbing thought. She put it out of her head for the moment and went to find Macy.

He was up and dressed and in unusually good spirits. While he sifted through emails on his laptop, she explained her plans to interview Carina. He wanted to go back to Coventry that day and offered to meet her in Harrogate at lunchtime to take her back with him and, since she had no transport home, Jo had little choice. She gave him the keys to Antonia's Mazda to hand to the police, as he was intending to pay DCI Gammon another visit, and hurried out to meet Petra.

They cruised along the A64 in Petra's little Nissan, Jo facing a series of questions about her other career, how she came to be interested in astrology and how she had managed to become a professional astrologer. Jo was happy to explain, finding it a welcome distraction from thinking about Antonia's death.

'I'd love to have the guts to do something like that,' Petra said, contemplating the dual carriageway with a serene expression. 'To give up the tedium of being a wage slave to do something you really love. It's what I'd like to do really. As you can imagine, an old hippie like me doesn't fit in with the whole IT scene. But I've got a good steady job and it's hard to take the risk.'

'You would get on well with my friend Hanni — she is a crystal healer and she might have something to say about auras too,' Jo said. 'You maybe just need to decide on what it is you want to do. I'll give you her number, she might be able to help.'

'I'd love that,' Petra said. 'Although of course, I do rate astrology,' she added. 'But to be a crystal healer, that must be amazing.'

Jo laughed. 'Hanni is pretty amazing actually. She's running her own business literally from her kitchen table on a farm in the Cotswolds, offering crystal healing sessions. I'm not quite there yet, running my own business as a full-time professional astrologer, but that's what I'm aiming for.' She told Petra about working for Macy and, as they were coming into the outskirts of Harrogate, this reminded her of the job in hand. She asked for more information about Carina Rutledge, knowing Petra could be relied on for an original description.

'She's a bit unenlightened and judgey. I mean, I've been on three of her courses altogether and she never takes me seriously just because I'm not your average computer geek. I happen to know she's a Capricorn — typically ambitious and a control freak.'

'That figures if this is where she lives,' Jo remarked. Carina Rutledge's house was situated on a new, upmarket development area where all the properties were built to look conspicuously different from one another.

'I believe they call this type of house "architect-designed" but I would have thought all houses had to be designed by *somebody*,' Petra commented. She pulled into the wide drive of an American-style ranch house with a low-pitched roof. 'I mean you're not going to get, like, a butcher or a baker designing your house, are you?'

Jo noticed that there were tidy lawns on three sides of the house, plants in the window and a new Volvo in the drive. She climbed out of the car and looked around. 'Pretty well how I imagined her place from what you said about her.'

They walked up the drive. 'My Life Path number is four so I have no trouble expressing myself,' Petra remarked. 'Are you into numerology at all?'

'Not a clue,' Jo admitted. 'Something else to talk to Hanni about. For now though, we need to decide on a story to tell Carina which would be more effective than admitting I'm a PI.'

Petra blithely went ahead and pressed the doorbell. 'Don't worry, I'll just tell her all about you. Leave it to me.'

The door was opened by a frowning woman, unquestionably the one Jo had seen with Sargent. She was followed by a Dalmatian, which sniffed at them idly, and a toddler of indeterminate sex, who was attached to the woman's left hand. Carina didn't noticeably warm up when she recognised Petra, who promptly took over.

'Carina, I hope you don't mind, I've brought my friend Jo to see you. She needs to ask you about something important,' Petra announced.

Carina did not smile back. 'Really, Petra, you know I can't solve your IT problems here. Or any other problems come to that. It's a bit bad of you, coming to my house like this. I told you to phone your help desk or look up the company policy—'

'Oh, it's nothing to do with IT or health and safety,' Petra said. 'It's more personal. Can we come in?'

'Obviously I'd love to chat, Petra, but I'm a bit busy at the moment.'

'It's about Oliver Sargent,' Jo said.

Carina's expression barely changed and her blue eyes, emphasised by her tan, flicked from Petra to Jo. But she held the door a fraction wider. 'Go straight into the kitchen. You could hardly have come at a worse time, I'm icing a cake.'

The round cake, covered in white icing, was on a raised stand in the middle of the kitchen table. A bowl of pink icing sat beside it and all the necessary kitchen equipment was laid neatly to hand.

'I just need to ask—' Jo began, but Petra interjected again.

'You see, Jo's in a difficult position.' She launched into an explanation. 'She was paid to look after Antonia Carlyle, you know, the one who died on the cliffs?' Here she paused, apparently to check that Carina was taking this in. 'You know Antonia? She's been on your course this week and now the poor woman is dead.' Petra emphasised the word with clenched fists and Carina, who had positioned herself behind the kitchen counter, almost flinched. 'So now you can imagine Jo's position. She feels very bad about it and just wants to get a few things cleared up.'

'I won't keep you long,' Jo said. 'I just wanted to ask about you and Sargent.'

'Wait.' Carina crossed to the kitchen doorway, picking up the toddler, who had sat down in the hall beside the dog. 'Kirsten!' she called. 'Come and take these two off my hands, will you?'

Jo briefly imagined that Carina was referring to herself and Petra, that Kirsten would turn out to be either a Rottweiler or a wrestler. In fact, a tall, willowy blonde woman loped down the stairs and took the toddler into her arms.

'Why don't you take Anna and the dog out to the park?' Carina said and closed the kitchen door firmly behind them. 'Kirsten's the au pair. She's Finnish,' she explained unnecessarily. 'Now I don't know what you're on about, Petra. Or you—' she threw a disparaging glance at Jo — 'but I don't want anything to do with it, so I think you should both leave before I call the police. Or my husband, I'm not sure which, but either one would ensure you left my property.'

Petra was so taken aback by this that she was rendered speechless for once. Jo took a hand. 'You see, I know you were with Sargent on Monday night,' she said in a quiet, reasonable tone, 'and I want to — no, I *need* to find out if he was still with you at around five thirty on Tuesday morning.'

Carina didn't respond immediately. She returned to her cake and stirred the icing. 'I don't know what you mean,' she said after a minute or two, 'and I suggest you show yourselves out.'

'Don't be like that, Carina.' Petra reached out to touch the other woman's arm. 'We just need your help.'

Jo admired Petra's open approach and had been prepared to give it a try because she knew how effective Aquarians can be simply by expecting the best from people. However, she could see it wasn't going to work on this particular hard-nosed Capricorn. There was no point in being devious now Petra had told the truth, she decided, so she would just have to out-tough Carina. 'You know who Sargent is, don't you? I've seen the two of you together — in the hotel bar and in the Bull.'

'He sometimes stays at the St George on business. I work there most weeks so I've got to know him a little. We've been for a drink now and again—'

'I'm not interested in your social habits,' Jo cut in, 'or in the lies you tell to preserve your comfortable lifestyle. I just want to know if you were with him on Monday night and Tuesday morning.'

Carina's chin jutted as she looked up from the cake mix. 'I thought you said you knew that.'

'I need to be sure,' Jo said. 'My friend is dead. It might be my fault. Can you imagine anything more important than that?'

'I can tell you that was nothing to do with Oliver.' Carina wiped icing off her fingers with a piece of kitchen towel. 'According to him, our whereabouts on Monday night are about to become public property and all because some silly girl threw herself off a cliff—'

'Antonia did *not* throw herself off.' Petra flung her arms in exasperation.

'The police are treating it as suspicious,' Jo added.

Carina pressed her lips into an angry line. 'I had a conversation with him about this. He's worried the police might suspect him, for God's sake. As if!' She gave a short laugh.

'Imagine Oliver tramping about on the muddy clifftop in the middle of the night to do in a member of his staff. I mean, it beggars belief. Why not just sack her?'

'So, were you with him all night?' Jo persisted.

Carina filled her piping bag with the pink icing and kept her eyes on the task. 'Yes, all night.'

'When did you leave?'

'About half past six to get home before eight o'clock when Kirsten gets the kids up. My husband is away at present so I rely on her.'

Still with her head down and one shoulder turned to them, she began to pipe small blobs of pink onto the smooth white surface of the cake. Jo watched the pattern emerge, mesmerised and when Carina spoke again, her tone was more conciliatory. 'Look, I knew this would have to come out because of what's happened. It's a pain, but it needn't ruin anything if you keep it to yourselves. That's what I'm going to say to the police too. Just because they need to know about it doesn't mean the world and his dog have to.'

'All right,' Jo said. 'Are you sure about your leaving time? Because Petra thinks she saw Oliver in the car park at quarter past five.'

'It couldn't have been. He was with me. I told you, I left at six thirty.'

'So you must have been there when I knocked at his door?'

'That's right, I heard you ask about your friend.'

Jo saw no harm in promising not to broadcast the information. The only people she would be likely to tell would be the police and they were going to find out from Sargent soon enough. Of course she'd tell Macy too, but he didn't count.

Carina dusted off her apron and showed them out. 'I told Oliver I didn't give a toss for his skin,' she confessed as they walked down the hall. 'All I want is to be kept out of it as much as possible.'

They walked in silence to Petra's car and then Petra spoke. 'I can't believe it, Jo. You were so horrible to her. It was marvellous.'

Jo was looking around in the hope that Kirsten would be returning with the dog and the baby. 'I'd like to see if the au pair can support Carina's story. Shall we see if we can find a park nearby?'

Petra was more than willing to try and they spent the next half hour walking round the neighbourhood looking for a tall blonde woman with a spotted dog and a toddler. They found a park not far away but there was no sign of Kirsten, and, as Jo was already going to be late to meet Macy, in the end they had to give up.

'I'll keep an eye open for her,' Petra promised. 'I'm in Harrogate at least a couple of evenings a week and most weekends. Then I'll ask her if what Carina said was true.'

'In any case, Sargent seems to have an alibi for the crucial time, assuming Carina is telling the truth.' Jo sighed.

Petra drove them towards the city centre. 'But she's not the sort to lie to protect him,' she pointed out. 'She's only told us this much because she knows he'll tell the police anyway.'

'I agree,' Jo said, 'but she might lie to protect herself, don't you think? What if Sargent told her to alter the time she left or he would tell her husband about the affair?'

Petra regarded her with wide eyes. 'Wow, you Virgos have such a down on human nature. Mind you,' she added with a grin, 'I'm not sure Carina is human.'

CHAPTER FIFTEEN

Jo had arranged to meet Macy at a pub in the centre of Harrogate. It was his idea — she would have preferred one of the cosy tea shops. However, the pub was apparently easy to find. Petra knew the place and gave her directions for getting there on foot before she dropped her by the Stray.

'You'll keep in touch, won't you?' she asked. 'I'd like you to do my horoscope for me. I've had it done once but it wasn't any good, it made me out to be far too sensible. And don't forget to send me the number of the crystal healer.'

'I will,' Jo promised. 'I'll give you a ring when I get home.'

'And I'll keep on the case,' Petra said. 'Who knows? I might remember something helpful.' By this time she was holding up a line of traffic, so with a quick wave, she drove off and Jo crossed the road as directed, reflecting that only an Aquarian could have cheered her up in the circumstances.

She was twenty minutes late by the time she reached the pub and she saw from the scaffolding outside that it was a bad choice. It was closed for renovations. Macy was waiting outside in his car, parked on double yellow lines. He leaned over to open the door from the inside.

'Sorry I'm late,' Jo said. 'I see the pub is closed.'

'I was late myself. I've been stuck at the police station — and then I couldn't quite remember where it was. I thought you'd got lost, are you OK?'

'Of course I'm OK.' Jo undid her coat and pulled irritably at the tangles in her curly hair. 'Why didn't you ask Petra to tell you where it was? She gave me precise directions.'

'I thought it was imprinted on my memory. It's not that long ago since I was there. Strange how places are always different from how you remember them.' Macy frowned as he waited for a gap in traffic speeding around a large roundabout.

Cancerians have notoriously long and romantic memories, and so Jo guessed the pub probably had some sentimental significance for him. Somehow this made her even more annoyed. Trying to sound rational, she said, 'I didn't know you'd ever been to this part of the world.'

'When I first started this job I used to travel about more,' he said, his eyes on the road.

'I suppose that's all you're going to tell me.'

Macy glanced across quickly. 'Why would you want to know more?'

'I don't,' she lied, 'but I enjoy seeing you squirm and I know how reluctant you are to tell me any of the sordid details about your past.'

'You're sure it's sordid, are you?'

'Well, it would be, wouldn't it? Anything to do with you is.' As soon as the words were out, Jo wondered why she had said them. It was almost as if she couldn't cope with the tenderness Macy had shown last night and wanted to press the self-destruct button. She closed her eyes and berated herself silently. Why couldn't she seem to do anything right at the moment?

The silence between them lasted for about twenty miles, by which time they were on the M1 and the idea of lunch seemed to have been abandoned. Jo supposed it would seem heartless to suggest food. Having settled herself in for a silent journey back to Coventry, she was surprised when Macy was the first one to speak.

'Don't you want to know what I was doing at the police station?'

Jo looked at his profile, apparently unconcerned, focused on the traffic, dark hair resting on his collar. She guessed it had cost him a lot to break the silence and had a sudden desire to touch him. 'Go on then, tell me. Did you get any more out of DCI Gammon?'

'Not really. But they had Oliver Sargent in for questioning all morning. One of the uniforms told me he has produced an alibi—'

'I know. That woman he was with in the pub last night. Carina Rutledge. I've been to see her and she knows he is going to give her name. She's braced for the inevitable interviews with the police but she still has hopes her husband need not know.'

'I suppose that might work out for her,' Macy mused. 'The police can be discreet. What did you think? Is the alibi genuine?'

'She's a sort of grim Superwoman type — runs a home and children, plus dog, makes them cakes for their birthdays and incidentally manages a business as well. I expect her husband is the kind who comes home in the evening, puts his feet up and says, "Christ, I've had a hard day, darling. Keep the children out of my hair, can't you?" As for the alibi, she must have been the person with Sargent at quarter to twelve, and if what she says is true, she was still there when I knocked on his door at half past six the next morning. According to her, that was roughly when she left.'

'It should clear Sargent,' Macy remarked. 'Especially as he doesn't have a motive unless you believe Antonia's story that he murdered her sister under another name and personality. That's how the police will see it, I'm sure.'

'But the times are crucial,' Jo pointed out. 'If Carina left only an hour earlier, he would have had time to kill Antonia.'

'So you think she's lying?' Macy said.

'Or maybe she *was* there all night but didn't know Sargent slipped out and came back—'

'Clutching at straws now,' Macy commented. 'If Antonia died between five and six as the police say, Sargent would have to have left his room between about four thirty and five thirty. Could he have done that without her noticing? And don't say she must be a sound sleeper.'

Jo ignored this for the moment because she didn't have an answer. 'It's bothering me as well that Antonia switched off the alarm and left her room in the small hours.'

'Maybe she couldn't sleep and didn't want to bother you so went for a walk by herself?' Macy said, but his sceptical expression showed he was far from convinced of this himself.

'It might sound feasible if you didn't know her, but she never did anything on her own.' Jo chewed her lip, going over again all the things she should have done. And what she might have forgotten.

'I do know she had an outsized persecution complex,' Macy said, 'which you might be in danger of forgetting.'

She looked at him swiftly. 'You're right about one thing. I am forgetting something or missing something — but that isn't it. And Antonia was right, wasn't she? Look what happened. She was right to be scared and maybe she was right to be wary of Sargent. Isn't it a bit suspicious that he didn't tell them about Carina straight away?'

'That works in his favour, though. If he'd murdered Antonia, he would have had his alibi ready but maybe he wanted to protect the lady's name. He had to ask her first.'

'What a gentleman,' Jo said. 'He had to get her to agree to lie about the time she left, you mean.'

'But a murderer would have planned all that.' Macy said. 'Anyway, the police have certainly worried him. I saw him in the canteen and he didn't look quite his usual suave self. He was on the phone to his solicitor and he sounded rattled.'

'Good,' Jo said, thinking of her last encounter with Sargent. 'I think he's a nasty piece of work under that charming exterior. Librans can be. They're very influenced by their Ascendant.'

Macy gave her one of his humouring looks. 'Don't start. You know it's wasted on me. Listen, why don't you come back with me tonight? I can't cook but I can fetch a mean takeaway.'

Jo looked across at him but his expression gave nothing away. She knew she wanted to stay with him. She was dreading spending the night alone for the first time since Antonia had died. But surely that meant it was the worst possible time to get involved with Macy?

She put out of her mind the fact that she had enjoyed last night. She told herself that if things were ever going to work out for the two of them, this was not the right time and decided to turn down his offer.

But it was one of those decisions that gave her no pleasure. Whichever way it had gone, she would have thought she had done the wrong thing. Ideally, she thought, Macy should have tried to change her mind — but of course he wouldn't do that. He dropped her at her flat without any argument — in fact, without saying much at all. He drove off pretty quickly too.

She let herself into her flat on her own and her mood finally dissolved into feeling thoroughly miserable. She sat on the sofa, still wearing her coat, and sobbed her way through half a box of tissues. Although she had known there was not much more she could have achieved in Yorkshire, she couldn't help feeling that she had given up too early and had left Antonia behind.

Her orgy of self-pity lasted a good hour, after which she roused herself to take off her coat and wash her face. All she really wanted to do was go to bed. But it was too early for that.

When she began to unpack, she realised that a lot of her belongings were still in Antonia's cottage. They would have to be collected sooner or later and, having turned down Macy's suggestion that they spend the evening together, she definitely didn't want too much time to think. A trip to the cottage would take her an hour or so, then she could pick up a takeaway on the way back, eat it in front of the television and go to bed early.

She went out before she could start talking herself out of it. Her car surged into life at the third attempt, and the sound of the noisy old engine lifted her spirits. She drove towards Warwick, turning off the main road at Ashow and shooting down the familiar lanes in the village. As she drove up the curling drive to the cottage, she tried not to think of anything sentimental. It was after five but it had been a bright day and the twilight lingered so the cottage was not in total darkness when she parked outside.

Inside, the cottage was just as they had left it. A magazine was folded open on the sofa with a pen beside it — Antonia had loved sending for offers and filling in surveys — and the cat's dishes were in their usual spot in the kitchen. The sight reminded her to tell Antonia's solicitor about poor Wilf, who was still in the cattery, and she switched on the kettle to make herself a cup of coffee while she sorted out her things.

It was as she was reaching for a mug from the draining board that she thought she heard a floorboard creak upstairs. She looked up at the ceiling. Antonia's room was partly above the kitchen.

She measured out the coffee with a slightly shaky hand. She had been jittery ever since Antonia's death and consciously reminded herself that no one but herself, Antonia and the landlady had keys to the cottage. Antonia's set would be with the police and if the landlady were here, her car would have been in the drive.

Jo poured water into her mug and stirred it, flicked the room light on and glanced round the kitchen to see if anything was hers. She soon found a small pile of items that she had brought with her or bought since she had arrived, like the hot water bottle that she had needed because there was no proper heating upstairs. In a couple of minutes, she had checked the kitchen and was ready to tackle the living room.

The soft, delicate thud from the room next door was unmistakable. Jo stopped breathing. Fear shot through her body like an electric shock. She listened hard.

The cottage was quiet again, seeming to breathe around her, familiar and now strangely cloying. She set down her mug silently and let out her breath.

In her mind's eye, Jo saw herself going purposefully into the living room and switching all the lights on. She imagined how the room would look, perfectly empty. Maybe she would put on some music to calm her nerves. But she couldn't make herself do any of these things. She just stood there, terrified, listening, waiting, while seconds went by that felt like hours. Finally, with the cottage still quiet around her, she walked softly to the door of the kitchen and made herself look through the gloom.

There's nobody there, she thought with relief. One sofa was a dark oblong under the window, the other almost lost in the shadows; the dresser and the table were familiar black shapes. But something moved in the corner of her vision and she turned towards the staircase.

At the bottom of the stairs, someone was standing very still. The dim light from the porch fell on sleek, reddish-blonde hair.

CHAPTER SIXTEEN

Jo felt weak. Her eyes were fixed on Antonia, who made a move towards her, putting out a hand. 'Jo, it's you—'

Involuntarily Jo took a step back and found herself holding onto the doorpost. The other woman waited, frozen there in the dim light, her hand extended. Antonia's face was so pale it seemed to float in the darkness.

'Listen, don't worry, I know what you're thinking,' she said.

'What—?' Jo's voice came out in a whisper. 'What are you doing here? Are you—?'

'No, no,' Antonia said in a sort of groan. 'It's not what you think. Wait, wait.' She crossed the room uncertainly. 'Where on earth is the light switch?'

Jo felt disorientated and detached and this helped to clarify her thoughts. Something swept through her brain like the beam of a lighthouse, throwing into relief all sorts of questions that she should have been asking since Antonia died. One thing was absolutely certain anyway: Antonia knew where the light switches were in her own living room.

'You're not her,' she said. 'But how do you know me?'

In the same moment, the other woman found the switch and the room was suddenly full of warm, orangey light. Jo stared across at her. The woman looking anxiously back was Antonia — or someone identical to her. She was the same height and build with the same red-gold hair clipped away from her face and the same pointed chin. Even her worried, vulnerable expression was similar. But it couldn't be her. It wasn't her.

'You're not, are you?' Jo said.

The woman put her hands to the sides of her face just as Antonia did when troubled. 'No, I'm not,' she said in a low voice. 'I wish I was and I suppose you do too.' She dropped down onto the sofa and buried her head in her hands.

'Who — who are you, then?' Jo asked, still keeping her distance.

Antonia's double looked up, hazel eyes full of tears. 'I'm sorry, I must have scared you half to death. I keep doing it to people but I can't help looking like her. I'm her twin.'

'Her *twin*?' Jo repeated, her voice rising. 'She never told me about you. This can't be . . . I mean, you're so *alike!*' For once, Virgo rationality deserted Jo and she felt close to hysteria.

'Yes, I am,' the other woman insisted calmly. 'I'm Theresa Vane, Toni's identical twin. Most people call me Tess. Toni and Tess, you see, it sounds so nice—' Her voice broke and she started to cry.

Watching Tess's shoulders shake with sobs, Jo took a deep breath. She stepped forward and offered her a handkerchief. Tess took it wordlessly and went on crying. Jo sat down and stared at the empty grate as her heartbeat returned to its normal pace. She waited patiently, not saying anything. What could she say? *I'm sorry I failed your sister* was patently inadequate.

'I know I scared you,' Tess said after a while between sniffles, 'but if it's any consolation, you gave me a bit of a fright too.'

'But you knew who I was,' Jo said.

'That's right. I'll explain about that.' She heaved a shaky sigh. 'But I didn't know it was you moving around down here. I'd fallen asleep on Toni's bed and when I woke up I heard a tap running in the kitchen.' She paused to blow her nose on the handkerchief. 'Thanks for this, by the way.'

'You know what happened to her?'

Tess nodded slowly, balling the handkerchief in her hand. 'Yes, I've been up in Yorkshire most of the day at the police station. I know how she died.'

'I know too. It's awful.' She watched Tess for a minute, sitting with her head down and her arms, very tense, resting on her knees. 'She never told me she had a twin,' Jo said at last.

Tess seemed to be gathering herself together, although she was still white-faced. 'That doesn't surprise me. It's quite like her to disown me until she needs me. We didn't always get on brilliantly, you see. It's hard to explain but she never quite got over the fact that I left home, took my civils and — luckily for me — happened to walk into a very good job. The fact that it was hundreds of miles away didn't help either.'

'Took your what?'

'Civil engineering exams. I work for a consultant in Edinburgh. I'm a partner now, as a matter of fact. It wouldn't be exaggerating to say Toni saw my career as a bit of a betrayal. She never wanted to leave home. I think if she'd had her way, we'd all still be living in the same house in Kent.' Tess paused. 'Maybe there was something to be said for that after all. Listen, can you spare half an hour? It must be odd for you but I feel as if I know you already — through Toni. Anyway, there are things I should tell you.' Tess looked up hopefully.

Jo remembered her coffee, which by now would be cold, but there was a bottle of wine in the kitchen cupboard that she had bought and never got round to opening. She fetched the bottle and two glasses, already thinking that she could stay the night rather than drive home — assuming Tess wouldn't object.

'How did you get here?' Jo asked. 'I didn't see a car in the drive.'

Tess had settled herself in the corner of the sofa just as Antonia used to do. 'I don't drive. It's one of my little foibles. I get taxis everywhere.' She hesitated and added matter-of-factly, 'Actually, we were in a terrible smash once — me and Toni. I've still got the scars to prove it.' She waved a hand towards her legs, which were clad in jeans.

'Was Toni driving?' Jo asked. That would explain Antonia's reluctance to drive anywhere.

'Yes. In fact, Toni got over it better than me. At least she carried on driving.'

As she poured out two glasses of wine, Jo had that sense of satisfaction that comes when a problem that has proved too difficult suddenly starts to fall into place. Her own thought processes, thrown by Antonia's death, seemed clearer than they had for days.

'I've worked out how you know me,' she said, making herself comfortable on the other sofa. 'It was the night of the ball, wasn't it? I thought Antonia was behaving oddly, even though she said she had a cold.'

Tess shook her head resignedly. 'Yes, I let her talk me into that. It was her idea to pretend to have a cold because our voices sound different and she said you wouldn't notice the other differences between us if I put my head in a bowl of menthol and pretended to be ill. We are both allergic to certain chemical smells, so she sprayed air freshener at herself to make her eyes and nose run.'

'She had been to visit Paul.' Jo recalled how Antonia had breezed in, strangely alert for someone coming down with a cold as she had claimed.

'She phoned me about the plan. We do call each other now and again. Usually when one of us wants something. She said she was going to the ball with you and at ten thirty she would go to the lavatory. I was to meet her in the end cubicle. She had even gone so far as to check out the hotel ladies' in her lunch hour,' Tess added with a rare smile. 'I was mad to agree to it, of course. I know she's obsessed with finding who killed Monique, but I also know she was really frightened of somebody. That was why she found you.'

Jo was eager for more details. 'So, on the night of the ball, you met her as planned, exchanged clothes and you came back with me?'

'That's right. She told me to say I had a cold and wait up to let her in. She came back here at about two o'clock by taxi and arranged for another one to pick me up in the lane at six, in time for me to get my train from Birmingham.'

'I heard you leave,' Jo remembered. 'But Antonia said she was changing the porch light bulb.' *She had probably removed it, so I wouldn't see any of these comings and goings if I looked out of the window*, Jo realised. 'Was Paul the obliging taxi driver? And why did Antonia go to all this trouble? What was she up to?'

'No, no it wasn't Paul. Despite what you might think, Toni didn't entirely trust him. Can't you guess what she was doing while I pretended to be her? You know the whole John Brooke/Oliver Sargent saga, don't you?'

'Well, I thought I did, but it seems Antonia didn't entirely trust me either,' Jo remarked. She couldn't help feeling let down.

Tess sighed. 'That's what she was like — devious, independent. It was force of habit with her never to tell anyone the whole story.'

'I know that,' Jo said. 'I knew it as soon as I saw how strong Scorpio is in her chart. But I didn't realise she would go to these lengths to pull the wool over my eyes. Why would she do that?'

'She wanted to break into Sargent's office. She had spent months getting friendly with one of the cleaners and she found out where they kept the keys. So she borrowed them and got a set cut for herself, so she could get into the place at night—'

'She did what?' Jo couldn't help interrupting.

Tess simply shrugged and sighed. 'That's my sister for you. She was absolutely driven. But the whole scheme was fraught because she had to switch alarms off and reset them.

Anyway, she said she could only do it once but she needed to get into Sargent's own office, where he kept his files. Being at the ball was her alibi in case the break-in was discovered.'

'But I might have been able to help. I probably wouldn't have objected to a spot of breaking and entering.'

'She couldn't take the chance. You have to realise,' Tess said, her head on one side and her tone gentle, 'this was like a crusade for Toni. She has been obsessed with it for years. Getting the keys was a major breakthrough, as she saw it. She had a chance to look for evidence to prove Sargent really was Brooke.'

'Did she find anything?'

'Apparently not,' Tess said, 'but I'm not a hundred per cent sure she'd have told me if she had. Perhaps she learned the hard way not to trust people. Things didn't seem to work out for her. What with finding Monique like she did and then the relationship with Guy broke down—'

'You don't know where Guy is, do you? I've been trying to get in touch with him.'

'You know about him, I suppose? How he lost his job?'

'Yes, I know he was a computer hacker and he was convicted. I assume that's when Toni left him?'

'Yes — not so much because of the crime but because he went totally off the rails. He became impossible, from what I can gather. Poor Toni tried to have nothing more to do with him. But he'd turn up every so often. When he was looking for Toni, he used to ring me, would you believe? And it's not as if we were close. I hardly knew him really. Once he even asked me for money.'

'When did he last ring you?'

'Only last week. He just wanted Toni's new address. I didn't give it to him, of course.'

'All the same, I think he found out,' Jo said. She sipped her wine and began the slow process of revising everything she knew about Antonia.

Tess broke into her thoughts. 'I'll never understand why she married Guy. He had bad news written all the way through him. And yet I think she really loved him. She was a strange girl and we used to fight like cat and dog, but now that she's not here, I feel like I've lost a limb. I feel unbalanced.' The other woman looked down, focusing on her wine glass.

In the silence that stretched out between them, Jo remembered that Antonia's horoscope had shown a rift between siblings. She'd naturally assumed this meant Antonia and Monique. Looking across the room at the woman, trying to get used to the fact that a single tilt of her head or a little downturned expression with her mouth was disturbingly familiar, she wondered what it must be like to lose someone you'd known even before you were born. 'Who is the elder twin?' she asked.

'Me. By forty minutes.'

'Not long.'

'It's a long time to be out there on your own.' Tess glugged another gulp of wine. 'And now I'm on my own again.'

As Jo sat back against the sofa cushions, her new clear-headedness took away some of the strain of the last few days, coupled with the fact that Tess was a more relaxing presence than her sister and seemed happy with silences. It was hard not to make comparisons between the twins. Tess seemed the quiet, practical one, and although they were undoubtedly identical, she was in some indefinable way not as pretty as Antonia. Jo pictured them at school. Toni would always be the one to pick things up more quickly, being more imaginative and sensitive, but maybe more inclined to jump to the wrong conclusion. Whereas Tess would probably never have put her hand up unless she knew the answer to the questions. And yet they had both been bright, Jo guessed. Fast thinkers and good communicators — typical Gemini twins.

'It was wrong of me to do anything to encourage her obsession with finding John Brooke,' Tess was saying, running a finger around the rim of her wine glass. 'It literally blighted her life.'

'But was she right about him?' Jo saw that Tess was capable of leaving the question unanswered and knew Antonia wouldn't have wanted that. 'I don't know if you're up to this yet, but there's a strong possibility that Antonia did not leave the hotel on her own. Or if she did, it was to meet someone, who might have meant her some harm—'

'You're saying she was murdered? The police hinted at that too. Well, I'd rather believe that than think that both my sisters killed themselves.' It was meant to be a dry remark but it sounded slightly hysterical. 'I think that would be enough to make me crack up.'

'Let's look at the murder possibility, then,' Jo said. She leaned forward. 'I think Oliver Sargent had the opportunity although I can't prove it yet because he's produced an alibi. But if Antonia had found the link proving he was John Brooke, he had a motive.'

'Not really. Even if he really was John Brooke, would he kill Antonia to stop that becoming public? It's not a crime to take another name.'

'But if the same man was close to both Antonia and Monique and both died suspiciously, it looks distinctly odd though, doesn't it? Enough to make the police look at both deaths very closely.'

'That was all Antonia wanted, a full police investigation into Monique's death . . .' Tess let this sentence tail off, then added with more vigour, 'When I heard Sargent was staying at the same hotel as Toni, I thought it was a bit weird. Do you think he deliberately planned for the training courses to be somewhere remote, so they had to stay miles away from home?'

'Well, he was in a position to engineer that,' Jo said.

'I've never met him so he's an unknown quantity to me. When Monique had her fling, I'd just gone up to Edinburgh for my Master's and I always seemed to be in the middle of research and studying in those years. I was thoroughly out of favour with Toni then — although Monique and I used to talk on the phone, so I knew all about the big romance.

I've been gradually creeping back into Toni's good books ever since.'

'You've seen Sargent though, haven't you?'

'Once or twice. I saw him at the ball and again, briefly, today.' She paused. 'He doesn't exactly strike me as Monique's type. I also bumped into Toni's friend Paul at the hotel and he seemed friendly — once he'd got over the shock of seeing me, that is. He bought me a coffee and we had a long talk. He's taken it really badly.' Tess sighed.

'I know,' Jo said with feeling. Tess looked at her as if waiting for further explanation but Jo didn't want to waste any time on Paul Bakewell. She was filled with a new determination. 'What I need to do is simply to prove that Sargent is Brooke. That would be enough to make the police look again at both deaths—'

'I don't want you getting obsessed too,' Tess interrupted. She considered for a minute. 'Mind you, if you really are serious about this, I think you should have a look at Toni's laptop. It's upstairs—' she indicated with a glance upwards — 'Toni sent me the passwords using a code we've always had. It was the kind of cloak-and-dagger thing Toni was always doing, so I didn't think much of it. Now I think she must have wanted me to take over where she left off — but quite honestly, I couldn't do it on my own.'

'Antonia had a folder with some cuttings in,' added Jo. 'I found them when I was checking the contacts she'd made when she put an ad in the personal column of the local paper. She had loads of news cuttings about recent attacks on women but she wouldn't say why she kept them.'

'That's only the tip of the iceberg of all the stuff she's got upstairs.' Tess got to her feet. 'We may regret this.'

* * *

Jo sat on the side of the bed in Antonia's room, while Tess tapped through the layers of passwords on her twin's laptop, until the screen displayed a list of files. 'She's got a file on Uncle Tom Cobleigh and all,' Tess said.

'Including me, I see,' Jo remarked, as her name jumped out from the list on the screen.

'Feel free.' Tess moved over so that Jo could access the keys. The information in the file on Sargent seemed basic — age, appearance, address, et cetera — but there were references to other documents and Jo set about trying to retrieve them, hampered by her modest IT skills and occasionally needing help from Tess.

'I'm nowhere as good as Toni on this stuff,' Tess said, breaking off from her slow job of sorting out belongings into bags.

However, between them, they found more details about Sargent, including a diary about him that Antonia had written every day since she started at Callendar.

'We will have to give this laptop to the police tomorrow,' Jo said. Macy would insist on it.

Tess nodded. She pointed to a neat pile of box files, unlabelled. 'And these too, I think. I found these under the dressing table.'

Glad to have an excuse to leave the tortuous process of sorting through the maze of Antonia's records on the small screen, Jo picked one up and opened what looked like a batch of invoices from Callendar Exports. 'What the heck was she doing bringing these home?'

'I'm realising how deeply obsessed she was,' Tess said, her hands on her hips and shoulders sagging. The bedroom floor was now scattered with half-filled black bin bags and piles of documents.

It was half past ten when Jo, sorting through one of these files, realised the significance of the bunch of forms in her hand. 'I bet these are what Antonia took from his office the night you impersonated her. They're copies of Sargent's claim forms for business expenses over the past five years.'

'Was she trying to prove he was embezzling as well, then?' Tess rubbed her eyes and looked away from the diary on the screen.

'Maybe? Or maybe she was more interested in the dates he was away from the office. She's marked a few of the forms showing long trips abroad. I wonder if they coincide with his courtship of your sister?' Jo had pulled out a batch of forms with new-looking orange sticky notes at the top of pages.

'Let's do a search on those dates.' Tess returned to the laptop. 'Read them out.'

As they went through them, they found that Sargent was claiming business expenses for being in France around the same time that John Brooke was in Kent. His forms showed he had travelled by ferry and car to Normandy several times in the year Monique fell in love with John Brooke. There were no details about where he had stayed abroad. He had just claimed a standard nightly rate.

'On its own, it's not enough,' Jo said. She stifled a yawn. 'But we're sending all this stuff to the police, that's for sure.'

'Just because he wasn't at work, doesn't mean he was seducing Monique.' Tess turned away from the screen and picked up one of the forms. 'I mean, he might actually have been in France, as it says here. Presumably he would have had to produce ferry tickets and petrol receipts to back up these claims. And what about the work he was meant to do over there? Wouldn't he have had to have something to show for his trips?'

'Not if they were just speculative trips touting for business from the French antiques trade,' Jo said. 'He is the managing director, after all. If he wants to take a bit longer than he should over business trips, who's going to ask questions? And I'm sure he could get round the receipt if he chose.'

'You're getting one-eyed about this, just like Toni.' Tess sighed and flicked through the paperwork. 'Look, there are other forms here showing trips to France. He went after Monique had died. Toni hasn't flagged these because they didn't fit her theory.'

'I know, I know.' Jo accepted the forms back and packed them away in order. 'We're still going to take them to the police. Because if Sargent knew that Antonia was getting this close to proving the link, it's a motive, isn't it?' She took the next box file from the stack. 'But while we've got our hands on them, there's still work to do.'

The two women finally gave up about midnight and even then, Jo took a box file crammed with papers to bed with her. 'I think Antonia kept every bit of paper that had ever passed through Monique's hands,' she commented from the doorway.

'But there's nothing about John Brooke.' Tess looked down at the litter of papers on the floor that she had just tipped out of a carrier bag. 'Not a love letter or a birthday card.'

'Antonia told me your sister burned everything to do with him.'

It seemed to be tacitly accepted that Jo would spend the night in her old bedroom but before she could say goodnight, Tess, white and frowning, put out a hand to her. 'Jo. It's the inquest tomorrow and I've got to go back to Yorkshire for that. The following week, it's the funeral in Chartham, where we used to live. You will come, won't you?'

'Yes, of course. I'll drive you, if you like?'

Tess nodded, her mouth compressed so she wouldn't give in to tears. Jo patted Tess's arm and, at a loss about what else to say or do, murmured goodnight and crossed the landing to her old room. Having got to know Antonia, she seemed to have been able to skip some stages of friendship with her sister, even though the twins were very different. Anticipating how she would compare Tess's chart to Antonia's, Jo got into her cold bed, cocooning herself in the duvet for maximum warmth.

It was one of the coldest nights of the year and Jo was repeatedly awoken by funnels of icy air reaching her body under the covers. At 3.10 she got up, put on the shirt she had been wearing that day and her socks and got back in. She lay still with her head under the duvet and thought of Macy and his well-disguised kindness. She wondered at her own stubborn independence for turning down his offer to spend the night at his place. *It would have been a darn sight warmer anyway*, she thought regretfully, lifting her head out to see her phone.

It was only half past three and she turned over again, her mind like a demented film director scanning the last few days of takes and pouncing randomly on scenes to replay. The sight of Tess in the darkened room downstairs, Antonia lying below the cliff with her head in the crook of her arm, Paul Bakewell's look of angry shock when he heard the news, Yvonne walking away from reception to give her time to read the list of Antonia's phone calls, Oliver Sargent's glacial blue stare as he stabbed his finger at her and warned her to watch what she said.

Something about Paul Bakewell was needling her and she kept replaying that few minutes in the foyer of the hotel when she had stood between two uniformed police, feeling dazed, and watched PC Kenny tell him that Antonia was dead. She felt the same surge of guilt, remembering how he had blamed her for Antonia's death. Then something else occurred to her. He had said he knew Jo was employed to protect Antonia. And yet, as far as Jo was aware, Antonia had gone to some trouble not to tell him. Had she changed her mind? That would not exactly be unknown for a Gemini but somehow it seemed unlikely, given Antonia's tendency to keep things to herself. So how had Paul known she was a PI?

CHAPTER SEVENTEEN

It was with that question in mind that Jo paid Paul a visit the next morning. She dropped Tess, subdued by the prospect of the ordeals ahead and nursing Antonia's laptop, at Coventry police station and drove towards Warwick. It occurred to her that as Paul worked late he might not appreciate an early visit, so she stopped in town, bought a newspaper and looked around for somewhere to have a coffee.

Out of curiosity she walked past the neat, painted house where Antonia had worked. The street was quiet, most of the people in the solicitors and court offices already behind their desks. She turned down the road next to the churchyard as the clock chimed. The tune sounded familiar and she puzzled about it as she continued her search for somewhere to sit and wait.

After half an hour or so sitting in the corner of a café, which was none too warm, sipping tentatively at a cup of coffee that was the colour and temperature of old dishwater, Jo decided that she had been sufficiently considerate to Paul Bakewell. It was ten o'clock and time any decent self-respecting person was up, she decided as she grudgingly paid for her coffee, even if they had been at work until the small hours.

She noticed that his taxi was not parked outside his house but she rang the doorbell anyway and waited, looking around at the quiet estate. A woman ambled by pushing a baby in a pram, and some workmen drew up in a van and parked on the corner.

Eventually Rachel's tall figure became visible through the frosted glass front door. She opened it ponderously, turning the mortice lock, drawing back a bolt and then appeared in the narrowest of gaps, sandwiched between the jamb and the edge of the door. She looked down at Jo, being half a head taller, her expression unwelcoming.

'Hello, Rachel. I'm Jo, Antonia's friend, I don't know if you remember me? Is Paul in?'

'He's at work,' Rachel answered, stony-faced, almost before Jo had finished speaking.

'Oh, I just wanted a quick chat with him.'

'Well, he isn't here.' Rachel regarded Jo with her round fish-eyes, the length of her face accentuated by the lank white-blonde hair hanging either side of it. She moved as if to close the door.

'Do you know when he'll be back?' Jo asked, seeking a toehold on the cliff-face of Rachel's hostility.

'I never know when he'll be back.' Her tone was clipped and cold but a little tremor seemed to run through her as she spoke. Whether this was anger or impatience or maybe even just the chill day, Jo could only guess.

'I thought he worked regular hours,' Jo said. She hadn't come here to see Rachel, but when someone so obviously didn't want to talk to her she had a perverse instinct to stay. 'You know, ten till two in the morning or something like that.'

'No, he does what he pleases. He doesn't always work nights. That's only one of his shifts,' Rachel said, not blinking.

'What shift is he on today, then?'

'Eight till eight — or until he gets fed up.'

The long face in front of her was still hatchet-like but Jo persevered. 'You must hardly ever see him some days.'

'That's right.' Rachel managed to say this without sounding at all conciliatory. Still the door didn't budge a centimetre and Jo realised that she was not going anywhere with this.

'Where can I find him, then?' Jo asked.

'At work, I told you.'

'OK, thanks for being so helpful.' Jo stepped back quickly as the door slammed. 'Nice to meet someone who's so hospitable,' she murmured and headed back to her car.

'Talking to yourself? First sign of madness, you know.'

Jo looked around and saw a window cleaner grinning at her from the bottom of a ladder on the lawn of the house next door. He placed his squeegee mop and bucket on the driveway and prepared to move his ladder.

'It's well past that stage,' she called back. 'Do you do this whole street?'

'Why? You just moved in around here?'

Jo went up to him so she could speak more quietly. 'No, but I've just been to see the woman who lives next door and she was so rude to me, I couldn't believe it. Is she always like that?'

'Ah, you obviously don't know her.' The window cleaner paused, folded his arms and beamed at her with all the superiority of additional knowledge.

'I've only met her once before and she was all right then. But today she seemed to be in a terrible mood,' she said. 'I wondered if something had happened to upset her.'

'Upset the Cold-fish? I doubt it, she hasn't got any feelings that I've ever seen. Never given us a hello yet anyway and we've been doing her windows for five years. The hubby's all right, though. Do you know him?'

'Yes, he's a friend of a friend, you could say.'

'Under the thumb, know what I mean?' Another grin of good white teeth split his face and without any encouragement from Jo, he went on, 'He's a pleasant enough bloke though, which is more than I'd be if the wife made me sleep in the back room.' He drew a breath, shaking his head. 'Separate beds. Bad sign, that.'

Jo laughed. 'It takes all sorts.'

'It does indeed.' He grinned and would probably have gone on to reveal more professional secrets but for an icy draught of wind, bringing the first smattering of sleet with it. He regarded the ominous sky. 'Lovely weather for it.'

Jo agreed and went back to her car, pondering on this snippet. Ten to one it didn't mean anything. But no wonder Paul had wanted a 'romantic friendship' with Antonia. And she had always kept him at arm's length — or so she had claimed. Jo had never been certain that she was being completely honest about that. But it was indisputable that Rachel's behaviour was distinctly odd. Jo had caught her rifling through Antonia's handbag — was that just the action of a jealous wife, or was there something more to it?

A thought came to her that all at once made her pulse race and she reached for her bag and pulled out her notebook. The top page had a Warwick telephone number scribbled on it, which she had memorised from the hotel phone log. Someone had called Antonia's room from this number at 2.10 a.m. on Tuesday. She punched in the number on the mobile phone and waited, her eyes on Rachel's frosted glass door.

The phone rang and there was movement through the glass. She pictured the phone on the hall table and guessed Rachel was standing over it. Finally she answered, her voice brusque as ever.

Jo cut off the call and sat unmoving for a minute. She had proved that either Paul or Rachel had called Antonia from the house but she had no idea why. The obvious explanation was that Paul had rung to confirm his expected time of arrival later that morning. But surely he would have called from his cab on his mobile?

It made speaking to him even more imperative and Jo looked up Paul's taxi firm on her phone. It had a Stratford number but no address. She had to call them to ask where exactly in Stratford and while she waited for them to answer, she saw the vertical blinds in Rachel's front room window shift and imagined the tall woman behind them watching her make calls. Belatedly, she dropped the phone and drove away, berating herself for being such an amateur. *I need to go back to astrology and what I know*, she thought, as she negotiated the many lights on the M40 junction and took the exit towards Stratford.

She was reminded of her conversation in Petra's car only twenty-four hours ago, but it seemed like days. Petra had been open about her ambitions to escape her nine-to-five job and Jo reminded herself to send on her friend Hanni's number. It would be good to talk to Hanni herself, she reflected, although she could almost hear the challenges her friend would put to her about her current series of bad decisions. In that delicate, roundabout way she had, Hanni would be bound to make her aware that she would do much less harm as an astrologer than as a PI. *Where can you spread more loving kindness, Jo? Where can you grow compassion in your life? Not by tangling with people who lie and deceive for a living.* That was the sort of thing Hanni might say. And yet, Hanni also seemed to have an instinctive understanding of what Jo needed to do. And for her own peace of mind, Jo knew she needed to find out what had happened to Antonia. Astrology would just have to wait.

* * *

The taxi office was located above a junk shop a long walk from the smarter shopping streets in Stratford-upon-Avon town centre. Jo ascended a dirty staircase, turning at the top into a low-ceilinged, untidy room where a woman had her nose in a paperback.

'I'm looking for Paul Bakewell,' Jo said.

'Friend of his? Or for work?'

'Friend,' Jo answered. 'Do you know where I can find him?'

The woman, who looked grimy under her make-up, flicked her earring while staring Jo out and then pulled on her headphones. '608? Come in, 608. State location.'

She lifted the headphones so Jo could hear a tinny version of Paul's voice respond, '608. Hello, Kim, I'm at Sainsbury's in Warwick.'

'Friend of yours here to see you. Name of . . .?'

Jo supplied her name. It was hard to discern any expression in Paul's voice but he didn't quibble about coming back to the office to see her as soon as he could.

There was a plastic-covered bench against one wall and Jo asked if she could sit down to wait. The other woman shrugged and hunched her shoulders over her book. It seemed an obvious opportunity to find out more about Paul.

'Must be a boring job?' Jo asked after a minute or two.

'Not really. Get lots of reading done.'

'Has Paul worked here long?'

'Longer than me.' She flicked over a page.

'Oh. How long is that?'

Kim lifted her head with its topknot and regarded Jo as if begrudging every second not spent in her book. Jo tried and failed to see the title. 'Only a couple of months, why? You've not come after this job, have you?'

'No, but I wouldn't mind a job like this.'

'Oh, you wouldn't, would you?' Kim snorted. 'Well, you can't have it. Is that what you've come about? 'Cause if so, Paul can't do anything. He's the lowest of the low round here — even I've worked that one out.'

'He told me he virtually ran the place,' Jo said, managing an indignant tone in order to play up to the role the younger woman had invented for her. Unfortunately her piece of acting was interrupted by a call from one of the other drivers to say he was starting his shift and Kim had to turn her attention to her screen. She spoke briefly into her headset and scribbled a note in a battered old book on the desk.

'Paul's full of bull,' Kim said when she had dealt with the call. 'And don't think I wouldn't say that to his face, because I would. Run this place?' She gave a derisory laugh. 'More like he could be on his way by the end of the week!'

'He might be sacked?'

Kim sniffed. 'Paul sometimes gets a mate to do his shift for him. Well, he's done that once too often. Plus the police were round yesterday asking questions about him, and Terry, that's the boss, doesn't appreciate it.'

'What did the police want?'

'They looked at the records. It was a good job I filled them in right, both sets. We're running two systems at the minute, so it's double the work. Because they don't trust this piece of shit—' she tapped her screen with her pen — 'I have to do the paperwork as well. It's not a picnic this job, you know.'

'I'm going off the idea. Paperwork isn't my strong point. Let's have a look.'

'It's complicated at first.' Kim clicked on to a programme on the screen, which showed a list of numbers, each one presumably a driver, giving times and locations. 'This lot has got to be backed up by this—' she pointed from the screen to a ledger with columns and the same numbers on each row — 'and this book doesn't go anywhere except from me to Terry, 'cause it's needed for tax reasons.'

'Wow, that does seem a lot of work,' Jo murmured. She scanned the week's entries for Paul's cab number. She suspected some sort of double-accounting scam was going on but was more interested in locating Paul's whereabouts on Monday night.

'There's a lot of detail here,' she added admiringly, flipping back a page or two until her eyes fixed on the date. But from a quick glance, it seemed that his fares were remarkably similar to other nights — a couple of short trips between clubs and pubs, restaurants and hotels, and usually one trip every night from the theatre.

'You know you said Paul sometimes gets someone to stand in for him?' Jo asked. 'Did he do that on Monday night?'

Kim took the ledger back and closed it. 'That's what the police asked. As far as I know, he was here.'

Jo returned to her plastic seat. *It fits*, she thought. Paul had called her at five thirty saying he had just finished his shift. But what about the 2.10 call from his home? According to this ledger, he couldn't possibly have made that — it was clear that taxi drivers had to account for their whereabouts all the time they were on duty, which must have been handy for the police. Focusing solely on Paul's driver number, she saw there were no fares booked in for him over the last few days. *That made sense*, she thought, as obviously he'd been in Yorkshire. In fact the last record of working, before today, seemed to be on Monday night.

'Sunday's his regular day off and he's been taking a bit of leave the last couple of days,' Kim explained when Jo asked.

No doubt Paul had told the police his movements, Jo thought, and they had been here to check. 'So the copper went away a happy man, did he?'

'Who knows with them?' Kim said. 'They were looking for something on Paul and they usually find what they're looking for, don't they?'

As she finished speaking, Paul came noisily up the stairs and into the room. Although he didn't look overjoyed to see Jo, he greeted her civilly, which was an improvement on their last meeting. She wanted a chat with him on their own and suggested they go for a cup of tea. He agreed after a moment's hesitation and told Kim he was signing off for a break.

She made a note in the ledger. 'I've only allowed twenty minutes,' she called after him as they descended the narrow staircase.

'You heard her, this better not take long,' he said when they were out in the street. 'I assume this is because you've finally found something useful?' He offered her some sugar-free gum, which she politely refused. He took some himself and chewed as he strode along. With his car keys clutched in his hand and his shoulders back, he looked tense and defensive and altogether different from Jo's first impression of him as a jovial, good-natured man.

She glanced around and saw a convenient café, the kind that is no more than a row of Formica-and-chrome tables down one side of a baker's. It looked as if it had seen better days but she was in no position to be fussy. She bought Paul a pot of tea and herself a weak frothy coffee.

'I'm not going to change my mind, you know,' Paul said as soon as she had sat down. 'I'm going to sue your firm if I can and it's no less than you deserve.'

It wasn't a promising start and the coffee tasted only slightly better than the dishwater effort she'd had earlier. Jo sighed. 'It's dreadful what's happened to Antonia. If I could have prevented it, I would have—'

'She was *paying* you,' he muttered, glaring at the table, '*paying* you to look after her. I thought it was funny at first that you two spent so much time together, if you were just her tenant. Then I realised and I couldn't believe it.'

'How did you know?'

Paul disposed of his gum in a paper napkin and stirred sugar into his tea. 'I followed you,' he said with a certain amount of pride. 'I saw you go into the office.'

Jo hoped it wasn't obvious that this made her feel uneasy. At the same time, she felt strangely pleased that Antonia hadn't told him. 'Well, at least I can ask you not to rush into this lawsuit,' Jo suggested. 'The inquest is today and the coroner may decide that Antonia killed herself, which doesn't leave you with much of a case—'

'I don't give a fuck what the coroner says,' Paul cut in. His voice rose, but there were no other customers to notice. 'We both know who killed her,' he went on, 'and he's still walking around scot-free. If you had any sense of what's right, or any feeling for Toni, you'd be trying to get the person who killed her locked up. But no, you were just happy to take her money.'

'I *am* trying to find who killed her, which is one of the reasons I'm here,' Jo said. She folded her hands on the table in front of her, aiming for an appearance of calm although her heart had started to hammer.

'What do you mean by that?' An expression of stubbornness mixed with malice came over the man's face and Jo felt glad they were in a reasonably public place. She took a moment to think and a sip of the revolting coffee.

'Only that I've been looking into your movements on Monday night. Did you ask someone to do your shift for you?'

Paul shook his head with disbelief. 'What are you like? You have the cheek to come here after making such a cock-up of things and accuse me of having something to do with it?'

Jo decided to brazen it out. 'Well? You were at work when she rang, weren't you?'

'Yeah, I took the call on my mobile. Toni was obviously upset. Someone had locked her in the sauna and she wanted me to go and see her. I said I would as soon as I finished work and I did . . . Look, I went through all this with the police. I think you've got a bloody nerve coming here and interrogating me.' He got to his feet, chair scraping on the hard floor, his colour and his voice rising again.

A woman behind the counter in a lemon-coloured uniform looked across and called, 'You all right, love?'

'Yes, thanks,' Jo said automatically but she could see it was time to leave. She pushed her half-empty cup away and picked up her bag.

'You're not going to get away with this.' He moved closer as she rose from her chair and although he was not much taller than her, his physical bulk was intimidating. 'I'm going to take you and your lover-boy boss to the cleaners,' he said at the sort of volume that was meant to be heard.

'It'll probably cost you more in solicitor's bills,' she said. She could feel herself flushing, and kept on walking out of the place.

How could he know about her and Macy? The thought that he had followed her made her skin creep. And maybe not just to the office. She wasted no time finding her car and driving home.

About to let herself into her flat, looking forward to a bath and a change of clothes, she heard music coming from inside. She hesitated, instantly tense. It seemed unlikely that burglars would want to play Van Morrison but, after the morning she'd had, it didn't take much to unsettle her. Nothing in the living room was out of place and she wondered what freak electrical fault could have started the music. She was still standing doubtfully by the door when Macy strolled out of the kitchen eating an apple.

'Make yourself at home, why don't you?' she said, a harsh edge to her voice.

'I thought you might still want me to feed the cat.' He shot her a disarming smile. Claudius appeared on cue and rubbed his head disloyally against Macy's leg.

'I am quite capable of feeding my own cat, thank you, now that I am living here again.'

Macy, still munching, made himself comfortable on one of the armchairs. Claudius promptly jumped onto his lap and Macy stroked the tabby fur. 'You weren't here last night,' he said with deceptive mildness.

'I beg your pardon?' Jo put down her bag and began to undo her coat. Her calm actions belied the anger building up inside her.

'I called to see if you were OK. You weren't here.' Macy held her gaze. 'Where were you?'

With the last question, Jo's temper surged. 'What do you mean, where was I?' she demanded. 'Just because we have had sex twice does not give you the right to let yourself into my flat, to stroke my cat, listen to my music and to presume you can ask me to account for my whereabouts.'

'You don't want to tell me. That's fine.' Macy finished the apple and threw the core across the room. It landed neatly in the bin by the desk.

'Yes, it is fine!' Jo said. 'If I don't choose to tell you, it is absolutely *fine!* Actually, I was working on Antonia's case and spent the night in her cottage but it is really none of your business.'

'Surprising you should say that, because it is my business, which you would realise if you thought for a second before you opened your mouth.' Macy's eyes became fixed on a point in the middle distance. 'I have received one piddling payment for this case, which covers maybe one tenth of the costs.'

'Well, you're hardly likely to receive any more now Antonia is dead.'

'Exactly, which is why I'm asking you to drop the case.'

'You can ask away—' Jo struggled to keep her voice from rising — 'but I will not drop it. It means too much to me.'

Macy got swiftly to his feet, ejecting the cat. 'I'm telling you, I'm losing money hand over fist. You can talk about what it means to you, but to *me* it means I'm running at a loss—'

'And now we come to it. That's what matters to you, isn't it?' Jo said, dimly aware her temper was mixed up with the earlier tension and her tone had turned nasty. 'That's what really touches your heart, isn't it? Money?'

'Of course it is!' Macy countered, his dark eyes fiery. 'Why else do you think I do this job? And it's not only the expenses bill you've been running up, but a letter threatening a negligence suit landed on my doormat this morning.' His voice became quiet but menacing. 'And if you think I'm going to let my business go down the pan just so you can ease your conscience, you're way off the mark.'

They were standing close now and Jo was shaking with anger. She exerted icy control as she faced him out. 'Two things — one, I am not dropping Antonia's case. Two, I want you to leave my flat.'

Macy was already walking to the door. 'You can do what you want in your own time but not in mine. And don't count on me for a job when you're fed up with your little crusade.'

He slammed the door behind him.

CHAPTER EIGHTEEN

Jo stared sorrowfully at her scanty breakfast of toast and coffee, drawing up a mental list of Macy's shortcomings and the reasons why she would be better off without that job. A week had gone by since she had told him to leave and they had still not spoken. She had to remind herself that she was determined not to call him. To distract herself, she had found plenty of astrology work to catch up on over the week, but in her quiet moments she still felt miserable. And she couldn't help dwelling on Antonia's case. Later that day she was due to drive to Kent for her funeral and was no closer to knowing what had happened to her.

Her phone vibrated on the kitchen table and Petra's name flashed up on the screen. With so much to think about since her return, Jo had almost forgotten about her.

'Jo, have you got a minute? I've been doing some digging for you.' Petra, as ever, launched straight into the middle of the conversation, dispensing with any small talk. When Jo was slow to respond, she added, 'You do know who's calling, don't you? It's me, the woman who took you to sunny Harrogate to meet Carina, superwoman, who juggles a job, a solicitor husband, four kids, a one-night stand and an au pair, and ices cakes while she's being interviewed about a murder.'

Jo laughed involuntarily. 'That was very cool of her, wasn't it? How are you, Petra? Back at work now?'

'That's where I'm calling from. But what's wrong, Jo? I can tell from your voice you are really low. You're not still on that guilt trip about Antonia, are you?'

'I suppose so — I'm going to the funeral later today. Not a cheerful occasion.'

'No, it's not just that. I'm getting terrible vibes. Something else has upset you, hasn't it?'

'I did have a really bad row with Macy,' Jo admitted. 'He sort of sacked me — but I wouldn't say it upset me, just made me angry.'

'Oh no, you didn't? I thought he was sexy, in a rumpled sort of way. He had a wonderful cool green aura, you know. I should try to make it up with him. I think you're both a bit mixed up — but listen, I didn't ring you to be your agony aunt.'

'I'm sorry, what's happened? Have you managed to bump into Carina's au pair?'

'Unfortunately not, but I've spoken to Carina again. Remember she told us she'd spent the whole night with Sargent and left at half past six? Well, I didn't believe her somehow. I watched her lips as she was speaking and she kept licking them. It's always the lips that give people away, you know, not the eyes.'

Aware that she had to pick up Tess in an hour, Jo urged Petra to come to the point.

'All right, but these details are important. You know what an ambitious cow she is? Perhaps you don't, but I can assure you she is. I think she'd forgotten that I make all the training bookings for my firm. And if her name should accidentally be deleted from my list, her little one-woman business would take a bit of a hammering. Anyway, the long and the short of it is I called her up to sort of remind her about this, in a diplomatic way.'

'You threatened her, you mean? I hope you don't get in trouble.'

'Who? Me? Nobody dares tell me off because no one else can do my job. Anyway, Carina didn't say much at the time but she rang me up at home last night and said she hadn't told us the full story. She didn't stay the whole night with Oliver Sargent. She had to leave earlier because she wanted to slip into the house and go to bed before anyone got up.'

'So what time did she leave?'

'Five fifteen. Oliver saw her to her car — the age of chivalry is not quite dead — and that must be when I saw him in the car park from my window. Remember I heard a car driving away? That must have been Carina.'

'So he would have had plenty of time to get to Antonia's room and somehow tempt her to come with him. Although God knows how he did that. Or maybe he just met her and took his chance. But why did Carina lie to us? Don't tell me she was protecting him?'

'Not likely.' Petra snorted. 'Protecting number one, more like. Carina said at first Sargent didn't mention her to the police at all but then they turned the screws on and he got nervous. He warned Carina that he was going to have to give her name. He told her to say she had stayed all night or he would tell her husband as well.'

'So she would protect a possible murderer?' Jo turned over her doubts in her mind.

'Sod the possible murderer,' Petra said, her voice triumphant. 'She was protecting herself, more like! When I asked her, she just said she knew Sargent couldn't do anything like that. Pretty sure of themselves, these Capricorns, aren't they?'

Jo agreed. 'It sounds bad news for Sargent. You'd better tell the police. And listen, thanks so much, Petra, this is a bit of a breakthrough.'

'Only a bit of one? But yes, I will,' she promised. 'I'm just making sure you know first. I should be thanking you anyway because now I know there is something other than the nine-to-five for me. I just have to work out what it is. Oh, and Jo,' she added, 'make it up with your man, won't you?'

'He is *not* my man,' Jo said, but Petra had already ended the call. However, she was smiling for the first time in days, grateful for Petra's friendship and enthusiasm, as well as for the information. Now she only had to find a definite link between Sargent and John Brooke to prove that Antonia had been right all along.

* * *

Jo had promised to drive Tess to the funeral in Kent and, although the prospect made her feel almost as sad as the falling out with Macy, she was determined to see it through. As arranged, she picked Tess up at the cottage. The funeral was at three o'clock and they left plenty of time to get there. Tess had arranged for them both to stay at her aunt's house afterwards and Jo would return to Coventry the following day.

Both women were quiet on the journey. Jo was mulling over her earlier conversation with Petra. She had already told Tess about Sargent's lack of alibi and now, as she sped along in the fast lane of the M2 in her old Renault, she reminded her of the need to prove that Sargent and Brooke were the same man.

'If Antonia was right and if we can find some evidence, then his proximity to both deaths must make the police dig deeper into both cases,' Jo said. 'And while we're in Kent, I might take the chance to ask around near where you used to live. I know Antonia has already done it, but I think it's worth another try — if you don't mind?'

Tess roused herself from her meditative silence. 'Of course not, I'll help if I can. We'll go over there after the funeral and I'll show you the house where we used to live. There aren't any close neighbours but I could introduce you to some of the people who knew Monique — if they're still there.'

'Right, I'll need instruction from here,' Jo said, spotting the signs for her exit from the motorway. As she followed Tess's clear directions to her aunt's house, she remembered

Antonia telling her how she had stayed there after their mother's death and how she had longed to go back home.

There was nothing wrong with the narrow, newly painted house. It was one of many others in a row of garden walls and gates and oblong lawns. Maybe the sisters had felt claustrophobic in the cramped, low-ceilinged rooms after their big house in the country, Jo thought, following Tess in.

Aunt Win was a softly spoken little fusspot, who made them tea while fastening clips into her curly white hair. With a clip in her mouth, she ran through the arrangements for the funeral and handed them a plate of chocolate biscuits. They were still drinking their tea and Tess answering Aunt Win's string of questions when more mourners arrived.

Jo and Tess had to get changed together in the back bedroom. Jo shook out the creases in the ankle-length black dress she had brought and hoped it wasn't too dressy for the occasion. Tess was buttoning herself into a severe black suit, which seemed more appropriate. They assured each other they looked fine and Jo put on some lipstick with a slightly trembling hand, wishing this ordeal over.

The house was bulging with people when she came downstairs. Jo didn't have time to work out who they all were because the hearse arrived as she was putting on her coat and giving herself a quick once-over in the hall mirror. She went straight out and waited, shivering on the pavement while the other guests straggled gradually down the path. She tried not to look at the coffin, which showed through the gaps in the wreaths and flowers.

By tacit agreement, Jo travelled to the church in Aunt Win's son's car, sandwiched in the back between his two teenage kids. Jo asked how well they had known Antonia and was told they weren't close and hadn't met more than twice in the last five years. 'Still, it's family, you know,' he said as if he felt he had to justify his presence.

There were a few more people waiting at the church, including a blond man, who Jo noticed simply because he looked under forty, unlike most of the others. She was surprised to see that Paul and Rachel Bakewell weren't there, until she realised guiltily that they probably hadn't known about it and she should have told Paul when she'd met him in Stratford.

What had seemed a crowd in Aunt Win's house looked a pitifully small group in the church. Jo followed the service unfalteringly with memories of being taken as a child to funerals of distant members of her mother's family, none of whom had seemed very long-lived.

She steeled herself to watch the coffin being lowered into the grave, standing in the mud while the icy wind whipped the skirt of her dress round her legs and stung her exposed fingers. She felt oddly lonely and realised that, although she had not known Antonia long and the woman had been frustratingly devious at times, still she had begun to see her as a friend. She admitted to herself that she was also regretting her recent argument with Macy, but there had been a finality about the way he had slammed out of her flat. It seemed increasingly unlikely that he would pick up the phone or seek her out again.

'You must come back to the house, dear, I've done a bit of a spread.' Aunt Win patted her arm as they filed away from the church. She didn't seem to have much idea who Jo was and probably thought she had been a friend of Antonia's. Jo wondered if she would be quite so pleasant if she knew she had been employed to look after her niece.

Tess, on the other hand, seemed to understand. 'I never want to go through anything like that again,' she murmured.

'Do you know all these people?'

'Yes, mostly, but I haven't seen them for years. Our French relatives have come, which is very good of them.' Tess nodded towards a foursome in dark coats, standing on their own. 'I'd better go and say hello.'

When she had piled a plate with vol-au-vents and egg sandwiches she didn't want, Jo found herself talking to the man she had noticed outside the church.

'It's all part of the ritual, isn't it?' he said by way of introduction. 'The religious service and the wake. People need it.'

'It's strange how something so gruesome can be comforting,' Jo agreed politely.

'Are you talking about the sausage rolls now?'

Jo grinned back at him and asked him how he knew Antonia. Almost as soon as the question was out of her mouth she had a sudden insight — this must be Guy. She stared at him as if she expected him to be familiar. A shock of untidy, curly blonde hair fell onto his face, which was drawn and thin. It was hard to tell his age. Somewhere between thirty and forty was as close as Jo could get. He had a glass of whisky in one hand and a half-smoked cigarette in the other and, close up, his dark suit looked shabby and his collar not very clean.

'I was married to her,' he said, confirming her guess. 'A short and sweet affair that should never have got up the aisle.'

'So you are Guy? I've been trying to find you.' He was the kind of man who might have been attractive once, she thought, but definitely not now. Unlike Macy with his unreadable dark brown eyes . . .

He was staring back at her. 'It worries me that you know my name.' Jo dragged her attention back to him. 'It can only mean Toni told you some awful things about me. Are you a friend of hers?'

'We met in Coventry, where I live. She had a rented cottage near Warwick.'

'I know. I finally tracked her down, thanks to a sweet girl in the office.'

'After trying her landlady and her sister?'

He nodded.

'In that case, I think you and I have spoken on the phone,' Jo added coolly.

'Oh?' He had the grace to look abashed. 'That's right, we probably have. I was too late though, she'd gone off to somewhere in Yorkshire by the time I turned up at that funny little tumbledown cottage.'

'What did you want from Antonia?'

Guy sucked on his cigarette. 'Just to say hello, old times, you know.' His eyes roved round the room as if he had trouble concentrating. 'Can I get you a drink?'

Jo agreed and watched his thin figure weave through the room to the sideboard where Aunt Win had set out a few bottles. He helped himself to a whisky and drank it down while he poured Jo a sherry. He refilled his own glass and wandered back, bringing the bottle.

'It's terrible, isn't it? What's happened to her. I can't get my head round it at all. I knew she'd been made redundant. That was why she moved to Warwick, wasn't it?'

'Only partly.' Jo eyed him curiously, finding it hard to believe he didn't know the real reason. 'She was following John Brooke, her sister's boyfriend.'

Guy groaned. 'She wasn't? Oh no, poor Antonia. It was a total obsession with her, you know. She never forgot him and blamed him for Monique's death.'

'I don't know, she may turn out to be right.' Jo watched his face carefully. 'Don't you think it's a bit strange that both sisters should die in suspicious circumstances?'

'I never thought of it.' He shrugged.

Jo almost made some biting reply to this but she held her tongue. Some instinct told her to keep on Guy's good side. 'Antonia was convinced she had found John Brooke, only he was using another name.' When he didn't react to this, Jo sighed. 'I suppose she *was* obsessed but that doesn't mean she was wrong. I feel I have to follow it up somehow. I don't suppose you ever met *the* John Brooke?'

Guy rubbed the stubble on his chin. 'I did, actually.'

'You've met him? Would you recognise him?' Out of the corner of her eye, she saw Aunt Win bearing down on them with a plate of shop-bought fairy cakes. Jo grabbed his sleeve as unobtrusively as she could and led him out of the room.

There was a cluster of guests in the kitchen and another group on the upstairs landing, who seemed to be speaking French, so Jo settled for the hall as a way of gaining a modicum of privacy. 'Go on, I want to hear everything about him. But first, did Antonia know about this?'

'No,' he said. 'I'm afraid I never told her.' He shot Jo a guilty look.

'All right, when was it? When did you meet him?'

Guy had the jittery look of the compulsive drinker but he was biddable enough. He settled down on the stairs, taking a moment to collect his thoughts and to top up his glass from the bottle he had picked up on the sideboard. 'It was just after Antonia and I got engaged and she and Monique were living in the family house. They were so close and I never felt included in the whole family thing. Never was and never will be now,' he added, making an expansive gesture with his glass to take in the little gatherings around them. 'To be perfectly honest, I wasn't very sure of Antonia at all in those days. She seemed so elusive — even though she'd agreed to get married, I still never knew where I was with her.'

'Sorry to interrupt, but would you mind telling me what Zodiac sign you were born under?'

'I'm Pisces the fish,' Guy said amiably. 'Is that significant?'

With an afflicted Neptune, I bet, Jo thought. But at least it tallied with what Antonia had told her. 'Maybe,' she said. 'Go on.'

'It so happened that I wasn't too busy at work that autumn, whereas Antonia had to work all hours. I had to be out of the office a lot and no one knew where I was supposed to be from one morning to the next, so I was just coasting along. The upshot of it was I had a lot of time on my hands and Antonia always seemed to have something better to do than to see me. When she wasn't at work, she was rushing home — Monique needed her help putting up some shelves or it was Monique's birthday or she wanted to "bury herself in the country for a bit".'

'Tiresome,' Jo agreed. She was rapt, leaning on the banister, pleased that Pisceans told such good stories.

Guy took another drag of his cigarette. 'I resented this quiet family life of hers, to be honest, and this clinging sister, and out of curiosity I drove down there one day. Antonia had taken me to the house a couple of times but always as some part of walking or cycling trip she was encouraging us to go on and I'd not had much time to really see the place — or the mysterious Monique.'

'Was she mysterious?'

'Not at all.' Guy gave a laugh. 'Very nice actually, softer than Antonia and a real homebird. She made me tea and gave me homemade carrot cake and we had a long chat. She was a good listener and I probably bored her to tears with my problems. She didn't tell me much in return—'

'Typical Cancer.' Jo grinned. 'Sorry, go on.'

'But while I was there, he turned up — the boyfriend. Monique was most embarrassed because she hadn't introduced him to anyone yet but she was madly, badly in love.' Guy shook his head. 'She transformed from an awkward little dormouse to a sophisticated woman in his presence. I almost fancied her myself . . .' He let the sentence trail away into silence and Jo wondered for a minute what the outcome would have been if Guy had transferred his allegiance from Antonia to Monique. Probably happier all round, she supposed.

'It's amazing to find someone who has met him,' she said, returning to practicalities. 'Antonia never gave up trying to find John Brooke and eventually traced him to Warwick, where, like I said, she believed he was using another name.' She dug out her phone and showed him a blurry photo that she had managed to take of Sargent in the foyer of the hotel. 'Do you recognise him from this?'

Guy shook his head as soon as he saw the picture. 'You are joking! That could be anybody and we are talking five years ago since I laid eyes on this bloke.'

'But if you saw him, face to face? That would be different, wouldn't it?' Jo insisted. 'That could prove Brookes and Sargent are the same man once and for all.' Guy was still looking doubtful, but Jo persevered. 'We could be certain then.'

'Monique's death was — well, very sad, but it was years ago. What good would it do to drag the ex-boyfriend into it now? Even if it is the same man.'

'And you didn't have any doubt that Monique's death was suicide?'

Guy raised sceptical eyebrows, looking up at her as he lit another cigarette. 'When a depressed person is found in an unlocked garage with the engine running, how could there be any doubts?'

'Antonia had doubts,' Jo pointed out.

'She was entirely irrational about the whole thing.' Guy's face hardened. 'You didn't know her then. She had a breakdown over it. I wasn't going to encourage her obsession, was I? And I didn't know she'd finally found his *doppelganger*.'

'Would you be prepared to speak to the police now about meeting John Brooke?' Jo watched as Guy shook his head, staring into his glass.

'I really don't think—' he began and broke off, his face creasing with doubt.

'It's what Antonia was desperate to prove,' Jo went on and watched as Guy lifted his cigarette, inhaling smoke. Finally he met her eyes.

'I guess I could. If it'll get this poor bloke who happens to look like him off the hook, I suppose I'll have to,' he said.

At that moment Tess popped her head around the lounge door. 'There you are, Jo. Listen, I'll be able to get away for an hour or so to show you where we used to live. Do you still want to go? Oh hello again, Guy,' she added.

'We may not need to go now.' Jo chewed her lip thoughtfully and cast her eyes at Guy.

'Don't worry, I won't go anywhere. I can see I've got to spend an uncomfortable hour with the police. If I don't go and see them voluntarily, I'm sure you'll see they find me somehow,' he said. 'At least that will put this whole bloody nonsense to bed.'

'That's how I feel,' Tess said. 'I don't know what Guy's on about but I've psyched myself up to see the old house and I want to go.'

'All right.' Jo abandoned her paper plate and followed Tess to the front door. 'Don't go away,' she said to Guy. 'I'm going to drive you to Yorkshire myself. We can start as soon as I get back.'

'What was all that about with Guy?' Tess asked as soon as they were in Jo's car. 'You two seemed to be getting on very well.'

'We have some firm evidence at last,' Jo said. 'Guy can prove that Sargent is — or isn't — John Brooke.' She explained briefly as she drove along the winding country lanes towards Chartham. 'This could be the corroboration Antonia was looking for.'

'Well, at least Guy is going to do something for her,' Tess commented. 'For once.'

'I'm sure Guy was after Antonia for money, as you thought. He says he didn't see her before she died, though. By the time he located the cottage, we'd left for Yorkshire.'

'Well, at least she was spared that, it's something anyway,' Tess said when Jo had finished. Now that the ordeal was over, she seemed more relaxed and in between giving directions, she expounded on her relatives. 'From the outside, we must seem a strange family. We're close but also we need our distance too. I suppose it's partly because only Dad's family is in this country.'

Jo slowed down to pass between parked cars along a narrow street. Even under the grey, lowering sky, the close-packed timbered cottages and black-and-white pub looked idyllic. The end of the high street was the end of the village but Tess directed her up a lane on their left and they drove on past a squat stone church. 'Park here—' she indicated the grass verge — 'and we'll walk up to the house so you can see it at least from the outside. I'm not sure who lives there now.' She unlatched the wide gate and they walked up the long, slightly rising drive just as it started to rain.

'I couldn't work out why my French relatives were giving me the cold shoulder,' Tess said. 'I finally had to ask Jeanne, who's married to my cousin, and she told me something I didn't know. Apparently when Mummy's sister died she left everything to Monique, and Monique went over to France, cleared the apartment and took the money. They never heard from her again, so they felt a bit miffed. I tried to build some bridges today by telling them that Monique was depressed and probably would have got in touch. All this happened just before she died, you see.'

Jo stood still despite the rain. 'Was there much money, do you know?'

'According to Jeanne, about twenty thousand euros.'

'Of course, it could have just been swallowed up by her debts,' Jo said, 'but if it wasn't — if Monique managed to get hold of the cash and keep it out of the banking system — maybe a greedy man would have—'

'Murdered her for it?'

CHAPTER NINETEEN

The house, red-brick and rambling, stood on its own with a paddock to one side and a small copse at the back. A battered estate car was parked beside it and a yellow toy truck was upturned in front of the door. Jo was still grappling with the latest information about Monique when a door flew open and a slim, athletic woman strode out, heading purposefully across a side lawn. Through the open gate, Jo saw her starting to take down the washing on the line. It seemed the perfect opportunity and Jo ran up to help, with Tess following.

The woman gave them a surprised look over her shoulder but carried on unpegging the washing. When Jo followed her to the doorstep with her arms full of slightly damp nappies, she thanked her and asked her into a square utility room. Tess followed carrying a bundle of sheets.

'Thanks for your help.' The young woman eyed their black funeral clothes, now less smart for being wet. 'Who are you? Have you broken down nearby?'

'Actually my friend was just showing me where she used to live,' Jo explained. She introduced herself and Tess, who was wiping the mud splashes off her legs.

The woman opposite them was thin-faced, dark and probably in her early thirties. She gave them a brusque nod and turned to sort out the washing. 'That's right, there was a lady called Monique Vane who lived here before us. Are you her daughter?'

'Her sister.'

'I'm Sue Langton. We've lived here for five years — me, Billy and the two kids.'

'I spent my whole childhood here,' Tess said, 'and the house looks just like I remember it.'

'We can't do anything to it because we only rent it from the building society. If we could, we'd like to build an extension so Billy can have a proper music room. He plays the drums, which is why we need a house with no neighbours,' she added with a rueful smile. 'Anyway, you'll have to come in and dry off. I can't let you go out in this rain.'

Jo had been hoping for this. She readily accepted the offer of a cup of tea and wondered how to get Monique into the conversation. Any information about the months immediately before she died would be useful. 'Did you know the owner at all?' Jo asked as Sue Langton led the way through a hallway. 'Tess's sister, I mean.'

'No, she'd — er — gone when we moved in. There is one thing, which is a bit embarrassing . . . You obviously know your sister died in — well — difficult circumstances—' She looked at Tess helplessly.

'I know she was found in the garage, yes,' Tess said.

'It's just that Billy — my husband — doesn't know. The people in the village made sure I knew about it but I've never told him because he's funny over things like that and I thought he'd want to move out straight away.'

'Don't worry, we won't mention it,' Jo assured her, although this cast a blight on her hopes of discussing Monique further.

Sue made them cups of tea, which they took into a big sitting room, where her husband and two small children were all watching a medical programme on television. In between sips of tea, Jo gathered it was showing a casualty ward in a hospital and she felt slightly on edge knowing that any minute something gory could come up on the screen. This didn't seem to bother either of the children, however. The eldest was clearly fascinated and the baby was falling asleep.

Conversation was strained and polite. Billy turned out to be a music teacher. With one eye on the television, he told them he used to play drums professionally but now worked in a comprehensive school in Canterbury. Sue seemed inclined to leave the talking to him.

Glancing around the room, Jo decided that most of the furniture probably belonged to the Langtons. It was mostly new, flimsy and out of keeping with the house. She asked what the house had been like when they moved in and discovered it had been unoccupied for three months after Monique's death while the building society had it on the market. The Langtons were new to the village and had been looking to rent just such a place. They had never met Monique or her boyfriend. Jo was ready to leave once she had discovered this much but they waited until the rain eased off.

Billy showed them out. He stood with them on the wet gravel and looked up at the sky as he and Tess discussed the possibility of more rain. Jo's eyes strayed compulsively to the detached brick garage, more modern than the rest of the house.

'Gruesome, isn't it?' Billy said, following her gaze. He had an open, cheerful face, which looked too young for the paunch below his stretched white jumper. Turning to Tess, he added, 'Your poor sister must have been very unhappy.' Tess nodded and he went on, blithely, 'I hope you didn't mention it to Sue because I've always kept it from her. I found out from the landlord of the White Lion the week we moved in, but I think it would upset her . . .'

Jo and Tess exchanged glances. 'We never said a word about it,' Jo said. 'I can understand how you feel, though. I expect you cleared out everything that belonged to Monique.'

'Well, there was no personal stuff,' he said. 'Only some old furniture, which wasn't our style. We couldn't sell it, of course, because it came with the house. We just locked it up in the garage.' He jerked his head in that direction.

Jo glanced at Tess, whose expression was wary. 'Do you mind if I have a look?' she was addressing Tess as much as Billy.

'Why don't you?' Tess said firmly. 'Seeing as we're here.'

'Monique had one or two interesting bits of furniture, which I might persuade the building society to sell me,' Jo added by way of explanation to Billy.

He headed towards the garage. 'I'm sure they would,' he said. 'They're no good to man or beast where they are.'

'I think I'll pass on this.' Tess hung back. 'I'll wait here but you go,' she added, giving Jo a meaningful look. She took the hint and pressed on.

Billy opened the doors after a struggle with the lock and she stared in at dusty stacks of old furniture. 'Creepy, isn't it?' He threaded his way between an old sideboard and a pile of chairs. 'There's a light switch here somewhere.' He found it and turned round to stare at the piles of furniture. 'They told me down the White Lion that she was found slumped in her car. She was drunk and the garage door was closed, with the engine running. The thing is, they were never one hundred per cent sure it was suicide because she wasn't sitting in the driving seat and she was half out of the car — so local legend has it anyway,' he finished.

'I know,' Jo said.

'The garage doors were unlocked but they are very stiff and difficult to open from inside,' Billy went on, 'so if she'd had second thoughts and got out of the car, she'd have had trouble getting out of the garage. I reckon that's what happened.'

Daunted by the amount of furniture and the dust, Jo looked half-heartedly in the drawers of a bureau. It would take days to inspect all this stuff and she could hardly keep Tess waiting in the cold. She wondered if it was worth staying in Kent for a while and asking Billy if she could come back to search properly. But what for?

'There's nothing in any of the drawers,' Billy said over his shoulder. He was working his way round to a pile tied in plastic sheeting. 'I don't know which bits of furniture you like, but this stuff is interesting. It was in the middle of the living room floor, tied up like this when we came here. Our nearest neighbour said he'd helped her unload it from a van. Monique told him she'd got it all from France.'

He lifted a corner of the plastic sheeting to reveal an ancient settee, standing on one end. Jo explained that Monique had been left the contents of a house in France. A jagged tear in the plastic caught her eye and she bent for a closer look.

'I know it's ripped but we didn't do that,' Billy was quick to explain. 'We just lifted the whole bundle exactly as it was and put it in here.'

Jo saw that not only was the plastic sheeting ripped but the fabric was roughly slashed. The stuffing was falling out, and it looked effectively ruined.

'Funny thing to do, isn't it?' Billy said, his good-natured face baffled. 'Fancy going to the trouble of bringing a knackered old thing like that all the way back from France. Showed she was a bit lacking, really, doesn't it?'

'It might show she had plans,' Jo said. She felt around in the dry old horsehair but all she found was a substantial hole. 'Especially if it wasn't ruined when she brought it back. Did this trip to France come up at the inquest? Did the police speak to your neighbour who helped her get it out of the van?'

Billy had moved on to stack some chairs to make a clearer passage to the door. 'No idea.' He shook his head. 'And the neighbour's gone now so he wouldn't be able to help you. Arthur Hatfield, a widower. He moved to Broadstairs a couple of years ago. Why are you interested in all this?'

'I don't know, but if you look at this sofa, it almost looks as if something had been hidden in there and someone has slashed the fabric to get it out.'

Billy had a closer look, frowning. 'Maybe,' he said, 'but what would she want to hide?'

'I don't know,' Jo said again, 'it's just an idea.'

They left the garage together and Jo watched him lock it up. 'I suppose most people would have moved on by now,' he said looking moodily up at the house. 'Five years is a long time to rent a place. But it seems to suit us. I suppose it's not very financially sensible is it, renting?'

'I'm the wrong person to ask.' Jo grinned. 'I rent my flat — and it suits me too. That's what matters, isn't it?'

Tess was standing forlornly on the drive and Jo apologised to her as soon as they were on their own again. 'I wasn't being macabre, honestly,' Jo explained on their way back to the car. 'I had to have a look and I think I've found something Antonia may have missed. Because she didn't know about the legacy, did she?'

'Monique seems to have kept it to herself, which is strange because I thought she told us most things. By the way, this had better be good because I'm absolutely freezing now.'

'Monique didn't tell Antonia she'd started going out with John Brooke straight away. So she was not always so transparent as you may have thought.' Jo looked at her watch. 'I know we have to be getting back to Aunt Win's soon but let me buy you a coffee first. I want to test a theory on you. Where can we go?'

Tess directed her to an ivy-covered hotel on the way to Ashford, where they ordered a coffee and went into a quiet lounge with an open fire at one end. Jo chose seats by the fire and launched into her hypothesis.

'From what you and Antonia have told me, I've got a picture of Monique after John Brooke disappeared. She was obviously depressed and in debt — the extent of which, incidentally, was another thing she kept from the two of you. She almost stopped going out and didn't even go to work for a few months. If she'd been tempted to kill herself, she might have done it then. I know—' Jo went on as Tess was about to object — 'I know a lot of suicides happen just as the person appears to be over the worst. But in this case, I think Monique had a plan because of an unexpected stroke of luck.'

'You mean the legacy?'

'Yes. When did she hear about it?'

'Tante Marie died in January 2011 but apparently it takes months for these things to come through. My cousin Jeanne said Monique went to Quimper to clear the apartment in April. She didn't give me an exact date but I could ask her.'

'April fits,' Jo nodded, thinking it through, 'especially if it was late April. She may have heard about the legacy maybe a month beforehand? She was getting over John, but it gave her an idea. By then, she must have known that he was after her money. When she knew she had inherited twenty thousand euros, I think she used it to get him back.'

'But how could she if she didn't know where he was?'

'Just because he wasn't answering her calls or messages, doesn't mean he wasn't receiving them,' Jo pointed out. 'I expect she contacted him saying she had come into money. Then she went across to France to get it. I saw a bill somewhere among all those papers Antonia kept for the rent of a van for the weekend. We could check the dates, but say she drove to your aunt's place — which is where, did you say?'

'Quimper, it's in Brittany.'

'OK, what's that — most of a day's drive, then. She emptied the house of all the stuff she had inherited and piled it into the van. I don't know what she would have done about selling the house—'

'It was a rented apartment.'

'So all she had to do was to draw out her inheritance from the bank or the solicitors in cash. She would have wanted it in cash, because if she had paid a cheque into her building society or bank account, it would have been like throwing it into a black hole. I know about this, I've been there,' Jo added feelingly.

She paused to think about Monique. The quiet, desperate Cancerian with her heart set on something would not have been easily deterred. She would have understood John Brooke's obsession with money because money was important to Cancerians too — but they would not put it before love. Her last, furious conversation with Macy came into her mind with a twinge of regret. She pushed it to one side as Tess was speaking.

'She wouldn't have had any trouble getting the cash as long as she could prove who she was.' Tess's sharp face was intense. 'So she brought the money home — and then what?'

'Wait, wait, you're rushing ahead. First, before Monique left France, she hid the money in the back of the sofa. I know this sounds fanciful but she had to do something with it. Twenty thousand euros is a lot of notes to stuff into a carrier bag. And she wouldn't have wanted the Customs people asking questions.'

Tess was looking at her sceptically. 'She could have locked it into a briefcase, it would have been more secure. All this sounds so unlike my sister. She was actually just an ordinary, quiet sort of person—'

'Look, just bear with me for a minute or two more,' Jo said. 'Anyway, I bet she didn't own a briefcase.'

'True,' Tess agreed with a sudden smile.

'Possibly she didn't consider how to carry the money until she got it,' Jo said. 'In any case, the sofa was not a bad idea. It kept the cash out of sight, which was her main aim, and no one would have suspected she was carrying anything valuable with that pile of old furniture.'

'She was handy with a needle too. Actually, I *can* imagine her doing that part,' Tess said. 'But what I don't see is how you worked all this out. Or is it just hypothetical?'

'Hypothetical, of course.' Jo grinned over her cup. 'But it fits with her character, which I feel I know from doing her chart. And it explains the great big hole in the base of the sofa. But I haven't got to that yet.' Jo finished her coffee and resumed her exposition. 'The lure must have worked even better than she had expected, because Brooke turned up before she had even got round to unpacking it. Within a day or two of her return, he probably turned up on the doorstep with a bottle of champagne and a bunch of flowers.'

'So he got her drunk and stole the money — but why kill her?'

'Because Monique was a bit more cunning this time. She probably wouldn't tell him where it was. She put a plan to him. She offered him a fresh start, somewhere far away and, crucially, the two of them together. This was not what he wanted, but he did want the money. The opportunity for killing her must have suggested itself. They were pretty isolated in that house, she was a bit drunk and the money was there somewhere. He must have known it would be in cash. Perhaps they went out for a drive . . .'

'A picnic, maybe with more wine,' Tess said and suddenly her eyes teared up. She pressed her thumb and forefinger to her face and dropped her head.

Jo fell silent. 'I'm sorry,' she said eventually. 'I'm getting carried away with my theories here. You've had quite a day.'

Tess raised her chin, dabbing her eyes with her knuckles. 'No, you know, the horrible thing is, I can just see it. I bet he tempted her out of the house and plied her with champagne. She would have been quite giddy—'

'Her plan was working.' Jo nodded, more to herself. 'But then when they got back, maybe he just drove straight into the garage, got out of the car ahead of her, left the engine on and locked the garage door. He could have pulled her into the driver's seat and for good measure bashed her head against the steering wheel, which would have dazed her, if it didn't knock her out altogether. Even if she had tried to get out of the garage, the gas would have made her drowsy quite quickly and she'd had a bit to drink. She must have felt weak and sat down in the car.' Jo stopped and sighed. 'And there she was when Antonia found her.'

'And while he left her in the garage, he looked for the money?' Tess busied herself pouring out the dregs from the cafetière as if glad of the distraction. 'I suppose the furniture was the obvious place to look, if he knew the cash had come from France.'

'Yes,' Jo agreed, 'but I think he did something else as well. I think he made that bonfire in the garden and burned everything he could find about himself — and, if he'd been careful, he'd know what evidence there was. After about an hour, he had to go and unlock the garage and return the key to the ignition. He did make one mistake in not positioning Monique's body properly in the seat, but perhaps he didn't dare spend too long in there in case he was overcome by the fumes.'

'The bastard.' Tess was white. 'And we still have no proof that he and Sargent are the same man.'

'Not yet, no,' Jo admitted, 'but we know they are because Antonia recognised him. She pursued John Brooke and became convinced she had found him when she found Oliver Sargent. I think she was trying to build her case, looking for proof, which is why she kept all those records. But now Guy should be able to confirm they are the same man. If Antonia was right—' Jo paused. It was important for her to find the words for how she felt. 'And I really want her to be right, don't you? I want to do this for Antonia. I've got to get him in front of DCI Gammon first thing tomorrow. Guy's evidence could make the police reopen the case.'

'We know Sargent had the opportunity because he was meant to be out of the country at the time,' Tess pointed out. 'Don't forget those trips that were also in those papers Toni saved.'

'I expect the police will want to go through all of them,' Jo agreed. 'And they'll need to trace the neighbour who helped Monique unload the furniture.'

'So you're going to tell the police your theory?'

'Yes, I'll phone them tonight. They may not believe me but I think — with Guy's evidence — we can cast sufficient doubt on Sargent now to make them take it seriously. Anyway, we've got to leave something for them to do, haven't we?'

CHAPTER TWENTY

'You're the second person this week who's wanted that room. What's wrong with the St George Hotel and Bloody Conference Centre all of a sudden? Have they been slaughtered by TripAdvisor?' The landlord of the Bull proceeded to pepper her with more rhetorical questions as Jo checked in. 'What is it about our single room that's so attractive? Is it to do with that poor girl who fell off the cliff? Do you want cooked breakfast in the morning?'

It took Jo a few moments to realise that this last question required an answer. She smiled. 'Toast and coffee will be fine.'

The landlord handed Jo the key to her room. 'You look all in. Have a whisky and soda on the house to take up with you.' He was already holding a glass up to the optic and she gave in. He was quite right — she was tired. She had spent most of the day driving Guy from Kent to Yorkshire. After hanging around at the police station for half the afternoon, she had decided she couldn't face the journey back straight away. The idea of a room at the St George didn't appeal either and so she had come to the Bull.

The landlord had not been encouraging about it but in fact the room was cosy and warm. She put the whisky and soda down on the bedside cupboard and sat down with a sigh on the single bed. It was too soft and the bathroom was tiny but she didn't care.

She didn't envy Guy, who was still at the police station as far as she knew. He had said he would get a room at the St George and catch a train back to London when the police had finished with him. He had been churlish and quiet for most of the journey. After a pub lunch, he had been more talkative — and had surprised her by asking for her phone number before they parted. He had suggested they meet up in London sometime — go to a club, he'd said. He could probably be charming, Jo thought, despite his dissolute appearance. So why did she find herself thinking he was shallow compared to Macy?

She shook her head at herself and took a sip of the whisky. It tasted better than she'd expected and she lay back on the bed to enjoy the warming sensation. She told herself not to think about Macy, who was a lost cause if ever there was one, and reminded herself that at least the case was turning out well. With Guy's evidence, Sargent would clearly have to account for his whereabouts at the time of Monique's death and Jo felt a certain amount of satisfaction that Antonia's doubts about him were being proved correct.

She had seen Sargent briefly at the police station, sitting on a hard plastic chair outside one of the interview rooms and looking unshaven and unusually unkempt. When he had noticed her, he hadn't bothered to disguise his intense dislike. She had met his gaze levelly but his very presence had made her feel uncomfortable and she had left as soon as she could after that.

She had a good night's sleep at the Bull and woke up to a thin rectangle of lowering yellow-grey sky framed by the narrow sash window, wondering where she was. Once she had come round properly, she decided she ought to make tracks for home. She packed her few overnight things together and, after she'd showered and dressed, did her usual thorough check of the room. She had once left a favourite necklace in a hotel room and this now drove her to look in all the drawers and cupboards before leaving even if she had never used them.

Under the bed she noticed a scrap of white paper and, thinking maybe she'd dropped a receipt, reached for it. Picking it up delicately between thumb and forefinger to avoid the dust, she found herself looking at a wrapper for sugar-free chewing gum.

She stared at the wrapper, remembering clearly that Paul Bakewell had offered her a stick of this gum the morning she'd met him in Stratford. Perhaps he had stayed here? And if so, which night?

There must be hundreds of packets of this stuff sold every day, Jo told herself, but all the same she asked the landlord at breakfast about the person who'd had the room before her.

'Stocky chap with a beard. Stayed for one night like you—'

'Monday?' Jo asked.

'No. Sunday night, it was. He was a pleasant chap. Jolly, talkative — was in the bar most of Sunday night, chatting away.'

'And was he well built, blue eyes and fairish hair?'

'Aye, do you know him then?'

'I think I do,' Jo said. Why would Paul have been here? Sunday was his day off, so maybe he had paid a brief visit to check on Antonia — with or without her consent.

The man who had asked for Antonia at the reception desk could have been Paul — Guy had insisted it wasn't him — and it had come as a surprise to Antonia. So maybe she hadn't asked him to come up but he had taken it into his head to do so anyway. That seemed to make a sort of sense. Of course, on the crucial Monday night he had been back at work, but it still seemed worth another visit to the police station in case it was an avenue they had not followed.

DCI Gammon seemed more frustrated by the information than pleased. Jo got small thanks for doing her duty and, feeling slightly disgruntled, she started her journey south later than she had hoped. Despite Gammon's discouraging reaction, Jo couldn't get out of her head the possibility that Paul had followed them up to Yorkshire. It gave her the same uneasy feeling she'd had when he had admitted to following her to the office and it dogged her thoughts all the way back to Warwickshire.

The persistent rain turned to snow as predicted and it was almost dark by three o'clock in the afternoon. Watching her windscreen wipers ineffectually shove the snowflakes about, she debated whether or not to go and see Tess, who was at the cottage packing up the rest of her twin's belongings. In view of the weather, it seemed more sensible to go straight home than drop in to tell her the latest news. 'But we Virgos do the sensible thing too often,' Jo said aloud. She sped past the Coventry junction and drove on towards Warwick.

The lanes around Ashow were slippery with wet snow and the glimpses of trees and hedges caught in her headlights showed a fairly thick covering. The cottage was heaped with snow, blue-white against the almost dark sky. Chinks of light glowed between the downstairs curtains.

When Tess opened the door, the cat shot out to stand, bemused, in the middle of the lawn with snow past his paws. She called him back but Wilf, though not overkeen on the snow, seemed to want to stay out in it. 'He must be mad,' Tess said. 'Come in and get warm. I've got the fire lit.'

'Wonderful.' Jo made straight for an armchair close to the warmth.

'I've just been carrying on with the sorting out,' Tess said from the kitchen, where she was fixing them both a coffee. 'Everything is left to me. Even the cat.' Tess waved around the room at the half-filled boxes and packing cases. 'This is pretty well all she owned apart from the car, which I'll sell. If there's anything of hers you'd like, please just take it.'

Jo shook her head, resting back in the armchair and taking in the cosy room for the last time. 'No, nothing, but I do think you should consider learning to drive Antonia's car.'

'Maybe,' Tess said. She carried their coffee over. 'I've got to get all this sorted out soon because I can't have too much time off work.' She sighed and looked up at Jo. 'But I want to hear what's been happening with you.'

Jo accepted the hot coffee gratefully. 'I've just had a horrendous journey down the M1 after spending part of yesterday in a very chilly police station.'

'So did you find out if any of our theory was right? Did Guy identify Sargent? Have they got him?'

'They were interviewing Sargent again when I left and I think they'll charge him for Antonia's murder. Once his alibi faded away, he was left pretty vulnerable and Guy told me he picked him out of an identity parade yesterday afternoon, which just about finished off his chances of getting away with it.' Jo noticed how tired her voice sounded. She sat up and took a long drink of coffee.

'I've been through all Monique's bank statements and there's no record of her legacy. Once the police have been in touch with my aunt's solicitors in France, they should have proof that she withdrew the money in cash,' Tess said. She shook her head and half smiled at Jo. 'Amazing how people you think you know can surprise you.'

Jo nodded but her mind was occupied with proving what they knew. 'That will help and things will look even worse for Sargent. Gammon — that's the inspector — told me the Kent police have reopened Monique's case, so I suggest you give all Antonia's notes and files to the police. It will make their job easier. They still have to find more evidence.'

'But you're sure they will?' Jo managed to force a confident smile. 'There's no problem about the files,' Tess went on. 'I'll be glad to get rid of them. Toni would have been overjoyed about all this. She was right all along.'

'I know.' Jo sighed. 'We've solved it but it's taken us too long and that's what makes me sorry.' She pushed her hair out of her eyes and stared at the fire, thinking she would never be as confident or as optimistic as she had been when she first set foot in this cottage.

'I feel I let her down too,' Tess said. 'But it was only when Toni died that we realised just how far Sargent was prepared to go. And it threw all these other things into the light — like Guy's evidence and Monique's legacy — which Toni didn't know about,' she pointed out. 'Anyway, Toni didn't come entirely clean with you. She kept a lot of what she did know to herself. By the way, I'm aware she owed your firm money and that will come out of the estate.'

Jo wondered if that would make Macy change his mind. When she had called at her flat the day before, she'd found a cheque for her outstanding wages and her P45 waiting for her in an envelope. She didn't want to mention any of this to Tess, so she just thanked her and said she would let the agency know.

'I'm going to send Mr Macy a note of my special thanks to you,' Tess said. 'I know astrology is your thing but I hope you don't give up the PI work altogether because you're really good at this, you know?'

'It might have given up on me,' Jo started to say, but as she was speaking the home phone rang and Tess reached over to pick it up. She listened for a few moments and put it down with a clatter.

'Another funny call,' she said, her eyes flicking to Jo's. 'I've reported them and I'm going to have the line disconnected.'

Jo put down her mug. 'Still? How many have you had?'

'Two or three a day. Mostly at night. I've told the phone company and they said not to respond at all and to keep a note of the times.' She got up, searched for a notepad, jotted the time down and handed it to Jo.

'Does he say anything?'

She shrugged. 'The usual run-of-the-mill obscene things, I suppose. What he would like to do to me.' She grimaced and avoided Jo's eyes. 'You don't think it's still Sargent, do you?'

'Well, he's not actually in police custody so I suppose it could be. Nothing else has happened to you, has it?'

Tess shook her head. 'Just the calls.' She seemed restless and got up to poke the fire. 'The sooner they lock him up the better. Do you think I should tell the police?'

'Yes, definitely. Keep a note of anything else that happens and I'll come with you to the police station tomorrow. Why don't you stay at my flat tonight? My sofa's very comfy.'

'No, thanks.' Tess looked around. 'I've got so much to do. I want to finish packing tomorrow and this will be my last night here, so I think I'll stay.'

'Well, I'll stay too, then. It's a pity I didn't leave my things here. I'll go home and feed Claudius and get some more overnight stuff.' Jo got to her feet, intending to leave straight away. 'If I go now, I'll be back before eight o'clock.'

'I must admit, it would be nice not to spend another night on my own in this place. Last night I drove myself mad thinking I could hear people prowling around in the bushes.' She laughed. 'I'm not used to somewhere as quiet as this and I've got an overactive imagination.'

Jo gave Tess instructions not to answer the phone or open the door and went out to her car. She suspected she was being overcautious but after her experience with Antonia she was determined not to take any risks. The snow was a couple of inches deep and cushioned her steps down the garden path. It was still falling, which would slow her down on her journey home.

Once in the lane, where the road was kept fairly clear due to passing traffic, driving was easier but even Jo was forced to keep well within the speed limit. Peering through the irregular clear patches on her windscreen and whirling white flakes in her lights, all she noticed about other cars was their distance in relation to her.

Coming out of a bend on a shadowy stretch of road, Jo saw headlights in a lane off to her left. The car was moving fast and shot out of the junction in front of her. Her foot went to the brake.

The tyres hardly gripped the wet road and she was half-dazzled by the car as it turned towards her. Her Renault slid to a stop and stalled. The other car screeched off in the opposite direction.

Shaken, she restarted the car. She had only seen the other car for a couple of seconds but something about it had looked familiar . . .

She stopped as abruptly as she dared and pulled into the side of the road to do a U-turn. The road was only just wide enough and she was halfway through the turn when she saw a car coming towards her. She couldn't rely on it to stop in time, and pressed her foot on the accelerator. The nose of her car scraped the hedge, flinging snow onto the bonnet and windscreen. The back wheels skidded round and she was heading back to the cottage faster than was safe.

She slowed down again when she came to the drive. By this time, she had convinced herself that there was nothing to worry about and that Claudius was going to do without his tea and breakfast simply because his owner was neurotic. Her headlights lit up car tracks, but they could easily be the ones she herself had made a quarter of an hour earlier. She had succeeded so completely in reassuring herself that when she saw the large dark shape of the car parked outside the cottage, it was like a jolt to her brain.

Her car skidded slightly when she stopped but she got out quietly, leaving the door ajar to avoid any noise. The cottage looked exactly as she had left it with a pencil of light spilling onto the snow from the living room window and the upstairs rooms in darkness.

She crossed the white lawn, leaving a trail of footprints behind her, and peered in through the gap in the curtains. Inside, the fire was blazing away in the grate and the boxes, packing cases and piles of wrapped ornaments were just as she had last seen them, but the room was empty. Maybe Tess was in the kitchen?

Jo crept round to the back of the house. The uncurtained kitchen window formed a lighted rectangle and she approached it cautiously, keeping to one side and craning her neck to peer in. The two mugs that she and Tess had used were standing upside-down on the drainer. The kitchen clock read 7.10. She waited for a minute, but from this oblique angle, there was no sign of Tess.

Jo felt in her pocket for her key ring, fingering each one until she found the long shaft of the mortice key. Treading carefully in the soft snow, she came to the back door, which was covered by a storm porch and in complete darkness. By touch she found the lock and silently brought the key to it. Just as she was about to try it, she heard a soft thud behind her.

She flattened herself against the door and raised her arm to strike. Something shifted to her right at shoulder height and moved again, dropping to the ground. It was Wilf travelling from the roof to the porch and now to the snow at her feet.

'You scared the shit out of me,' she hissed and the cat flattened his ears at the hostile sibilant sounds.

There was still no noise from the cottage and Jo turned her attention back to the business of getting in. The key moved easily in the lock and the door opened with barely a creak. Jo slipped in, looking around her quickly, but the cat hung back. She closed the door softly on Wilf and paused, listening.

She could hear muffled sounds from upstairs, small squeaks and thuds. She selected a long-handled knife from the rack on the wall, unlatched the door at the bottom of the stairs as softly as she could and crept up, her heart pounding. She stopped on the landing. The sounds were more distinct now and she distinguished a high-pitched whimpering overlaid by laboured breathing.

She took the two steps to Antonia's room. In the darkness, she could make out the door, which was half open, and at the same moment she realised that a voice was hissing a series of obscene instructions.

She stepped into the doorway, knife raised. In the pallid light from the window, she saw Tess's face, gagged by a pair of tights, and her hands tied over her head to the wooden bedpost. The broad back of a man was bent over her, his trousers half off. The fear in Tess's eyes made up her mind.

'Stop!' Jo cried, her voice shaky but clear.

He turned round.

It was Paul Bakewell, red with excitement and anger. Even in the shadows she could see his eyes gaping with rage.

The next few minutes were chaotic. All the time she could hear Tess struggling violently to get free. Paul lunged towards her. Jo kept the knife out of his reach and kicked at him. He flung himself at her and they both fell, his full weight on top of her, grunting. She caught him with the knife, ripping his shirt and sinking the blade into something tough. He tensed and she struggled out from under him, still clutching the knife.

Jo turned on her knees to face him, the room swaying around her. He was nursing his upper arm, which was running dark blood. Her knuckles were still locked round the handle of the knife. She pointed it at his chest. 'Stay there. Don't move.' She steadied herself with a hand on the bed. At the same moment, Tess wrenched herself free, picked up the alabaster lamp beside the bed and raised it with both arms.

'Don't. Don't.' Paul put his arm up to cover his head. 'You fucking women. Always trying to get me. You're gonna kill me like you've always wanted — just what you've wanted—' He seemed smaller as he cowered beneath his arm.

'Call the police,' Jo said to Tess in an unrecognisable, harsh voice. 'He won't move.' She kept her eyes fixed on Paul, who stared at the floor, a pathetic, flabby man, half undressed. And yet he had been utterly terrifying.

'You were after Antonia, weren't you?' Jo addressed him directly, her breath catching in her throat so that her voice still sounded alien. 'You made her life a misery, breaking into this place, stealing her briefcase, writing her anonymous notes—'

'I loved her!' Paul shouted, and Jo tried not to flinch. 'I worshipped her.'

'You harassed her. You tried to make her dependent on you. You fiddled with the fuse box so the lights went out at night and she would call you to fix them. Good old reliable Paul would come along to make everything all right.'

'She *loved* me.' Paul's disturbing round-eyed gaze bore into Jo.

'You poisoned her cat and offered her a shoulder to cry on.' Jo spoke without knowing what she was going to say next, drawing on information that had been buried inside her for weeks. Behind her she could hear Tess speaking to the police and her normal, rational mind began to reassert itself. She knew she had to keep Paul like this, at bay, cowering.

'When you knew she was at the St George, you trapped her in the sauna. How did you manage that?'

Paul dropped his head into his hands. 'It was me. I was there. I just kept out of your way.' His large, rounded shoulders hunched closer to the ground. 'I kept an eye on her the whole time she was in that bloody hotel. I stuck a towel under the door of her cabin to make it stick and whipped it away before they let her out. I only wanted her to have a fright. To recognise who really loved her.'

Jo remembered seeing a man in a jogging suit and a baseball cap who had kept his back to her. She let out a breath in disgust. 'To make her *need* you. But she was too bright for you, wasn't she? You didn't expect her to employ a PI, did you?'

'You didn't help her in the end. No one could help her then. You women killed her, bloody pushy women.' He looked up. Tess had come to stand behind him, silent and shaking but still holding the heavy lamp base in her hand. Paul stared at her as if he scarcely recognised her and sank back against the wardrobe.

Jo did not dare look at her watch but she wondered how long it would take the police to get there in the snow. 'What are you talking about? You killed her, no one else.'

'Rachel did it,' Paul hissed, his eyes blazing, and for a moment, Jo believed him. She had guessed Rachel had been jealous of Antonia — afraid they were probably having an affair, she could have been the one doing the dirty tricks to frighten Antonia away — but it was Paul who had easy access to the cottage, who Antonia trusted and who could have stolen the spare key any time he had been 'fixing' the electrics.

And if Rachel had killed Antonia, who had made that call from her house in Warwick? Not Paul. He had just admitted to following them into the sauna.

He was speaking again. 'That was why she refused to marry me — because of Rachel interfering.'

'But Antonia couldn't marry you. Not at the moment anyway — you're married to Rachel.' Jo was trying to keep her voice rational and quiet. She shot a quick glance at Tess, who was still blocking his exit. She returned the look stoutly, still white-faced.

He gave a scornful laugh. 'You're not half as bright as her. She knew I wasn't married. I don't know how but she wasn't surprised when I told her Rachel was my sister.'

'So why do you tell people she's your wife?' Jo forced herself to keep her attention fully on the man in front of her.

'That's Rachel's idea. When I came out of prison she had it all arranged. She had moved into that house, told the landlord and her employer and the world and his dog that we were married. She said we'd move to a place where nobody knew us and pretend we were married for respectability. She said Mother would have wanted it. I know now it was to keep me under her thumb. Silly cow, she thought it gave her a sort of control over me. I was in no position to argue when I first came out, but then I met Toni. She changed everything.'

'She'd never have married you.' Tess spoke unexpectedly. Her voice was low and level.

Jo's brain had become slow but horrifyingly clear. She remembered Antonia collecting cuttings from the local paper about sex attacks. 'Rachel knows all about you, doesn't she? And when she got desperate, she rang Antonia in the middle of the night and told her it was you who attacked those women—'

'Poor Toni didn't know what to think.' Paul shook his head sadly. 'She thought Rachel was just jealous, making things up to keep us apart. Toni still trusted me. I turned up at her room like I'd said I would. I told her not to tell you, and she switched that alarm thing off so you wouldn't know I was coming to fetch her.' He sneered suddenly. 'I said you were panting for Sargent and just wanted to get in his bed, so you couldn't be trusted.'

'And yet *you* could?' Jo whispered.

'She let me in and said she wanted to go home. I said I'd take her, there and then. She'd packed her stuff ready but she was in a right old state, crying all over the place. I said we should go for a walk to clear her head. I had something important to say . . .' His voice dried up.

Jo was just about to ask another question to keep his mind occupied when he looked up, tears running down his puffy face. 'She trusted me,' he repeated, 'but I couldn't trust her. I knew she'd never let it rest there. Toni kept files on people, you know. On you, me, she had a file for everyone she knew and she'd have followed up what Rachel told her, checking dates, times. She might even have told you.' He stared at Jo with loathing.

'So you killed her?' Jo asked matter-of-factly.

Paul shook his head in anguish. 'No, no, I confessed. Once we were outside on the cliffs, I told her about those girls. How I had to do it because they had no respect for me. One of them was just a shop girl and she treated me like dirt, wouldn't serve me, ignored me. I had to show her.' It was obvious that he was working himself up. Jo felt herself start to shake and struggled to keep the knife still. She and Tess exchanged quick glances.

'So what happened?' she said, trying to make her tone conversational.

'She didn't understand.' Paul looked miserably from one woman to the other. 'She didn't see why I had to do it. She just got angry and started shouting. I tried to calm her down but—' Sobs strangled his voice. He pushed his fingers into his eye sockets, and Jo and Tess exchanged another cautious glance. Paul seemed to have broken down completely and although he was no longer threatening, Jo didn't know if either she or Tess could stand it much longer.

'She wouldn't listen to me.' Paul was speaking again, almost in a whimper. 'She ran away from me. It was black as pitch, I didn't know she was so near the edge.' His voice caught on a sob. 'She only screamed once. Not like the others, they went on screaming and screaming.' He clutched his head. 'But not Toni. Just the once. And that was all.'

Paul fell silent, sitting trance-like, staring ahead until it became almost unbearable. Jo had to speak. 'You got someone to cover at work for you that night, didn't you?'

Paul looked at her, his eyes bloodshot and blinking. 'A call to a mate and another asking for a cab to Heathrow, prepaid. That's all the trouble that took.' He regarded Jo steadily, accusingly. 'You're the cause of it all. I had to get her away from *you*,' he repeated. 'You were poisoning her mind against me, but I thought I'd won her round.'

'What did you do after it happened?' Jo asked. Her arms ached with holding the knife. The bloodstain was seeping down Paul's side and across the polished floor. 'You pretended you'd just arrived in Yorkshire when I saw you.'

Paul nodded slowly. 'After I'd seen her fall, I had to go back to the hotel first with her holdall and to get rid of the note she'd left you. But that didn't take long.'

Jo swallowed hard. She remembered the hotel room looking oddly tidy and yet in the drawers, Antonia's clothes had been rumpled and stuffed together. The pad of hotel stationery had been left open on the desk.

'I drove away and came back later — after I'd rung you.' He turned to Tess suddenly. 'I did love her and when I saw you I thought she'd come back from the grave. I couldn't believe my luck. That I had a second chance.'

Tess shuddered. At the same moment, the police sirens sounded their plaintive wail. Jo waited a minute then said to Tess, 'Go down and let them in.'

Jo shifted to take her place in the narrow doorway, still pointing the knife at Paul. He didn't flinch, however, just sat, slumped against the wardrobe. They waited there, motionless, until she heard the heavy footsteps on the stairs and even when the men in uniform pushed past her to fill the little bedroom, she still didn't move.

* * *

Two hours later, Jo stood in the kitchen stirring hot chocolate in a pan on the stove. The muscles in her arms were still shaky, partly from relief and partly from tension. The swirl of the melting chocolate was mesmerising but occasionally she glanced across at the back window to watch the snow falling. Upstairs she could hear the familiar, domestic sounds of the shower running.

The police had required some persuasion to leave the two women on their own. As all of Tess's contacts were either in Kent or Scotland, it had been down to Jo to call someone local, but Jo had been adamant that wasn't necessary. Her parents were elderly, she'd said, a description for which they would not have thanked her, and her sister had young children, which was perfectly true. Both women had assured the officers that they would be absolutely fine and here the snow had helped them as it had become increasingly obvious that any form of transport, including moving their own vehicles, parked at angles across the drive, was not going to be easy. Eventually the officers had left with instructions to the women about when and where to report in the morning. Meanwhile, the snow had kept on falling and now the chocolate was ready to pour.

As Jo lined up the two largest mugs she could find in the cupboard, Tess appeared, pink-faced and wrapped from head to toe in thick towelling. 'That feels better,' she said but Jo could hear the underlying grimness in her tone. She saw the chocolate, made a little appreciative noise and accepted a hot mug in a shaky hand. 'Amazing,' was all she said.

'I wouldn't be surprised if we were snowed in tomorrow.' Jo looked up again at the window, where the starless sky was being gradually obscured by white flakes.

'As long as both Oliver Sargent and Paul Bakewell are behind bars, I don't care,' Tess remarked. She led the way to the front room and immediately started to bank up the fire with a fierce energy as if she was stuffing the logs in Bakewell's face.

'Well, Bakewell definitely is and Sargent is under police guard, so they tell me.' Both women sat down somewhat gingerly on either side of the fireplace. 'How are you feeling?' Jo asked. 'Any injuries?'

'Only my wrists and ankles. I'm glad you convinced them we didn't need to go to A&E.' Tess fingered her left wrist. 'I suppose I deserve that for being daft enough to let him in.'

'I don't think so,' Jo said with emphasis. 'Paul was very good at playing the nice guy.'

'Thank God you came back when you did.' Tess had put down her mug and was cradling the bottom half of her face in her hands. 'Why did you decide not to go back to your flat after all?'

'Paul passed me and it took me a minute or two to realise it was his minicab. At the time, I thought it could have been Rachel. I was never sure about her. She's almost as weird as him.'

Tess suppressed a shudder. 'Do you think their relationship was incestuous? Is that what he was saying?'

'God knows. But it was peculiar anyway. Rachel was certainly as possessive about him as any wife could be. I once caught her going through Antonia's purse. She must have been looking for some proof they were having an affair. I reckon she was terrified Antonia would take him away.'

'That's a bit more than just sisterly love,' Tess remarked. A silence fell after this. Jo's thoughts turned to Antonia.

'You know the Kent police think they've found that neighbour of yours who recognised Sargent as John Brooke from a photograph,' Jo said eventually.

'I know. If only Toni had had their resources.' Tess sighed. 'Still, we got them for her in the end. Thanks to you. How're you feeling?'

'Sore, but just bruises I think.'

Tess dropped her hands to her lap. 'You really have been amazing, you know. I'm so glad Toni found you. But what about you, Jo? This whole business hasn't brought anyone any luck, has it?' She gave Jo a long, steadfast look. 'There's no need for you to still feel bad about it all, you know. You did everything you could and you never gave up.' Jo nodded silently and applied herself to her hot chocolate. 'I notice you didn't call your boss when the police asked for a local contact,' she added 'I would have thought him the obvious choice.'

'Well, that's a bit complicated at the moment.' Jo stared at the fire, where the flames were now flickering around the fresh tinder. 'I suppose I'll tell him in the morning.'

'I hope you're not thinking of giving this work up? You're so good at it,' Tess said. 'I mean, I know you like the astrology stuff. I don't really get that, to be honest, but I do think you should stick with helping people in this more practical way too.'

'I'm not sure it's still an option,' Jo said. 'Macy and I had a bit of a falling out.' She left it at this and Tess had the sense not to pursue it. They drank their hot chocolate in silence. Tess took hers to the front window to watch the snow.

Jo sat back in the comfortable old armchair and wondered if she would make that phone call to Macy in the morning. On the drive back from Yorkshire, she had called her friend Hanni. Ostensibly, Jo had phoned to ask her about Petra and her crystal healing session but, although grateful for the new business, Hanni had not wasted long on that. She had instantly sensed that all was not well and soon Jo was telling her about the argument with Macy and the fact that he had apparently sacked her.

Hanni had simply listened and carried on listening while Jo went through all Macy's many failings and why she didn't need the PI work. This had taken at least two junctions of the M1 until finally Jo had admitted to Hanni, 'I don't know whether I should ask for my job back.'

Hanni hadn't given her any advice on this and, even if she had, Jo reflected, she probably wouldn't have taken it. Hanni had never understood why she'd taken on the PI work in the first place, as she always maintained that the Universe would provide. 'There are plenty of people who need your advice on the movements of the stars and planets to help us live more harmoniously,' she had said. 'So there will always be work for you as an astrologer. But, Jo, maybe you should make your peace with Macy first.'

After the shock of the last few hours, this was the one thing Jo found she remembered most clearly from their conversation. Now she looked towards Tess, still standing at the window with her back to her.

'I think you might be right. I've still got my astrology work but—' She paused as her tired brain tried to articulate her sudden realisation. 'I don't know that I want to give up PI work altogether. I think I'll always want to do some sort of detective work — with the help of astrology, perhaps.'

'That's good,' Tess said. She drew the curtains and replaced the fireguard. 'So you just need to make it up with your boss.'

As this was probably the only thing that Tess and Hanni would ever agree on, Jo reflected with an inner smile, it must be right. 'That's where it gets complicated,' Jo said. 'Or rather, it's Macy who is complicated. I've done his birth chart, so I should know. He's a Cancerian and his Moon is in Sagittarius like mine. I should understand him, but I don't.'

'But you don't have to understand him to work for him, do you? Or is there more to it than that?'

'There's more to it. And you're right, I shouldn't need to. But it might help if I understood myself half the time. I've worked out one thing though — it's my fault we've fallen out.'

Tess gave a little shrug. 'That's easy, then. You just have to eat humble pie.'

Jo looked across at her in the gloom and nodded slowly. 'Yes, I'm going to go and see him. Of course,' she added with a wry smile. 'I'll wait until the Moon is in Libra, making a favourable aspect to my Sun. Because I'm certainly going to need all the help I can get from the stars.'

THE END

ALSO BY LINDA MATHER

THE ZODIAC MYSTERIES
Book 1: FORECAST MURDER
Book 2: A SIGN FOR MURDER
Book 3: MURDER AS PREDICTED

Thank you for reading this book.

If you enjoyed it please leave feedback on Amazon or Goodreads, and if there is anything we missed or you have a question about, then please get in touch. We appreciate you choosing our book.

Founded in 2014 in Shoreditch, London, we at Joffe Books pride ourselves on our history of innovative publishing. We were thrilled to be shortlisted for Independent Publisher of the Year at the British Book Awards two years in a row.

www.joffebooks.com

We're very grateful to eagle-eyed readers who take the time to contact us. Please send any errors you find to corrections@joffebooks.com. We'll get them fixed ASAP.

Printed in Great Britain
by Amazon

62839339R00128